life
ON THE
leash

life
ON THE
leash

VICTORIA SCHADE

GALLERY BOOKS
New York   London   Toronto   Sydney   New Delhi

G

Gallery Books
An Imprint of Simon & Schuster, Inc.
1230 Avenue of the Americas
New York, NY 10020

First Gallery Books trade paperback edition September 2018

GALLERY BOOKS and colophon are registered trademarks of Simon & Schuster, Inc.

For information about special discounts for bulk purchases, please contact Simon & Schuster Special Sales at 1-866-506-1949 or business@simonandschuster.com.

The Simon & Schuster Speakers Bureau can bring authors to your live event. For more information or to book an event, contact the Simon & Schuster Speakers Bureau at 1-866-248-3049 or visit our website at www.simonspeakers.com.

Design by Bryden Spevak

Manufactured in the United States of America

10 9 8 7 6 5 4 3

Library of Congress Cataloging-in-Publication Data

Names: Schade, Victoria, author.
Title: Life on the leash / Victoria Schade.
Description: First Gallery Books trade paperback edition. | New York : Gallery Books, 2018.
Identifiers: LCCN 2017055245 | Subjects: LCSH: Dog trainers—Fiction. | Dogs Training—Fiction. | Triangles (Interpersonal relations)—Fiction. | GSAFD: Love stories
Classification: LCC PS3619.C31265 L54 2018 | DDC 813/.6—dc23 LC record available at https://lccn.loc.gov/2017055245

ISBN 978-1-5011-9167-1
ISBN 978-1-5011-9168-8 (ebook)

For all the dogs like Cooper, and the people
who work tirelessly to save them

ONE

Cora waved sheepishly at the car she'd just cut off and mouthed "Sorry!" to the driver. She had three minutes to make it two blocks, find parking, and dash to her client's house. In DC, on the wrong side of rush hour, two blocks could take hours. On this day the traffic gods were on her side.

She'd told Madison Perry she'd arrive at her home at eleven thirty, and her phone read eleven twenty-nine as she snagged a serendipitous parking spot in front of the brownstone. *Military precise,* she thought as she speed-walked to the front door. She hoped her new client would notice. Though she was chronically late for every other part of her life, Cora always managed to make it to her clients' homes on time, even if it meant breaking a few traffic laws along the way. The illegal U-turn she'd made in the middle of the street to snag the prime parking spot? Just part of the job.

The Perry brownstone was in a beautiful section of Georgetown. Close to Montrose Park, a few streets up from the shopping on M Street, and storybook charming on the outside. The low wrought iron fence opened to a courtyard filled with precision-trimmed boxwoods, so perfect that they looked like the gardener had used a laser to sculpt them. Blossom-heavy window boxes anchored the four large front windows. *Looks like a* House Beautiful *centerfold,* Cora thought.

As she rang the doorbell she wondered who she was about to meet. Cora always tried to imagine her clients prior to seeing them face-to-face as a way to prepare for the all-important first session. Context cues, from the way the client's voice sounded, to the syntax of their e-mails, to the type of dogs they owned, all helped Cora paint a picture that was, more often than not, dead-on. Predicting canine behavior was her specialty, but predicting human behavior was a close second.

Madison's e-mail had detailed the challenges she was having with her new boxer puppy ("The nipping! The peeing! You need to fix this dog!"). Cora was always hesitant when a potential client asked her to "fix" their dog, because a dog is more than a piece of malfunctioning household equipment. Obedience training wasn't a business of quick fixes, despite what Doggy Dictator Boris Ershovich preached on his TV show.

Madison's e-mail signature had included her title at a prestigious DC law firm, so Cora assumed that she was an established attorney with a similarly well-connected husband, perfect children, and a new puppy to round out this year's Christmas photo. But the name Madison gave her pause. She'd never met a woman over the age of thirty with the name. Cora heard footsteps approaching and envisioned the polished woman she was about to meet.

The door opened. "Look at *you*—right on time."

Cora stood dumbfounded for a moment. The square-jawed Hillary-coiffed power broker she was expecting was actually a gorgeous late-twenty-something blonde in black yoga pants and a slouchy cashmere cardigan. The woman looked only a year or two older than twenty-eight-year-old Cora. Perhaps this was Madison Perry's daughter?

The woman extended her hand. "Hi, I'm Madison. Thank you for fitting me in so quickly. I swear, Oliver is the *devil*. He's really driving me crazy." Cora saw Madison's eyes flit up and down her body, taking in her frayed sneakers, work bag, and coat.

Cora swallowed her disbelief. *This* was Madison? This model-like creature was lady of the Georgetown manor *and* chief legal officer at Crandall, Quinn & Hawkins?

"Hi, hi." Cora was caught off guard by her miscalculation. "Nice to meet you."

"Please come in." Madison took two steps backward and then clasped her hands under her chin. "I hate to do this, but could you take off your shoes?"

"Of course. Murphy's Law." Cora laughed. "Today's the day I'm wearing old socks." She loved her neon unicorn socks and wasn't ready to toss them, despite the holes blooming on both toes. She kicked off her shoes, worried that her feet smelled.

"You know how it goes—white carpets," Madison said, gesturing like a spokesmodel toward the immaculate cream and white damask-print rug.

Cora nodded. White carpets indeed. She tucked a stray tendril back into her thick caramel-colored braid, a nervous habit that did no good because the strand always popped right back out. There were times, like when she met a successful, put-together career woman, that Cora doubted her decision to give up a fast-track corporate job to become a dog trainer. But, no matter that the salary wasn't cushy and the stock options were nonexistent, Cora was making good on her promise to Cooper.

She glanced in the mirror as they walked down the hallway and admitted to herself that she looked more like a homeless person than someone whose name and impressive job title used to appear on a weighty business card. She still kept one in the folds of her wallet as a reminder of the corporate drone she used to be. Holey socks and all, Top Dog was a dream manifested into reality.

Cora's button-down logo shirt was wrinkled and stained with dog slobber. A belt loop on the back of her three-year-old jeans had torn off because she was constantly using it to hike them up. Her old black jacket was flecked with a rainbow of dog fur. Disorder verging on frump had become a way of life.

But the truth was Cora could get away with the squirrel's nest of dark blond waves and makeup-free face. She looked like she belonged in a vintage soap ad promising velvety suds and a schoolgirl complexion.

"Did you have any trouble finding us?" Madison asked, sounding as if she was talking to a child.

"Uh, no. I've had quite a few clients in your neighborhood. Georgetown is sort of my backyard," Cora replied.

"Oh! You *live* in Georgetown?" Madison sounded surprised.

"No, I live in DuPont, but I have tons of clients in Georgetown. I get a lot of referrals around here, particularly—"

"Anyone I might know?" Madison interrupted.

Cora felt like she was in an interview for the Junior League. "Um, Ted Sullivan? He's over on P Street. Marjorie and James Klein? Uh, let me think . . . the Dunn family?"

Madison shook her head at each name but appeared comforted by the fact that Cora could rattle off a list of folks in her tony neighborhood.

Cora stole glimpses of the rest of the beautiful house as they moved toward the kitchen, averting her eyes from her reflection when they passed another oversize shabby-chic mirror.

"Well, here's the little monster," Madison said with a flourish.

Oliver the twelve-week-old fawn boxer puppy was curled up in a tiny ball, fast asleep in the corner of his faux rattan crate.

"Oh. My. Goodness," Cora exclaimed. "He's *perfect*. I'm in love!"

Oliver stirred, stretched, and then realized that he had an audience. He went from slumbering puppy to entertainer in an instant, leaping in circles and barking excitedly.

"Should I take him out of his crate?" Madison asked.

"Please! I have to kiss that little face right now." Cora saw Madison wrinkle her nose.

"It's gross, I know, but *j'embrasse mon chien sur la bouche*!" Cora said, unable to control the stream of French. She often broke into her second language when she was feeling uncomfortable.

"*Vous parlez français?*" Madison asked, raising an eyebrow.

"Oh, *j'essaye de parler français*," Cora replied with false modesty. Her minor in French guaranteed that she did more than *try* to speak the language, but it wouldn't do to brag in front of Madison. "Let's head outside for a potty break right away since he's just waking up from a nap."

"Really? He needs to go out after he wakes up? That's probably why he pees all the time after I take him out of the crate. I just thought he was mad at me for leaving him in there."

Cora switched to autopilot and began her standard dissertation about the misunderstood world of canine elimination as they walked Oliver through the kitchen toward the backyard. She surveyed her surroundings while well-rehearsed words tumbled from her mouth. The kitchen was large and formal, painted a warm Tuscan orange, with soft Vermeer light pouring in from the many windows. The giant circular table seated eight, and Cora envisioned the chummy dinner parties Madison probably hosted there.

Madison and *who else?* Cora could see rows of silver-framed photographs on the shelf above the fireplace behind the table, but she couldn't get close enough to them to make out the faces. Was Madison a second wife to some cigar-smoking DC backslapper?

The yard, once they exited through the French doors, was as impressive as the rest of the house, surprisingly large for Georgetown, and ringed on all sides with a tall privet hedge. Cora wondered how the burned-out urine spots to come would go over with Madison.

"Charlie's on the way," Madison volunteered. "He called and apologized for being late—he really wants to help with Oliver's training. I mean, he *better* help. Oliver was his idea. I've never even had a dog before . . . Charlie doesn't know it, but I'm really more of a cat person."

"Maybe Oliver will help you be both," Cora replied, starting to understand the scope of what she would be dealing with. She fretted that she'd eventually have to snake charm the woman into liking her in order for them to successfully complete the program. But for now, she focused on the dog, knowing that a puppy could blur the hard edges of even the most disagreeable clients.

So his name is Charlie. Cora checked Madison's left hand. Bare. Pretending to be a puppy person to lock down old Charlie?

Oliver stopped jumping on Cora long enough to find just the right spot to pee, and Cora chanted "Hurry up, hurry up," to him. She turned to Madison. "I like 'hurry up,' but do you already have a potty phrase?"

"A *what*?"

Cora started to explain how a simple phrase can become a Pavlovian trigger to get a dog to eliminate but was interrupted by the French doors opening to reveal the most gorgeous man she'd ever seen. Cora suddenly understood why Madison would lie about being a dog person.

He was Cora's kryptonite: tall, broad shouldered, with short sandy hair that swooped in a way that looked styled but not fussy. He radiated the kind of kick-in-the-gut good looks that made both women *and* men stare. He wasn't "pretty" but arresting. Manly, like he'd be at home chopping wood in a flannel shirt, even though he was wearing an expensive-looking suit.

There's got to be something wrong with him, Cora thought, steeling herself to remain professional. *Aside from the fact that he's dating someone who doesn't like dogs.*

He strode over toward Cora with his hand outstretched. "Hi,

you must be Cora. I'm Charlie Gill. Sorry I'm late. Can you believe that I hit traffic at lunchtime?" His ruddy cheeks and quick smile unnerved Cora.

Cora met his grip with a firm handshake and did her best to hide her immediate and unprofessional attraction to her new client.

"Nice to meet you, and I totally understand the traffic. It runs my life—I could tell you stories!" Cora said, smiling her biggest "I'll blind you with my teeth so you don't notice that I'm not wearing makeup" smile. She hoped that he hadn't heard the tremor in her voice or noticed the bright red splotches she could feel blooming on her cheeks.

Oliver rushed over and jumped up on Charlie. "There's my little guy!" He laughed and leaned over to pet his puppy. Charlie's voice went up. "Are you the best puppy in the world? Yes you are! Why, yes you are, little Ollie-by-golly!"

"I know this is going to sound totally bitchy, but can we get started?" Madison asked. "I have a one o'clock meeting."

"Of course! Sorry about that," Cora replied, embarrassed that she wasn't more on top of the lesson and avoiding looking directly at Charlie. She usually controlled the progression of the hour with a conductor's fluidity, but she had a feeling that the Perry-Gill household wasn't going to be business as usual.

"Let's start off with some Q and A."

They headed back inside and settled in the kitchen, Charlie and Madison sitting at the table and Cora taking up her usual position on the floor next to the dog.

"I just have a few questions that'll help me get to know Oliver better and help me understand what you want from training."

Cora launched into her standard questionnaire—Where did you get your dog? Who's your vet? What type of food is your dog eating?—and studied Charlie and Madison as they took turns answering. People revealed more than they realized during that simple twelve-question interview. Cora usually divided her time during Q&A interacting with the dog and gauging the people, so that when they stood up to begin the session she could predict how each party would react. The interview process was a holdover from her project management days, a part of her corporate arsenal that she used to set her apart from her dog training peers.

Madison was the easier to read. She'd almost come out and admitted that she didn't really like Oliver, and during the interview Cora began to realize just how deep that dislike actually was.

"There's so much wrong with this dog, right, hon? He's like, pawtistic I think." Madison put her hand on Charlie's thigh and laughed at her own joke. "But we've got our very own Doggie Dictator now. There's a ton of stuff to fix, but that's why we're paying you the big bucks!"

The corners of Cora's mouth turned down before she could help it. Equating the success of her program with the cost was a close second to the "fix my dog" request on her list of red flags. (Which was tied with people likening her to Boris Ershovich.) Sure, private training was expensive, but so was having a plumber show up when you've got an overflowing toilet.

Charlie sighed, as if heading into a frequent battle. "Mads, there's not a 'ton' of stuff wrong with Oliver. He's a typical puppy. It's all normal." He reached down to pet Oliver, who was chewing on his shoelace.

"What are the main challenges? I want to make sure we get to all of it." Cora focused on Madison, as unpleasant as she was, because her cheeks got hot every time she looked at Charlie.

"Where do I start?" Madison held out her hand and ticked off the problems on her manicured fingers. "The peeing, the drooling, the poop in my closet, the hair, the muddy paws, the smell, the nipping, the jumping, the destruction of my shoes, and the non-stop spazziness. I'm *over* it."

Charlie sighed again, crossed his arms, and leaned ever so slightly away from Madison.

"Wow, that's quite a list!" Cora said. "I've got good news and bad news. The good news is that I can help you with most of it." She paused. "The bad news is that muddy paws, drool, and hair are all a part of the deal when it comes to dogs. Maybe you should've stuck with cats?" It slipped out before Cora could stop herself, and it sounded unkind. She kicked herself for insulting the person who was about to write her a check.

"Sometimes I wish I had," Madison said, narrowing her eyes at Cora.

"I think we're going to be fine, Mads," Charlie said, defusing the mounting tension and finally reaching out to his girlfriend, giving her hand a squeeze. "I'm sure Cora knows how to help us, and she'll show you that Ollie-by-golly is a genius after all. Right?" He looked at Cora with a hopeful expression.

"I promise. You'll be *embrasser votre chien* before you know it!" Cora's French tripped her up yet again, making her think about kissing. She turned pink, and wondered how she was going to navigate the next five weeks without ever looking directly at Charlie.

TWO

On the drive home, Cora's cell phone jangled her out of her self-satisfaction for successfully navigating the Perry-Gill lesson. She struggled to dig through her overloaded work bag with one hand while managing the quirky back streets of Georgetown with the other. Of course the phone had to ring on the narrow cobblestoned street that was partially blocked by a moving van. Phone located and earpiece inserted, she answered, "Top Dog Training, may I help you?"

"Duuuude, where are you? Didn't you get my texts?"

"Hey, Mags, I'm just leaving my final client of the day. Haven't even had a chance to look at my phone. What's up?" Cora's roommate, Maggie Zabek, had a knack for reporting inane but entertaining gossip, so Cora didn't always rush to check when her name popped up on-screen.

"I'm guessing you didn't look at the *Post* this morning before you left, right?" Maggie's father was an editor of the local paper in Richmond, and though she was thirty years younger than the average newspaper reader, she defiantly subscribed to the paper version of the *Washington Post* as an act of solidarity for a dying medium.

"No, I was running late. Why?" Cora could tell by Maggie's voice that something was up.

"Um, when will you be home?"

"What's going on? You're freaking me out, just tell me what's up. *What* was in the *Post*? Is it something about my business? Is there a new Boris Ershovich training center opening up in Rosslyn or something?" The idea that the powerhouse dog training celebrity might franchise on her home turf was one of the many unlikely but still stressful thoughts that kept her up at night. After three years of struggle, she was finally established in her market, but she knew she could never compete with Ershovich's star power.

"No, it's nothing about you . . . per se. Jesus, C, I don't want to tell you on the phone. You kinda need to see it to believe it anyway. It's not *bad* bad, it's just . . . freaky." Maggie paused.

"I'll be home in five. This better be good."

"It's . . . something, all right."

Cora snagged a parking spot right in front of her building and raced up the stairs to their place. Her dog Fritz was waiting for her at the door.

"Hi, Fritzie. Hello, my handsome boy. Where's Auntie Maggie?" She leaned down and kissed him on top of his square head. Fritz did a little dance to welcome her home, and for a few seconds as she massaged his shoulders, nothing else mattered. Greeting complete, she stood up and shouted, "I'm here, now will you please tell me what's going on?"

"I'm in the kitchen," Maggie replied.

Cora rounded the corner and saw Maggie sitting at the tiny kitchen table with the newspaper spread in front of her and a pitcher of orange juice nearby. She was still in her leopard print flannel pajamas, her short white-blond hair sticking out from her head in wild spikes. She looked adorable even when disheveled. Maggie patted the pitcher and smiled. "It's too early for wine, but it's never too early for mimosas."

"You look awfully cheerful for someone delivering news that requires alcohol. Let me see this." Cora swooped down and tried to grab the paper from the table, but Maggie threw her hands on top of it.

"Can I at least point it out to you? Back off for a sec. I need to make a speech first."

Cora hopped up and down in frustration.

"Okay, Cora, my dearest friend. Here goes." Maggie cleared her throat and paused dramatically. "You've been through a lot of crap in the past, and since I know you pretty much better than anyone else, I think I'm qualified to say that you've finally put that all behind you. Put *him* behind you."

Cora's stomach dropped. The bad news was somehow related to Aaron, her ex-fiancé. "Oh no. Oh no. What is it? Is he getting married?" By this time Fritz had pushed his head beneath Cora's hand, sensitive, as always, to the slightest shifts in her mood. She touched it absentmindedly.

Maggie's expression changed from concerned to pained. "Please don't get upset, C. He's not getting married. Here, look."

Maggie pushed the newspaper toward Cora and pointed to a small photo near the TV listings. Cora leaned in and squinted at the group of smiling people in the picture. She picked out Aaron immediately, tanned and grinning.

" 'Meet the cast of *America's Hottest Landscaper*'?" she read the caption aloud. "Are you kidding me? Aaron is going on a reality show?"

It had taken her a year and a half, but Cora *had* put Aaron Affini behind her. Now he was going to be back to haunt her via the television. She'd finally lost the phantom ring sensation, when her thumb would unconsciously slide to touch the spot on her left hand where the delicate platinum engagement band had once sat.

Maggie studied Cora's face. "You okay?"

Cora nodded and shrugged at the same time, her mouth a tight line.

Maggie spoke quickly, as if to keep Cora from focusing on the photo for too long. "Look, I know it sucks, but maybe he'll get kicked out or voted off or eliminated on the first show. He'll disappear again in a few days. Gone, purged, invisible, just like before."

"You know that won't happen, Maggie. Aaron *always* wins. Always." Cora pulled the newspaper from the table and held it close to her eyes. "He's the best-looking guy in the group."

"But it's not just a beauty competition! It's also to see who can weed best, or mow fastest, or do whatever landscapers do. We both know he's lazy as hell. Don't worry, C, he's not going to make it far."

But Cora knew better. She knew that when Aaron had his eyes on a prize, nothing could stop him. And she knew that he was at his best when he had an audience.

Cora threw the paper on the table. "Whatever. It's fine. I'm fine."

Maggie eyed her skeptically.

"What? Who even watches the Garden Channel anyway?" Cora paused. "I'm happy for him." She raised her arms and gazed heavenward. "Universe? I'm totally fine with this."

"Look at you, all evolved and grown up! *Namaste,* y'all." Maggie placed her hands together and bowed at Cora. "Now, do you want a large mimosa, or an extra-large mimosa?"

She hoped that Maggie couldn't see through her tough-girl act. Cora's coping technique after the breakup was scrubbing every trace of Aaron from her life, both electronically and in real life, and then pushing any thought of him from her mind each time he dared to creep into her consciousness. The rejection was too painful to dwell on, so she'd erased him. Completely.

"I need to get out of here." Cora called to her dog. "Hey, Fritz, wanna hike?"

Fritz danced in front of her, then took a few steps toward the door. The word *hike* meant one thing: Rock Creek Park.

Their long walks in Rock Creek Park were the highlight of the week for both of them. The ritual gave Cora an opportunity to connect with her own dog after spending the majority of the week working with other people's, and it gave Fritz a chance to lay claim to the landscape by lifting his leg on everything vertical. On this day, with the warm spring air bringing everything back to life, a hike would be a hit of dopamine that could banish thoughts of Aaron for at least a few hours.

Maggie scrunched up her face. "Want me to come?" Since this

was the first time in all the years they'd lived together Maggie'd asked to come, Cora wasn't about to make her best friend go hiking.

"Nope, I'm fine. Don't worry about me, okay?"

There was a catch in her throat. She didn't have lingering feelings for Aaron, at least none that she acknowledged, so she couldn't understand why she was so unnerved by the news he might get famous. Perhaps because she could no longer control the Aaron narrative, she feared he might loom larger than life in her head once again, despite her best efforts to purge him forever. Maybe she was just being petty and didn't wish professional success for the man who'd jilted her.

Fritz gave a muffled "harrumph" in his polite indoor voice to speed Cora along, so she took the hint and grabbed his leash.

THREE

A day and two head-clearing walks later, Cora pulled
up in front of her client Fran Channing's house ten
minutes early. She dug out her phone and scanned
her e-mail, stalling so that she'd arrive on her client's doorstep
exactly on time. She scrolled past the junk mail and new client
inquiries until a message from her client Wade Cohen looked
interesting enough to open. "Thought of You, Cora," the subject
line read.

"Hey Miss Dog Lady," it said. "Saw this job posting and
thought of you immediately. You need to try out—let's talk."
Wade and his wife, Rachel, were always brainstorming ways for
Cora to grow her business, in between training sessions with their
adolescent golden retriever, Daisy, and unruly twin girls, offering
advice for everything from her social media presence to her flyers.
Wade's profession was filming corporate training videos, so she
couldn't imagine what sort of job would make him think of her.
She scrolled down to the forwarded message.

We're looking for a one-of-a-kind dog trainer! Are you outgoing? Do your customers and their dogs love you? Bolex Media is casting an exciting new show that will help viewers train their dogs in an entirely new way. See the attachment for program overview and submission details.

Cora stared out the window as her stomach started to churn. A TV show? Wade thought she should audition for a *TV show*? Cora was ready for *someone* to unseat the famous Doggie Dictator, but she had never considered, even in her wildest anti-Ershovich rantings, that that someone should be her. She was a worker bee, a boots-on-the-ground tactician whose sole purpose was to smooth the bumps in the canine-human relationship. Could she become a spokesperson? Be the "face" of positive dog training? It felt unlikely. Cora always ducked in the back of group photos, or offered to take the picture instead of being in it. She hated being the center of attention. When she factored in her lack of experience onstage or in front of a camera—she'd even opted to be crew in her third grade production of *Cinderella* instead of one of the mice—doing anything other than daydreaming about the opportunity seemed unlikely.

But still. The chance to do TV dog training *right,* to help people train with empathy and compassion, rather than barely camouflaged abuse, was tempting. Maybe she could summon the spirit to at least ask for more information about the show? Asking for more details was hardly a commitment to star in a TV show. Issue resolved, she dropped her phone back in her bag and pushed the thought from her head so she could focus completely on her clients.

Fran Channing and her gorgeous young Bouvier des Flandres, Sydney, were Cora's favorite new clients. Fran's Australian accent, giant black-rimmed glasses, and irreverent Louise-Brooks-meets-Helmut-Lang style were charming. Her oversize furry black dog, though, was an odd match for her, as Fran seemed better suited for a portable purse-size dog. Sydney's black mustache and beard made him look equally unique, but his herding dog work ethic didn't fit with Fran's lifestyle. She was overwhelmed by his energy levels, and it was up to Cora to help make the relationship work. A lot of pressure, yes, but she was up to it.

She lifted the heavy iron knocker on Fran's front door and heard Sydney start barking before it had even touched the base. Sydney had been wild at the beginning of their first session, but Cora knew there was a genius lurking beneath his exuberant attention-seeking behavior.

Fran opened the door immediately, as if she'd been waiting for Cora. She rolled her eyes as she tried to hold her dog back. "Hello, darling, please come in. What a *week* we've had. We need you so."

"Wow, looks like Sydney is ready to work!" Cora laughed as she struggled to get in the door and past the cheerfully lunging dog. "What's going on with you guys?"

"Let's chat a bit. Please come in."

Cora followed Fran down the hall. From the outside, Fran's home looked as stately and old-fashioned as the rest of the neighboring homes, but the inside was a revelation. Her take on interior design matched her sartorial sense; her home had a severe minimalist edge softened by the light pouring from the huge glass walls in the rear of the house. Sparsely furnished homes usually made Cora nervous—one misplaced paper made them messy—but Fran's managed to walk the line between museum-like and inviting.

"Darling, the things we worked on last week in class are amazing! Sydney knows how to sit when I ask, and he comes running when I call him. I couldn't be more pleased."

"I hear a 'but' coming . . ."

"But"—Fran cocked an eyebrow, dipped her glasses, and paused dramatically—"his front door etiquette is an embarrassment, as you just saw. I had a little cocktail party here over the weekend, and Sydney was the worst host. He jumped on everyone when they walked in the door." Fran placed her hand on her chest. "I died. This has to stop, you understand."

"Totally. Jumping up makes me nutty, too, because I'm normally on the receiving end. But remember, jumping up on people is rewarding for dogs . . . it feels good to vent some of that energy and make contact with us. You're going to have to work hard at this one, and give it plenty of time to sink in."

"How much time? Because I'm hosting my book club on Thursday, darling."

"Very cool! What are you reading?"

"Nothing! We call it a book club, but it's really just a bunch of saucy middle-aged ladies who like to sit around and drink. I'd invite you, but you're about thirty years too young. Call me when you have your first hot flash."

Cora laughed. "I can guarantee that Sydney won't be perfect in time for your book club, but I do have a quick trick for you."

Cora grabbed a thin cotton leash from her bag while Sydney

danced at her feet. She opened a nearby closet door and looped the leash on the inside doorknob. She held the leash then shut the door on it, grasping the clasp end in her hand.

"I think I see where this is going. I love it!"

"Remember the arm-cross sit I showed you last week? *This* is where we're going to use it. You'll leash Sydney before you let people in, and then lead them over to him and practice some arm-cross sits." The arm-cross sit was Cora's magic bullet, a way to clearly signal to the dog that he needed to sit no matter how distracting the environment. "Do you mind if I blog about this?"

"Be my guest. I'm ready for Sydney to become an Internet celebrity so I can retire in style."

Cora pulled her phone out of her back pocket and started snapping photos of Sydney on the tether. Her semisecret blog was a lightly trafficked photo-heavy diary of her work with her clients' dogs, solutions to typical training challenges, stories about the foster dogs that passed through her home, and frequent tirades about Ershovich's highly publicized but highly harmful techniques. Since she needed anonymity to speak her mind, her brother Josh had helped her to set it up so that readers would have to dig deep to discover her identity or location, and her profile photo on the site showed only Fritz's paws. She'd named it ChienParfait.com ("perfect dog") as a joke, acknowledging that many of the dogs she worked with were far from textbook, but in their own way each was perfect.

Fran watched Cora as she snapped a few photos of Sydney on the tether. "You need to write a book. This is *so* simple, but of course I never would have thought of it!"

"A book? Seriously? It's never crossed my mind. Maybe some-day." Cora considered Wade's audition e-mail. *First a TV show, now a book?* Cora mused. *Who do they think I am?*

"Write something. The world needs a sane training voice out there. You'd find your audience, I'm sure of it. And the press would go bonkers for those Botticelli curls and green eyes, so you'd have no problem promoting it. You'll be a hit, darling!"

Cora started to speak, but Fran was on a roll.

"I despise that Ershovich guy. Emphasis on the 'dick' in 'dicta-tor,' if you ask me. I tried reading his first book and I didn't learn a thing, all he did was brag. And his show is ridiculous. He seems so angry at those poor dogs." Fran waved her hand above her head, as if shooing away a bug. "If you ever decide to write something other than your blog, keep me posted. I know people."

Everyone in DC "knew people." Even though Cora was curi-ous, she knew better than to ask what people did for a living. It was too early in their relationship, and she made a practice of not pry-ing into her clients' lives. If they wanted to tell her about their jobs, families, or hobbies, she was an eager listener, but she never *asked* people what they did when they weren't training their dogs. Work-ing with people in their homes was an intimate business, and Cora did everything in her power to keep the relationships professional until invited to do otherwise. Cora wasn't sure what Fran did for a living, but she could tell that whatever it was, she did it well.

"That's really nice of you—thanks, Fran." She quickly changed the subject, ever the timekeeper, so her clients got their money's worth. "Have you been outside today? We've got a great day for leash walking, so let's get suited up and get out there."

FOUR

"Oh my God, I have to fart!" Maggie whispered. "Why do I always get gas right before Bikram? It's like farting in a Crock-Pot."

Cora stifled a giggle as they entered the yoga room that evening, which was already a few degrees warmer than the rest of the gym and had a permanent fermented odor. She was still trying to appreciate the benefits of yoga, but the "quiet mind" aspect escaped her. The only time Cora could ever recall having a quiet mind was as the anesthesia kicked in before her oral surgery. During class, she thought about her clients, particularly during Downward Dog. She thought about what she'd eaten that day, and how it might react in her stomach as she contorted herself. She thought about Fritz. She thought about her workout outfit and wondered if her black spandex pants stretched out and became transparent when she bent over, like the pants on the woman in front of her. She was happy she wore a thong, just in case.

"This isn't about competition," Ravi, the instructor, murmured each week at exactly the same point during the hour, when heels were touching the ground and asses were pointing to the ceiling.

Thank God, Cora thought in response. *I'd be in last place.*

"Now let's just . . . hang out in the pose for a while," Ravi intoned as he effortlessly flowed into Tadasana.

Hang out. Cora had come to hate the expression. No one dated, it was all "hanging out." She glanced over at the perfectly pretzeled Maggie, who was the queen of "hanging out," expertly juggling no fewer than three men at a time. Cora—who was hoping for something more than hanging—envied her friend's casual attitude toward dating. "There's enough of me to go around," she'd wink and say with a Mae West accent when Cora asked.

Cora attempted Eagle pose, wrapping one leg around the other like a twist tie, but the sweat dripping down the back of her calf made her foot slip off her supporting leg. She landed awkwardly as her sweaty foot hit the ground.

"Sorry! Sorry!" she whispered to the rest of the class. Her spills were so predictable that no one even bothered to look at her when the inevitable crash came. Maggie kept her eyes closed but choked back a giggle.

Even after Cora had started to recover from the blindsiding breakup with Aaron, she kept herself in dating sabbatical mode. His timing had been cinematically awful, at the end of a spur-of-the-moment getaway to Paris, Cora's third trip and Aaron's first, a trip that Cora had been calling their "engagi-moon" to anyone who would listen. Though Cora'd worked hard to help the city bewitch him—plying him with buttery croissants, taking him to the Pont Neuf at night, and initiating sex the moment they got back to their room no matter how tired she was—he'd been sullen and withdrawn the entire time. His sudden confession on the flight back that he didn't want to be married, full stop, no prologue or epilogue, left her questioning everything she thought she knew about love.

She could recall the rest of that flight like a highlight reel. Clawing off her seat belt and running to the bathroom, feeling like she was going to vomit. Trying to pry the ring off her finger so violently that she drew blood. She'd rinsed the trail of red off and dangled the ring from the tip of her finger over the toilet bowl, letting it sway back and forth just centimeters from a sky-high grave. Any turbulence would've done the job for her, but fate wasn't on her side.

When she'd emerged from the bathroom a flight attendant saw her tear-streaked, blotchy face and rushed her back to the galley for a dose of sisterhood and a shot of tequila. With a crew's worth of pep talks and a blanket from first class draped around her shoulders, she'd walked back to her seat next to Aaron with her chin high and refused to look at him for the remainder of the flight. She knew he could see right through her bravado, but she didn't care. She refused to show him any weakness.

Aaron never told Cora exactly what had happened to bring him to that conclusion, so she was forced to try to find the facts hidden within his platitudes—it's not you it's me, we're different people, you need things I can't provide—and map out her own version of their relationship implosion. Every possibility left her feeling like damaged goods.

It took her a long time to feel ready to put herself out there again. Her self-imposed dry spell was good for her brain and her bank account—it allowed her to focus on building her business and kept her too busy to worry about distractions like Tinder and Facebook stalking. Now, though, she was ready to dip her toe in the dating pool again. Her bed was starting to feel too big.

Cora glanced around the yoga room. *No comers in Bikram, that's for sure,* she thought. The gray-haired ponytail guy was a creepy close-talker who hugged without invitation. The decent-looking guy two rows ahead of her always wore Lycra bike shorts and a tight racer-back tank top. She didn't care how normal he seemed during their brief chats before class. She just couldn't come to terms with a guy who willingly exposed the outline of his package to everyone in the gym each week. Besides, it wasn't that impressive of an outline. The one gorgeous, yoga-chiseled, suitably attired guy in class? (Shorts of a respectable length every week.) Perfect, but gay.

Corpse pose. Finally. Savasana, Cora's favorite position. She couldn't quite master Balancing Stick pose, but she could lie on the ground, palms upturned, with the best yogis in the world.

"*Namaste,* people. See you next time." Ravi bowed to the class. Cora didn't even bother thinking impure thoughts about Ravi, he of romance-novel hair, tan skin, and perfect physique. There was the unwritten yoga instructor's code about not dating students, and then there was the problem of Ravi's stunning spin instructor girlfriend. Cora wasn't a poacher.

Charming Charlie Gill flitted into consciousness. *Off-limits,* Cora reminded herself.

"Hey, sweaty Betty," Maggie called to Cora, still resting on the floor. "I'm going out to get a smoothie with Gym Jack from the front desk."

"You mean Gym 'Jake' from the front desk?"

"Jack, Jake—close enough." Maggie shrugged. "Wanna come?"

"I'd love to be your third wheel but I've got to get home and let Fritzie out." Cora was timepiece precise about walking her dog.

"Okay, I'll see you tomorrow, then."

"Tomorrow? Maggie—you're all gross from class! Are you serious?"

"I'm sure he has a shower. Besides, getting clean is half the fun!" Maggie gave a little cheerleader kick and headed for the front desk, where Jake watched with a mooney expression on his face. Maggie hoisted herself up on the counter and planted a kiss on his cheek.

Hurricane Maggie strikes again, Cora thought.

She zipped up her hoodie and headed out to the street. Their gym was a bargain basement cement box in a seedy part of town, but the instructors were excellent, and Cora didn't need bells and whistles like Olympic-size pools and racquetball. She couldn't bear the thought of putting on makeup and fancy outfits just to work up a sweat.

The spring air was cooler in the darkness. She pulled the hood from her sweatshirt up onto her head.

"Hey, Red Riding Hood! Hey, girl!"

Cora looked around to see local eccentric Joe-Elvis emerge from an alley.

"Hey, Joe! Got a song for me tonight?"

A short, round African American of an indeterminate age, he

knew every single Elvis song ever recorded, and could sing like a human jukebox when asked. He didn't like to maintain eye contact, and he spoke with a slow, stilted delivery. No one knew where he lived—though he always wore a beat-up red windbreaker he didn't seem homeless, since his jeans were always clean and had a grandma-approved seam ironed down the front.

"What do you wanna hear? It's Friday night, where's your man? And where's my dog Fritz? Are you lonesome tonight?" He swayed back and forth as he talked.

"You must be psychic. I'd love to hear that song."

Joe paused to slip into character. He adjusted his stance to mirror the King's famous pose, lifted one arm in the air and sang the first chorus with conviction. He held his pose, and then peered at Cora out of the corner of his eye.

"I *loved* it—that was great!" She burst into applause, ignoring the people staring at the strange tableau as they passed by.

"Thank you, thankyouverymuch," he replied, still in character. Joe spotted a dark figure walking toward them briskly with two dogs and dropped his pose. "Hey," he called out to the man. "Hey, I like your dogs. Can I pet them? Yo, can I pet your dogs?"

The man slowed and pulled off his headphones, an angry expression on his face. "What did you say about my dogs?"

Cora sensed the misunderstanding before Joe did. "We just want to pet your handsome dogs. Is that okay?"

The man relaxed. "Oh, sure."

The muscular steel-gray pit bull and tiny Chihuahua wagged their tails and marched in place, eager for some attention. "Nobody loves dogs more than me. 'Cept maybe her." Joe hooked his

finger toward Cora. "Her boy Fritz looks like this big guy." Joe
knelt between them and placed a hand on each, and the pit bull
rolled onto his back on the sidewalk so Joe could scratch his belly.

"Lookit my big tough guy," the man said ruefully. "You a
killer, huh? Pepito is tougher than you, Beefy."

Cora laughed. "They're quite a duo. Do they like each other?"

"Like?" The man shook his head. "These two are in love.
Brothers from different mothers. They do everything together."

Cora thought of Fritz home alone and felt a pang.

"Allrighty, boys. Let's roll," the man said to his dogs.

"Thank you!" Joe called after the trio as they walked away. He
stood up and brushed off his knees. "Bye, girl, see you next time."

Cora had told Joe her name dozens of times but he never remembered it. "Bye, Joe, see you soon."

Cora arrived home to find Fritz curled up on the floor near
the door. He had three beds scattered throughout the small apartment, but he slept in them only when she was home. Otherwise
he took up the uncomfortable post near the door until Cora came
back.

He woke immediately as she came in but took his time stretching into his own Downward Dog before he walked over to greet
Cora. At eight years old, Fritz was starting to slow down, and
his mellowed greetings were a depressing reminder that her best
friend wasn't going to live forever.

Cora had adopted Fritz from the Humane Rescue Alliance
when he was a rangy teenager, her first dog as a grown-up. She'd
wanted to rename him Cooper to honor the dog that had inspired
her canine career, but she worried that she'd be reminded of that

dog's sad life every time she said his name. There were other ways to remember Cooper. To make sure that no other dogs ended up like him.

Fritz had been underweight from his time on the streets, and his brindle-and-white coat was dull and thin. He had a jaunty patch over his right eye that made him look a little like Petey from *Our Gang*. He'd been at the shelter for a month, and the environment was clearly taking a toll. When people came near his pen he responded by joyfully leaping up and down with an off-putting fervor. The card attached to the front of his pen described him as a stray with a "big personality," shelter code for "out of control." The combination of his square, pit bull face, athletic frame, and wild behavior all but guaranteed him a long stay at the Alliance. Cora fell in love the moment she saw him.

Core knelt by the door in front of Fritz and gentled him closer so that they were face-to-face. She cupped her hands behind his ears and leaned her forehead against his. They meditated together in silence for a few moments, each saying their own little prayer of thanksgiving for the other.

"*Mon amour, mon amour,*" she sang to him under her breath. "*Tu es parfait.* There's no way I'm lonesome tonight because I've got you. Let's walk, baby dog."

FIVE

Cora detoured to Politics & Prose after she finished with her rainy Saturday clients, soaked shoes and growling belly temporarily ignored. Time to stop thinking about thinking about the audition e-mail and actually do something about it. She wasn't ready to make any bold moves yet, but if she could find a book that would convince her that auditioning was easy and fun, and that anyone could do it, then *maybe* she could take the next step. She felt like she needed a sign.

She navigated the shop's narrow aisles, not sure what she was looking for. She passed an Ershovich endcap featuring his best seller and felt like his smug face was mocking her for even thinking about auditioning. How could she go head-to-head with a powerhouse like Ershovich?

But the details in the e-mail attachment that Wade had forwarded intrigued her. The program was going to feature dog-friendly techniques only and use spy camera footage to show what goes on in the typical household after the trainer leaves for the day. Cora often wished she could see what her clients were doing after she headed out at the end of a session. She could tell when people skipped their homework or practiced an exercise the wrong way for an entire week until she came back and worked on it with them. She could envision the spy cam footage of people on the show making typical mistakes, and a funny sports guy voice-over doing a play-by-play of what they should be doing instead, complete with corrective red ink on the screen. *This sounds different,* Cora thought when she reread the e-mail. *This isn't a heavy-handed dictator forcing dogs into submission while the owners stand by applauding. It's a collaboration between the pet parents and the trainer, which is more realistic. Maybe I could be the person they need.*

The store was packed with a mix of older hippies browsing the day away, handsome yuppies with their unruly children, and Georgetown students looking to escape the library. Cora kept her eyes downcast as she passed people. By the end of a four-client day, she was wrung out and tired of using her observational skills. She wanted to find some sort of inspirational "yes, you can do it," Oprah-style book and spend the evening on the couch.

"Hey, I know you!"

That voice made her stop in her tracks. There, not five steps away, stood Charlie Gill, looking as if he'd walked between raindrops.

"Oh my gosh—hey. It's Oliver's person!" It sounded like she had forgotten his name but "CharlieGill! CharlieGill! Charlie-Gill!" echoed in her head like a demented Greek chorus. Cora ran her hand over the top of her wet head, lamenting the frizz surely popping from her thick braid.

"Looks like you worked outside today. You're soaked!" He laughed sympathetically.

Cora did a little curtsy. "Yep. The glamorous life of a dog trainer. I now have raisins for toes." She felt the splotches forming on her neck. *Toes? Why did I bring up my feet?* Cora had planned on putting a little extra effort in her appearance the next time she was due to meet with Charlie and Madison—an ironed shirt and tidy ponytail at least—but here she was looking positively shipwrecked.

"I have an idea—want to warm up and grab some coffee with me downstairs? I actually have about a dozen Oliver questions I'd love to ask you . . . I'm buying."

She felt another splotch bloom near her ear. Coffee with Charlie? Was Madison going to join them? Could Cora use the opportunity to win Madison over so their remaining lessons would be conflict-free? But what if Charlie was alone? Would joining him for coffee be an ethics breach . . . especially because he looked even better than she remembered?

Cora wanted nothing more than to sit across from Charlie with a hot cup of coffee in her hands while a Sinatra-wannabe crooned a movie soundtrack in the background. She let her mind drift for a few moments, lulled by how perfect it would be if he weren't actually her client with a supermodel girlfriend. Maybe their feet would touch accidentally under the table. Maybe he'd laugh at all of her jokes, and tell her that he liked the way her one curl fell right above her eye. She could feel the blush splotch threatening to take over the side of her face.

"I wish I could, but I've got to finish up here and get home. Long day." Cora clung to her honor code even when she hated it.

"Understood," Charlie said, smiling and nodding his head agreeably. "So I'll see you in a few days?"

"Definitely. Good luck with Oliver's homework!" She waved awkwardly and moved away from him quickly, hoping to avoid running into Madison in her waterlogged state.

Cora had a hard time focusing on the books. She kept glancing around the store, trying to catch another glimpse of Charlie so she could study him from afar. What was it about him that unnerved her?

The books in the theater reference section weren't quite what she was looking for. They were too anchored in the intricacies of technique and offering tips for trying to survive as a "working actor." She shuddered. She didn't want to be an actor. She wanted to find a book that would give her the confidence to stand in front of strangers with Maggie's bulletproof self-assurance and Aaron's preening swagger. Even though she knew her dog training stuff, Cora had to admit she was in short supply of both self-assurance and swagger.

When the book titles on the shelves stopped making sense, Cora decided it was time to pack up and go home. One quick turn through the café wouldn't hurt anything, would it?

When she glanced around the room, her eyes were drawn to Charlie in a far corner, his head cradled in his hand, reading intently. There was only one cup of coffee on the table. She watched him for a moment, trying to decide if she should walk over or escape unnoticed. He looked up as though he felt her eyes on him and caught her staring. Her face went scarlet.

"Hi," she mouthed to him, waving again.

"Come sit," he mouthed back, gesturing to the seat across from him.

She shrugged and threaded her way through the crowd to him.

"Change your mind? Sit down, let's chat." He started arranging his belongings to make room for her.

"No, no, I really shouldn't." She looked down at the magazines in front of him, and he followed her gaze.

"It's all car stuff. I'm looking for a new car and wanted to read up. Now that we've got Oliver my Bimmer ain't going to cut it. And you can bet he's never going to set foot in Madison's little TT."

"You're buying a car just for Oliver? That's awesome! What kind?"

"I've pretty much decided on a Range Rover. Can't you picture it? Me and the O-man, rolling in our Rover?" He pantomimed being behind the wheel. "You can come for a spin with us!"

If Madison didn't exist, that might have sounded like a prelude to a date. Despite their professional arrangement, it still felt like the invitation was leaning more toward pleasure than business. She decided to clear up any confusion. "That would be fun, we could work on his car manners. Oliver's a lucky dog, you're really looking out for him."

"Yup, he's gonna be a baller in his new car. Hey, I'm excited for our next session. And of course Oliver is, too. He was totally in love with you."

"The feeling was mutual." Cora's face burned. *Were these double entendres?*

Charlie slammed his palm on the table, startling Cora. "I almost forgot! I meant to e-mail you after you left last week to tell you that Madison is going to be away for the next few weeks on an assignment. So it's going to be just you and me. Is that all right?"

"Yup," she sqeaked. "It's fine, it's great! I mean, it's better to have the entire household take part in training, but that's not always possible. We'll be fine. It's okay. Is she upset about missing it?" Cora was babbling.

"Yeah, she seemed like she didn't want me doing it alone, but I don't want to wait until she comes back—too much time for the O-man to forget his lessons."

"That makes sense. Okay. Cool," Cora answered. She knew she needed to make her face look normal but she couldn't stop grinning. "Anyway, I've got to head out, I'm sure my dog is sitting by the door with his legs crossed. You know how that goes."

"Actually I don't. Oliver pees whenever the mood strikes."

"I guess we need to focus on potty training next time!"

"Please. And is it okay if I text you with questions in between sessions? I promise I won't pester you, just once in a while."

"No problem, of course." There was no way that Charlie Gill could ever pester her. She pulled her cell phone out of her back pocket and tried to keep her fingers from trembling as she entered his number.

SIX

Cora arrived home to find Maggie and Fritz sprawled on the couch together, TV blaring. Fritz leaped from his perch to greet Cora, nailing Maggie in the gut as he dismounted. "Oof, dog! I'm gonna need a kidney transplant someday thanks to you!"

Fritz and Maggie were fast friends, and their bond made Cora love Maggie a little more, if that was even possible. Maggie was the sister Cora had always wanted—the perfect mix of partner in crime, cheerleader, sympathetic ear, and court jester. Cora was still slightly in awe that this petite force of nature allowed her into her orbit. Maggie was a postmodern pinup feminist, with the allure of Monroe tempered by the convictions of Steinem.

They had met at The Tombs in Georgetown four years ago while Cora was waiting for Aaron to finish a round of darts. Maggie was sitting at the bar trying to get the bartender's attention while ignoring an unsteady baseball-capped frat guy pushing up to her. Cora happened to be standing behind the guy and eavesdropped as he got to work.

"You're cute," he slurred to Maggie. "But you'd be so much cuter if you didn't have that thing on your arm." He ran his finger down her intricate elbow-to-shoulder mermaid tattoo.

Maggie pouted prettily. "You don't like Esther? I got her after I finished working as a mermaid in the Weeki Wachee show in Florida. She's very special to me."

The guy ignored Maggie's obvious opening to talk about mermaids and opted to insult her again. "Florida, huh? Most Florida people are white trash, but you're not so bad." He eyed Maggie from head to toe.

Cora picked up on what he was doing right away—cutting Maggie down with backhanded compliments to weaken her confidence and make her more open to his advances.

Maggie giggled. "Thank you!" She seemed oblivious, but her manner verged on sitcom southern belle, all flirty shoulders and fluttery hands. It was too much, too over-the-top. Couldn't the guy see that she was playing him?

"So what brings you to Georgetown? You here to try to score a rich guy?"

"Maybe . . ." She lowered her head and looked up at him through her lashes. This woman was candy-coated poison. "Is that what you are?"

Cora held her breath as the guy laughed and leaned in closer. *This is going to be good.*

"Or are you a prick who thinks negging is cool?" Maggie's demeanor changed from boozy flirt to strident in an instant. "Listen, fucker, I *graduated* from Georgetown and I just got accepted to Yale to get my MFA, so why don't you move on with your pickup artist bullshit, okay? You are a *douche!*" She cupped her hands around her mouth and shouted into the crowd. "Hey, ladies, be careful, this guy is a pickup artist loser!"

Maggie was attracting attention, the guy was grabbing at her menacingly, and Cora wasn't sure what was about to happen, so she stepped forward.

"There you are!" she playacted. "Come on, let's go!" She took Maggie's hand and threaded her through the crowded bar.

When they reached an open area near the men's bathroom Cora turned to Maggie. "I heard everything he said and you were awesome! But I didn't want it to get out of hand—he looked like he wanted to punch you."

"Seriously, right?" She shook her head. "Anyway, thanks for saving me."

Cora cocked her head. "I hate to pry . . . I heard pretty much everything you said . . . was *any* of that true?"

Maggie laughed. "What, I don't look like a Hoya to you? All of it is true, right down to the Weeki Wachee mermaid gig. I'm a theater major and I can play a pretty convincing idiot when I have to."

They spent the rest of the evening huddled together trading stories and laughing until their stomachs hurt. Skipping past the awkward new-friendship courtship dance, they progressed immediately to BFFs, becoming roommates six months later.

"It's on in ten minutes," Maggie said, pulling Cora from her reverie.

"What is?"

"Look at you, ignoring the obvious. Aaron's show, *America's Hottest Landscaper.*"

Cora had resisted researching the show for a week, staying true to her total Aaron blackout. When she finally gave in—at a year and a half post-breakup she felt she could handle it—she was pleased that she could find only the show's description and cast bios. It seemed that *America's Hottest Landscaper* would debut to little fanfare, which meant that she wouldn't have to watch the rest of the world fall in love with her ex. The twelve contestants fit all the reality show stereotypes: the underdog, the hot girl, the grizzled veteran, the sweet mom, the party boy, the spoiled brat, the fish out of water, the out and proud guy, and on and on until Aaron's category.

The dreamboat.

Aaron had his shirt off in his bio photo. The photographer had caught him mid-dig with a shovel so his arm muscles popped from the exertion. His dark hair was spiked up with sweat. His tanned face was turned toward the camera, and he grinned directly at it, as if he saw his best friend behind the lens. He looked friendly, happy, and absolutely heart-stoppingly beautiful. Bastard.

Cora joined Maggie and Fritz on the couch in their tiny family room. Her friend reached for her hand.

"You okay with this?"

Cora sighed. "Do I have a choice? I feel like I'm going to vomit. But better to see it than wonder about it, I guess."

The show unfolded in typical reality show fashion, with an upbeat adult contemporary theme song, quick cuts of the cast, and the introduction of the female host. Cora felt clammy the moment she saw Aaron. She watched him and exhaled slowly, like someone trying to calm down after a scare. Seeing her ex-fiancé in pictures was one thing, but seeing him in action, smiling and laughing and captivating everyone around him, made her head hurt. And her heart.

"This is what theater has become." Maggie sighed. "We watch each other do lawn work and go on dates and buy houses and flip tables on television. It's gross. I'm so glad I opted out."

Cora didn't reply. Maggie's "opting out" of her acting career was more a matter of never truly pursuing it. She was obscenely talented but lacked drive. She'd fallen into a part-time job at Saks that turned full-time and decided to stick with it, always making vague threats to chuck it all and move to New York or Hollywood. In the meantime she turned the sales floor into her stage, performing her butt off for the dowagers and dot-com wives to bring in better commissions.

"It's insane, but he wanted this so badly. I can't believe he actually made it happen," Cora said.

Maggie snorted. "A reality show? This was Aaron's big dream? So much for finishing his degree."

"He didn't say he wanted to be on a reality show, but he said he wanted to be famous. That was his end game—being famous. Didn't matter how. He *loves* to have people watching him. TV makes perfect sense." Cora waited a beat. "Wouldn't it be weird if I got on TV, too?"

Maggie threw her a perplexed look.

"You know my clients Wade and Rachel with the twins and the golden puppy? He e-mailed me about this new dog training show that's being cast and he thinks I should audition."

"Oh my God, you totally should!" Maggie screamed, waking

Fritz from his snoring slumber. "Wouldn't it be amazing if you could take out the doggy dickhole? You'd be perfect!"

"You really think so? There's a tiny part of me that wants to try, but you know I don't have that Aaron gene. The concept of being on TV freaks me out. But *somebody* needs to show people you can train dogs without hurting them."

"Yeah, and that somebody might be you. I think you'd be awesome, C. I can totally help you find your TV gene."

"We'll see," Cora answered cryptically, still warming up to the idea.

America's Hottest Landscaper was a new low in the world of reality programming, in Cora's honest opinion. The show's initial challenge involved a mulch installation, and the resulting close-ups of the contestants sweating, grunting, and grimacing coupled with the gritty soundtrack made it look like soft-core porn. The episode mainly revolved around Aaron's abs and Carly the hot girl's cleavage and it was clear that the editors wanted viewers to pick up on the simmering sexual tension between the duo. Carly was platinum blond, Aaron's favorite. He loved to tell Cora that she was an exception, since her hair color was three shades darker than what he normally went for.

Aaron won the challenge, and the attractive host ascended the steaming pile of mulch to congratulate him and ask him about his strategy. Cora was numb to the effects of seeing him on screen by the end of the program, more in awe of the train wreck of a show he was on.

"Tell us how you did it, Aaron," the host bubbled. "How did you move this mountain of mulch in just three and a half minutes?"

Aaron paused to wipe the sweat from his forehead with the back of his hand like a hardworking everyman. "Well, Brittany, I just gave it my all. I didn't expect to have such a fierce competitor in Andy," he said gesturing to the openly gay contestant. He turned back to the camera and lisped, "He's a skinny little f***—I didn't think he had any heavy lifting in him. Well, except for . . . you know . . ." He smiled his golden boy smile and elbowed Brittany. The camera cut to Andy, who stood a few feet away with an unguarded look of shock on his face. The word was bleeped, but there was no doubt about what he'd said.

Maggie and Cora turned to each other, agog.

"Holy shit, your ex-fiancé just made a gay slur on national television. He is going *down* the hard way."

SEVEN

Fran Channing asked Cora to hold their third lesson at her Old Town Alexandria office, as Sydney often accompanied Fran to work despite his less than stellar manners. Cora was excited that she'd finally be able to match a career with the woman she so admired.

Cora's phone pinged nonstop during the drive. Sixteen new texts, all about Aaron's embarrassing TV debut. "He looked gud but cnt belve wht he said!!!" and "R u ok? Did it make u sad to c him??" and "Better off w/out him!" Even her technophobe mother weighed in with a typically verbose text. "Hi honey. I watched the show and I can't believe what Aaron said. I'm worried about you. Are you ok? Love, Mom." The support helped. Watching his flirting from a distance brought back some of the old hurts she'd buried, even if the result was the firm conclusion that he was an asshole.

She found Fran's office on a quiet side street lined with cherry trees about to burst into bloom. The brick building was a small, re-purposed factory with the ghost of the former tenant's decades-old logo still visible on the side. When Cora saw the tall red letters on the front of the building, Fran's immaculately styled home made sense: The International Association of Boutique Lodging.

Cora entered the airy foyer and was met by four unmarked doors. She tried the first one—locked. The second one opened, and she found herself peering into a room filled with cubicles. No one looked up as she entered, and no one came forward to help her, so she backed out quietly. Flustered and fearing she was late, she speed walked to the third door and barged in right as a blur of a human was coming out.

"Sorry, sorry," the blur cried as he ran by her. "Gotta catch the UPS guy!"

Cora saw a secretary sitting at a desk just beyond the door and hoped that she was finally in the right place. Then, she heard the distant jangling of dog tags and knew that she was. Sydney rounded the corner like he was chasing a breakaway sheep and came to an immediate sit in front of her the moment he saw Cora's crossed arms. The dog was equal parts heart and brain, and she adored working with him.

"Would you look at that? Look at my good boy!" Fran's voice echoed down the hallway as she trotted out to meet Cora, her Asian-inspired silk duster trailing behind her. Fran turned to the secretary. "Lydia, do you see that? I *told* you he's a genius! Now if we could only do something about his leash walking . . ."

Cora and Sydney followed Fran into her expansive office, which had the same vibe as her home: clean lines, stark styling, and nothing out of place. Cora took a seat next to Sydney on the ground and leaned against the wall, hoping that the dirty paw prints on her shirt from her last jumpy client wouldn't transfer onto the pearl-colored wall.

"Darling, I'm sorry I'm so frazzled today! There's been drama with one of our properties. Have you seen the blogs? We've been Tweeting up a storm about it."

"I've been with clients all morning—what did I miss?"

"There's this horrid new reality competition, and honestly, what reality show *isn't* horrid, and one of the contestants called another contestant an unforgivable slur—don't make me repeat it, darling—and made some insinuation about gay sex. Who does that?" Fran rolled her eyes dramatically. "Anyway, it turns out that the show was shooting at the Hamish Hotel, and the owner, Roland Gibson, got wind of what the idiot said. Well, Roland is a force of nature, so he put a stop to the production right in the middle of it. Stormed the set and threw them out! Heroic of him, if you ask me. From what I hear, it was a miracle they could cut the premiere from the footage they got."

Cora knew what was coming the moment Fran said the word *reality*. She had a feeling that Aaron's comments would raise some eyebrows but she never imagined that he would be responsible for a Tweet storm about equality and gay rights.

Cora looked down at Sydney, who had rolled onto his back and was swatting her hand to encourage more belly rubs. "I have to tell you something. I don't want to but I can't *not* tell you now that you brought it up." Cora exhaled. "This is really . . . I don't know what to call it. Embarrassing? Horrifying?"

Fran pulled her glasses farther down her nose and peered at Cora.

"I know that guy from the reality show, Aaron. I was actually, um . . . I was engaged to him about eighteen months ago."

Fran stared at Cora for a few seconds, openmouthed. It was scary to see her shocked into silence.

"Oh my dear girl. Oh no. *Really?*"

Cora nodded her head sheepishly, as if his sin was suddenly hers.

"I don't know what to say, darling. This must be very uncomfortable for you on several levels."

"Honestly, I haven't given it a lot of thought. It was bizarre seeing him on TV, and what he said was awful, but I just sort of . . . put it out of my head. That's how I deal with stuff. I can't believe that he's even on TV—I'm just coming to terms with *that*, and now based on what you're telling me, it sounds like he's going to be everywhere. I don't know how to process it. Plus, I'm mortified that I was with someone who would say something so awful."

"Want my advice? Just keep it to yourself then. You don't need to insert yourself into his public shaming. He's a mistake from your past, and now he's dealing with his own mistake. You have no part in this—it's obviously not your fault, and he is not your responsibility. Okay? So let's move on, darling . . ."

Cora was grateful to end the conversation quickly. "Thank you, Fran. It seems like you have a lot to take care of today, so why don't we leash up and get outside?"

Fran turned to dig through her oversize bag for the leash, and Cora leaned in closer to Sydney, pushing his unruly bangs out of his eyes.

"*Mon petit monster,*" she whispered to him so that Fran couldn't hear her. "Are you going to be a good boy today?" Sydney tilted his head at her, as if considering the question. "Are you ready to learn some stuff?" Cora smiled at him, regarding the dog like a mischievous kindergartener, then cupped his head in her hands and planted a kiss on his forehead. She noticed a figure out of the corner of her eye and turned to find the lanky UPS-chaser watching her with a half-smile on his face. Cora went scarlet, sheepish that her pep talk with Sydney had a witness.

Fran's voice rang out. "Well, hello, Eli! Cora Bellamy, please meet Eli Crawford. Cora is helping me train my naughty boy, and Eli helps me train my naughty computer."

"Also known as an IT manager. Sorry to interrupt your conversation with Sydney. It looked important." Eli nodded at the dog and walked toward Cora. Sydney jumped up and ran to greet him, blocking Eli's path so that he had to acknowledge the dog before he got to Cora. Eli gave in to Sydney's demands, and didn't seem to care when the dog playfully nipped at his pant legs as he walked toward Cora.

"Just going over some last-minute tips before we get started." She struggled to stand, and Eli offered his hand in greeting as well as to help her up. Cora was impressed that he could focus on her completely, smiling reassuringly, while preventing Sydney from jumping on him.

"What can I do for you, Eli?" Fran asked.

"I just wanted to chat with you about the upcoming phone migration . . . do you have time later?"

Cora watched them as they discussed their schedules in a friendly shorthand. Eli was a head taller than Fran, but he leaned against the edge of Fran's desk so that he didn't tower over her as they negotiated. Sydney threaded between them as they talked, soliciting pats from Eli as he scrolled through his calendar. He made an indecipherable inside joke as they finalized their meeting time, and Fran doubled over with laughter.

Eli turned to leave and Sydney escorted him to the door. He leaned down and whispered something in the dog's ear.

"I talk to dogs, too." He winked at Cora and walked out of the room.

EIGHT

Cora's dog trainer friends were nearing the bottom of their first round of drinks by the time she arrived at their monthly gathering. Even though they called themselves The Boozehounds, they rarely made it to a third drink. Winnifred, the older Earth Mother dog trainer with butt-length white hair, was telling an animated story when Cora walked in, her gauzy sleeves dragging across the table every time she gestured. Vanessa, a stunning African American newbie trainer who was apprenticing with Winnie, was watching her teacher with her typical rapt expression, as if trying to absorb every bit of her wisdom. It was impossible to look at the varied trio of women and guess what drew them together, unless you looked close enough to see the dog hair on their clothes.

"Let's start with the gossip. Anyone have any juicy stuff going on? Cora, you want to talk about the Aaron stuff?" Winnie asked, assuming her role as the unofficial ringleader of the group.

"*Absolutely* not. Pass." Cora was doing her best to continue filtering Aaron from her life, but his comments had turned him into the handsome villain everyone loved to hate. Vanessa was probably dying for Cora to spill insider gossip about Aaron, since she lived for reality television.

"I'll let Winnie give you our updates. She's a better storyteller anyway," Vanessa answered with a shrug. She and Winnie trained in tandem until her apprenticeship was complete.

Cora considered asking them if they'd ever had a crush on a client, but kept her mouth shut. She didn't want to give voice to what was rattling around in the dark parts of her brain.

"So did any of you see the Animal Asshole last night?" Winnie asked, slamming her empty mug on the table. The group always tried to make each other laugh with alternate names for Boris Ershovich.

"It was awful," Vanessa replied.

"I didn't watch," Cora said. "What happened?"

Winnie pretended to gag. "Oh, the usual choking, kicking, hanging, and yelling, all gussied up to look like dog training. It was a young dog—a *really* young dog. I had to turn it off."

Cora shook her head. "It makes me want to throw up. Why can't people see that he's abusing those dogs?"

"If it's on TV, it has someone's blessing, right? If it's on TV, it has to be okay. We should make them do one of those disclaimers at the beginning of the show; 'using these techniques may cause your dog to freak the fuck out, bite people, cause property damage, develop redirected aggression, blah, blah, blah,'" Vanessa said.

"But what can we do to stop him? Aside from Cora's wonderful blog that she won't let anyone read and protest letters to the network, we're powerless to do anything," Winnie said.

Maybe this was her moment to tell her friends about the possibility of auditioning for her own show. But she didn't want pressure from them clouding her decision-making process. She stared at her mug.

"Spill it, Cora. You know something you're not saying. What is it?" Winnie's observational skills never turned off, even after a few drinks.

Cora took a swig of beer to buy a few seconds before she answered. "There's a casting call for a new dog training show. I'm thinking about auditioning."

"What?!" Vanessa shouted.

"Thank you, Jesus, we have a voice!" Winnie exclaimed, raising her hands to the ceiling.

"Whoa, there! I said I was *thinking* about it."

Winnie studied Cora's face. "Do you want to do it?"

Vanessa and Winnie stared at Cora. The scrutiny was intense.

"I don't know. Maybe. I mean, my rational brain is a hundred percent against it. You know I hate being the center of attention. But my heart . . . there's something telling me to go for it."

"If I were done apprenticing I'd do it in a heartbeat," Vanessa said. "This face?" she pointed to herself. "Ratings, baby!"

Winnie shook her head. "That ship has sailed for me. And even if I weren't a hundred years old I don't think I could put myself out there like that. People can be brutal. But you should definitely do it."

Cora thought of Aaron. His TV trajectory was a cautionary tale, and one that made Cora feel less confident about pursuing the show. She would never say anything as spectacularly awful as

Aaron had, but Cora knew that standing up to Ershovich would make her chum for his brainwashed supporters. She feared the backlash that would inevitably come. There were hundreds of opinions about Aaron on Twitter, less than a day later, the slur (#freespeech), what he meant by it (#homophobe), what he looked like (#smokin), if he was in fact gay (#closetcase), how stupid he seemed (#bagofhammers), and how people felt about the show (#fireaaron). Cora almost felt sorry for him.

Winnie placed her hand on top of Cora's and brought her back into the moment. "Clarity will come to you. Don't force it."

"You would be amazing, Cora. You've got to at least try out. For the dogs. And for me, so I can come visit you on the set," Vanessa said.

The three of them sat in silence, contemplating what it would mean if she decided to pursue the opportunity.

"Whatever you decide, we're here for you," Vanessa said. Then she threw her hand up to catch the bartender's attention. "Another round for the Hounds, please!"

NINE

Charlie Gill Day.

Cora tried to pretend like it was any other lesson, but she took a few extra minutes getting ready, pressing her apple-green logo shirt that complemented her eyes, wearing her most flattering jeans, and taming her waves before braiding her hair.

"Are you wearing *mascara*?" Maggie asked accusingly as Cora got ready.

"I don't know . . . ," Cora answered, using a jokey teenager voice thick with vocal fry, hoping to deflect the question. She hadn't told Maggie about Charlie Gill. Cora loved nearly everything about Maggie, but she didn't appreciate her cavalier attitude about poaching men. Maggie had had an affair with a married professor while she was in college, and she had occasional dalliances with guys in relationships. Cora was sure Maggie would push her to cross the professional boundaries she worked so hard to maintain. Plus, there was no reason to mention him. He was just a handsome client, nothing more. A very handsome, charismatic, kind, funny client that kept popping into Cora's head uninvited.

Fritz rolled onto his back to expose his freckled pink stomach as Cora dashed by, his catfish mouth grinning and his tail thumping a Morse code invitation on the hardwood floor. Fritz knew that no matter how pressed for time she was, Cora always responded to his entreaties for belly rubs. She bent over and gave the naked part of his stomach a few quick scratches.

Cora sped out the door in the haze, ignoring Maggie's demands for clarification. She checked her face in the rearview mirror as she navigated the end of the morning rush hour, not surprised to find a preemptive red blotch forming on the side of her neck. *Be cool, be cool, this is no big deal,* she told herself. *It's all about Oliver. We've got lots to accomplish with that little dog!* Cora wanted to make sure that Oliver's behavior was extra polished so that Madison would be impressed when she returned home.

Charlie and Oliver were outside on the front step when she arrived. Charlie was in a dark suit and jaunty orange-striped tie, leaning back against the stairs with his eyes closed and his face turned up to the sun, his hands clasped behind his head. Oliver sat next to him and chewed on his leash contentedly, using his fat puppy paws to clasp it with surprising dexterity. They were even cuter than Cora remembered.

"Hey, guys!" Cora called out. "Are you ready to work, or are you taking a nap?"

"Oliver, look who's here—it's your teacher!" Charlie straightened himself and grinned at Cora. "We are so ready for this lesson. Like, beyond ready." Oliver strained at the end of the leash, trying to reach Cora, making high-pitched whining noises. "Wow, someone has a major crush on you!"

Which someone are you talking about? she wondered. "Eager students are my favorite," she replied, trying to keep her voice steady while her stomach flip-flopped. "Let's start with a leash walk." She didn't want to go inside with him alone. She needed fresh air and the bleach of sunshine to sanitize the thoughts running through her head every time he looked at her.

Cora explained the mechanics of loose leash walking while Oliver dashed around them, investigating every inch of the world as only a puppy can. The sidewalks were empty on the quaint street near Charlie's house, but Oliver still managed to get distracted by every scent molecule that drifted by. When Cora took the leash from Charlie after watching his staccato attempt at walking Oliver, their hands grazed accidentally and sent a jolt up Cora's arm. She refocused and demonstrated how if she occasionally rewarded the dog with a small treat for walking near her without pulling, he would eventually choose to fall in line beside her, awaiting more goodies instead of pulling like a sled dog. The beginning stages of the lesson were easy but dramatic enough to make Cora look like a magician.

"This makes so much sense!" Charlie said. "Madison made me watch that awful Boris dog training show, and it was insane, like a church revival but with dog training. She still doesn't get it that we're not training the O-man like that. The dogs on the show looked miserable, he looked angry, and the whole thing was depressing to me. If you watch the dogs it's obvious they're hating every minute."

Boris Ershovich's TV show was shot in front of a live audience in various venues throughout the country, and there was indeed a religious fervor about them. He packed his audiences with acolytes that cheered and applauded madly any time he gestured to himself or the dog he was training. Many of the audience members brought homemade signs with sayings like BORIS IS FOR US on them. They waited in lines after the show for autographs and photos. Ershovich was every inch the celebrity dog trainer, and he seemed to care more about his fame than about the dogs he was supposedly helping.

"I love that you picked up on those points," Cora exclaimed, regretting the word *love* the second it came out of her mouth. "Ershovich's approach is outdated and really cruel. I always tell people to listen to their gut when it comes to training—if it doesn't feel right to choke your dog, don't do it!" *The way I train always feels right*, Cora thought. *I want people to know that.*

"How you train feels right to me." Charlie paused. "Did you hear he's coming to DC?"

Cora stopped in her tracks and turned to face Charlie. "Are you *serious*?" The show had crisscrossed the country over the years, never coming close enough for Cora to feel territorial. Now Boris Ershovich was bringing his black art to her backyard.

"Yeah, I saw it on my Facebook feed. He's live streaming the first fifteen minutes of it. Madison wants me to go to the show. I can't believe that she still likes him after everything you taught us last time! No way I'm going—I got my *own* dog trainer." He smiled and put his hand on Cora's shoulder, and she felt her neck blush bloom. "Plus I'd never hear the end of it at work."

Cora jumped on the opportunity to ask him about his career. Totally within bounds, since Charlie had brought it up first. "What do you mean?"

"I guess it's time I tell you what I do. I usually keep it quiet because the second it comes up the conversation gets ugly. I tell people I meet at parties that I'm an accountant."

"Now I'm scared to ask. Are you a hit man or something?"

He laughed. "No, you of all people will appreciate it. It's an intense job, and I love it, but I need to be able to turn it off sometimes. I'm general counsel for the Animal Legal Protection Foundation. We're a group that—"

"The nonprofit?" Cora interrupted him. "You're basically animal welfare superheroes! I read all about that horse-drawn carriage case in New York . . . you saved those horses."

"So you're familiar with my work."

"I donate to the ALPF every year. I'm in *awe* of you," Cora said, not holding back now. It was totally acceptable to crush on his job. "Can I get your autograph? You're seriously like a rock star to me."

Charlie chuckled and reached down to pet Oliver, who was lying on his side, chewing on a stick. "Hardly. But yes, it's a phenomenal organization, and I'm really proud to work there."

The three of them walked on, and Cora considered this new piece of the Charlie Gill puzzle. Was he trying to be irresistible?

"So are you allowed to tell me what you're working on?"

Charlie furrowed his brow. "This one is really tough. We're dealing with a roadside attraction bear that lives outside a restaurant in a cage. He eats whatever people throw to him—lots of candy and french fries and crap like that—and he hasn't been out of the cage in years. He looks half dead. The owner refuses to relinquish him, so we're going over his head and suing the state department of wildlife for issuing the guy a permit to exhibit the bear. It's a mess."

"Do you think you're going to get the bear out?"

"No question. I never lose."

"That confidence has to count for something," Cora replied.

"I'm serious. I pretty much always get my way." He looked at her out of the corner of his eye and smiled.

The comment felt loaded. Cora sidestepped. "Well, the animals are lucky to have you in their corner."

She realized that the lesson had taken an abrupt turn from business to pleasure, so she refocused on Charlie's leash technique. "You guys are getting it! Really nice work."

"Thanks, but I'm not the one you have to worry about," he replied, looking grim again. "I hate that Madison is missing training. We Skype every night, and she seems a little weird about all of this." He gestured broadly.

"Oh, she's concerned that he's not going to respond to her when she gets back?"

"That, and . . . well, I think she's a little . . . jealous . . . of you. She said you were cuter than she thought you'd be."

Cora tried to laugh it off, but it came out as an awkward high-pitched choke. "What? Oh my God! No. That's so crazy! Seriously? Oh my God, she's *gorgeous*! I'm just . . . just a dumb dog trainer."

"Please, Cora. You're a miracle worker—look at my dog!" Oliver was walking perfectly in step beside them. "And forgive me for saying this, but you're the total package. Seriously."

His compliment hung in the air between them. Cora opened her mouth to respond, wanting to thank him but not sure what words were going to come out. She hoped that he'd go on and explain which specific parts of the package he liked best. But she forced herself to focus on Oliver instead.

"Now this dog *here* is the total package! Look how great he's doing!"

Charlie noticed her dodge and responded in kind. "Yup, that's my boy! I'm so proud of you, Ollie-by-golly!"

By then they had reached Charlie's front gate. "I feel bad," Cora said, "we took up the entire session leash walking and we didn't have a chance to work on any inside stuff. Do you have a few minutes to go over 'stay'?"

"Actually I don't today, but I already know that I want to do more than just your standard five sessions, so no worries. We've got tons to do together, Cora."

More time with Charlie Gill and his adorable puppy. It didn't feel like work, but she needed to keep it strictly business, despite what was starting to percolate below the surface of their interactions. She'd handled boundary-pushing clients before, bored middle-aged dads and diplomats' lazy sons. But none of them, not even the very handsome and very married restaurateur who offered to prepare oysters for her in his Georgetown brasserie after-hours, had ever taken up residence in her thoughts the way Charlie Gill had.

TEN

Cora's ancient hand-me-down Volvo shuddered to a stop in front of the new high-rise just outside Old Town. The building looked like it wouldn't be out of place among the skyscrapers of New York, which made it stick out in quaint Alexandria. She was back in Virginia to meet with Beth Ann Devlin, a new client referred by Fran Channing. The dog in question was a year-old miniature poodle named Chanel that was barking at every noise in the hallway, a problem with no easy solution in a busy building, and on top of that, Cora's initial phone conversation with Beth Ann had been stilted and awkward, not a good sign.

She called Beth Ann when she was in the lobby, per her instructions. The call went to voice mail—Cora could barely hear Beth Ann's message over the pounding dance music in the background—so she typed out a quick text as well. When she didn't get an immediate reply, she took a seat on one of the fierce-looking wood-and-steel benches arranged in the lobby. It was an upscale, modern building with a disinterested young security guard and few defining features other than the gleaming marble floor and modern art on the walls that looked like neon honeycomb. The formality of the building made Cora feel like she was getting ready for a job interview, and her stomach flip-flopped reflexively. She would've rather been in Wade's cozy kitchen, or even Fran's posh living room, than in the unwelcoming skyscraper.

She was pondering Charlie's compliment for the millionth time when she heard someone call her name. "Cora, is that you?" She looked up and saw the Human Blur from Fran's office standing in front of her.

"Oh, hey! You're . . . Evan, right?"

"Close—Eli Crawford. Nice to see you again! I was hoping I'd run in to you today."

Cora was confused. "Wait, how did you know I'd be here?"

"I see Fran didn't tell you. Beth Ann is my neighbor down the hall, and I'm the reason you're here today. Chanel's barking is driving everyone on our floor insane, so I told Beth Ann to get in touch with you. I've never even met the dog, but she's made quite the impression on me." Cora remembered Beth Ann's rushed introduction on the phone, and that she had mentioned the hotel association but had mumbled something unintelligible after it. Cora had just assumed that Fran was the one who had referred her.

"Well, thank you for thinking of me! That's so nice of you." Cora looked down at her phone. "We were supposed to meet fifteen minutes ago, and I called and texted her but I haven't heard back. I might be getting 'porched.'"

Eli looked at Cora questioningly. "Porched?"

"Yeah, that's when you make an appointment with someone

and they don't show up—you end up sitting on their porch. Or in this case I guess I'm being 'lobbied.' "

"It's funny how every industry has its own buzzwords. I love that insider stuff. What are some other secrets?" He sat down on the narrow bench next to her.

"Umm . . . you put me on the spot, so of course I can't think of anything good right now!" said Cora, startled he actually wanted to keep her company while she waited. "How about the hotel world? What are some of your industry secrets?" There, back on solid footing, shifting the conversation away from herself.

"*Boutique* hotel. There is a difference."

While Eli launched into an animated overview of what qualified as a boutique hotel, and why the distinction was so important, Cora took the opportunity to study him. Tall and scarecrow-skinny, he was wearing a cornflower-blue button-down shirt with the sleeves rolled up and heavy canvas dress pants. His pants were narrow and slightly cropped, exposing navy argyle socks and scuffed bowling-style shoes. Cora couldn't tell if his geek-chic look was calculated or accidental. He was a tweed cap and vest away from a *Newsies* costume, but she supposed it worked for him.

"When we have more time, remind me to tell you about 'key bombing.' And did you know that you should never drink out of those glasses that are in your room at big chain hotels? They've got those little paper hats on so you *think* they're clean, but they don't actually wash them! They use"—he paused to let her curiosity build—"furniture polish! How disgusting is that?"

"Um, it's horrifying, because I drink out of them all the time."

Cora hid a grin, amused by the way Eli didn't just tell a story, but actually *lived* it as he spoke, gesturing dramatically like an actor.

"And you'll never guess what's all over ninety percent of the TV remotes in hotel rooms." The words were coming out quickly, as if he couldn't keep up with his thoughts.

"No clue."

"Urine and semen."

His words hung in the air for a moment before Cora burst out laughing.

"Wait, did I just say that?" Eli asked himself. "Did I really just say the word *semen* to you? Oh my God, I am the *worst*." He leaned back against the wall and stared at the ceiling.

"I get it, humans are gross, that's why I hang with dogs," Cora said, trying to ease Eli's embarrassment. She glanced down at her phone again and was surprised at how quickly the time had passed in his company. "Wow, she's over twenty minutes late. It's time for me to hit the road—"

"Not so fast," Eli said quietly, staring across the lobby.

Cora followed his gaze to a young woman staggering toward them, loaded down with shopping bags. Her dyed blond hair had what looked like a days-old blowout that was starting to go greasy at the roots. Attractive in a slightly puffy, too-much-makeup kind of way, she wore gold mirrored leather high-tops, tight jeans that emphasized her thick legs, and an expensive-looking chunky white sweater coat that was too warm for the temperate spring day.

"Are you Cora? You must be Cora. I'm so sorry I'm late!"

"Hi, Beth Ann. I was just about to leave, I thought you forgot about our lesson. We're really behind schedule, and I have another client booked right after you, so we can get started on Q and A and paperwork, but I have to leave on time." Cora had little patience for people who didn't respect her time. Plus, she noticed a blinged-out phone in Beth Ann's hand. She had her phone and didn't even have the common courtesy to text that she was running late.

Beth Ann furrowed her brow. "Okay, okay, that's fine. Let's hurry then." She turned to face Eli. "Thanks for helping with this."

Eli stood a few feet away, watching the women trade soft jabs. "My pleasure." He turned to Cora. "The entire eleventh floor thanks you in advance. And I'm glad that you weren't lobbied." He bowed, turned on his heel, and walked toward the door.

Cora followed Beth Ann to the elevator, trying to focus on her new client's disjointed monologue while digesting her thoughts about Eli.

"So what should I do about that?" Beth Ann asked.

Cora hadn't heard a word Beth Ann had said. She defaulted to her standard answer. "I think we have our work cut out for us!" The elevator opened, and Cora heard Chanel's keening barks and yowls the moment she stepped into the hallway.

Beth Ann turned to her and shrugged. "My baby doesn't like it when I leave."

The intensity of Chanel's barking put Cora on edge. She was overly sensitive to dogs going through trauma, and she could tell that what she was hearing wasn't just separation discomfort. The barks intensified as they got closer to Beth Ann's door and reached operatic heights when the key hit the lock.

Beth Ann opened the door to her small, dark apartment.

"There's my baby! Momma's home now! Yes, here I am!" Chanel panted and leaped at the pair as they walked in.

Cora had seen her fair share of unkempt dogs in her day, but Chanel was something to behold. The tiny yellow-white dog had dark tear stains that spread from the corners of her blackberry eyes to the tip of her nose. Her fur was matted tightly in some spots and patchy in others. The dog's nails were so long that some of them had started to curl under. Beth Ann had told her that Chanel was a purebred toy poodle with champion lines from a local pet store, which didn't seem possible, given the dog's un-missable underbite and wonky ears. She also knew that the store in question was known for passing off puppy mill puppies as dogs of distinction with "papers." People were so proud to say their dog was "AKC-registered," but Cora knew that high-volume for-profit breeders who kept their dogs in squalor could easily get papers, and that having a "registered" dog was no guarantee of anything other than a steep price tag.

Cora knelt down to pet Chanel, and the trembling dog urinated a small puddle.

"Oh wow, she really had to go," Cora said, looking up at Beth Ann. "Let's get her outside quickly before we start."

"I'll just take her to the balcony to save time," Beth Ann answered as she scooped up Chanel. Cora watched Beth Ann wind her way through stacks of boxes around the apartment, plop the dog on the balcony and shut the door.

"So she's . . . balcony trained? She knows to potty out there?"

"Sort of. She kinda pees wherever she wants!" Beth Ann gestured to the floor, which was dotted with dark stains.

"Okay, so I guess I should add potty training to the list of things we need to cover."

"Sure, we can do that! That would be great!" Beth Ann radiated a maniacal energy.

Cora nodded toward the boxes and stacks of clothing strewn around the apartment. "When did you move in? Unpacking is the worst part, right?"

Beth Ann giggled self-consciously. "I've been here for two years! I just can't get my shit together!"

Cora looked around the apartment again with a critical eye. Dirty dishes were piled in the sink and strewn on nearly every surface. She spotted bags of clothing from Nordstrom, Saks, and J.Crew stacked on top of the moving boxes, but from what she could see spilling from them, everything appeared to be tags-on brand-new and untouched. The couch was piled with dresses on hangers, and the one on top was a stunning frothy pink ballerina-style dress from Neiman Marcus. A small pile of petrified poop was next to it on the couch cushion.

The reality of what Cora was facing hit her.

Beth Ann was a budding hoarder.

Chanel hopped on her back legs and scratched at the glass door, barking a machine-gun riff-riff-riff-riff until Beth Ann let her in. Chanel immediately ran to investigate Cora.

"She's a cutie," Cora said, ignoring the fact that the dog looked like a "before" photo from an animal shelter. "She could use a nail trim, though." Down on her knees to get a closer look at the dog's ravaged body, she started with the most pressing need first because she didn't want to dump the laundry list of Chanel's ailments on

Beth Ann right out of the gate. She held the dog's tiny paw in her hand. "I bet it's uncomfortable for her to walk with nails this long."

"Oh my gawd, there's *no way* I could cut her nails! She's insane! She goes into beast mode when I try to do any grooming!"

Cora masked her disapproval. "Hm. Well, she seems fine with me touching her paws. Let's add grooming to the to-do list as well, and in the meantime maybe you can take her to your vet for a trim?" The list was growing longer and more complicated by the minute.

Just then Cora realized that her knees felt wet. She leaped up, and sure enough her jeans had blotchy circles on them. "I think I knelt in a pee spot," she said, gesturing to the evidence.

"Probably. It happens all the time. Don't worry, I'll clean it up later!"

Cora was beginning to feel claustrophobic. The disarray in the apartment, the dog in need, and the owner who seemed very lost were almost too much for Cora to take. She hoped that she'd be able to break through Beth Ann's veneer of forced cheerfulness and help her understand how to take care of her dog.

"Beth Ann, look at how Chanel is sniffing around. That's an obvious clue that she needs to go to the bathroom. I didn't see her do anything when she was out on the balcony, so let's get her outside before she has another accident. But I want to take her on a real walk, so get her leash, please."

Beth Ann nodded and chanted to herself, "Leash, leash, leash, where is her leash?" as she dug through various stacks. She clearly had no idea where it was, which led Cora to conclude that Beth Ann probably didn't walk her dog on a regular basis.

Chanel was sniffing and spinning more urgently, which meant that they needed to move quickly. "It's okay, don't worry about it, I have a leash in my bag. Just pick her up so she doesn't go."

Beth Ann acted as if she hadn't heard Cora and continued moving items from one pile to another, still chanting, "Leash, leash, leash." Cora ran to her bag to grab her all-purpose leash but was too late. Chanel squatted and dropped a giant runny pile of poop near the couch.

"That's okay, baby!" Beth Ann shouted to her dog. She looked at Cora and grinned. "I guess you *do* have your work cut out for you!"

ELEVEN

ChienParfait.com's top blog post was titled *Brûler en Enfer, Boris Ershovich,* with a whopping forty-two hits, the most of any on her site. Cora assumed the traffic was due to people trying to translate "burn in hell" into French and accidentally landing on her site. Her second most popular was *Vas te Faire Foutre, Boris Ershovich,* a post probably stumbled on by hapless folks looking to translate "Go fuck yourself." She had a hard time saying the words out loud, but she couldn't control what her fingers typed when she was on an Ershovich rampage. In her most recent post, titled *Ça signifie la guerre, Boris Ershovich,* she declared war after seeing him manhandle a puppy and challenged him to a train-off.

Though she sounded bulletproof when she wrote, she doubted that she could summon the same bravado on a TV screen. But still, she couldn't stop thinking about Wade's e-mail. Every time she looked at her inbox, there it was. She didn't want to delete it, and she worried that she'd forget about it if she filed it, so it sat there like a turtle in the middle of the road, awaiting her attention.

The titles of many of her Ershovich posts were inflammatory, but the content was scientific to a fault. She worried that her few readers might get bored by her endless methodology comparisons, but she had to vent her anger about the damage he was doing in the name of training. Ershovich was abusive, and Cora not only pointed out *why* in her posts, but she also described how to approach typical behavior problems with a dog-friendly, scientific, replicable methodology.

Most of her non-Ershovich posts came from her clients' lessons. Her series about leash aggression starred her long-term client Benson, the shepherd mix, whose incremental progress each week was enough to delight his guardian. Cora featured her client's cat Baby, who always tried to take part in training alongside her canine brother. She wrote about the front door trick she'd shown Fran and even included a photo of Sydney in his doorknob tether setup. She always asked her clients' permission before she wrote about their exploits, particularly when she took pictures of the dogs, but always managed to "forget" to tell them where to find the posts. Cora felt that she needed their blessing in order to write about them with a clear conscience, but she was afraid to get their feedback on what she produced. Her anonymity allowed her to express her feelings without judgment or repercussions. Something that wouldn't be possible if she stepped into the limelight.

She logged on after her session with Beth Ann to write about the importance of grooming upkeep. Cora had a feeling that unfortunate Chanel would provide plenty of fodder for the blog, from potty training to socialization, all handled with her typical diplomacy. She never said anything negative about her clients, but she was still glad that she hid her identity when she wrote. She'd read other trainers' blogs that spoke out against Ershovich and was shocked by the venom from his supporters in the comments sections. They claimed that trainers like Cora were just "jealous cookie-slingers" who couldn't handle "red zone dogs." Cora didn't know if she could handle the backlash.

She took a peek at the dashboard, curious to see which posts, if any, were resonating. She was shocked to discover that the traffic to her two top Ershovich posts had doubled in a week. Then she dug deeper and saw that *all* of her posts about Ershovich had received a significant increase in traffic. Someone in Maryland was watching her blog very closely, checking back a few times per day to see if Cora had added anything new.

Cora texted her brother. "Can u tell me what's up w CP? Traffic increase is weird."

Josh texted back after a few minutes. "So weird. Gimme a sec to ck IP addys."

Cora and her brother had nothing in common, but they found kinship in the tech side of her business. She was happy to hand him the reins, and he was happy to show off his skills and gain bragging rights to their parents about how much he was helping her.

She scanned the dashboard while she waited to hear back. Her posts mentioning Fritz all had a slight bump as well, but the majority of the hits were about Ershovich. Her phone dinged. "Almost all of them r the same IP addy. Don't be freaked out . . ." The text ended.

She waited and freaked out. Josh loved a good cliffhanger. Her phone pinged again with a link from him. She opened it and scanned the confusing "WhoIs" data, scrolling down until she saw the IP address of the mystery reader who had been all over her blog.

The *Washington Post*.

TWELVE

"**S**o did you forward your stuff for the audition yet?" Wade asked. He crossed his arms and stared at her, and with his shiny shaved head the pose made him look like a live-action version of Mr. Clean.

"You don't give up, do you?" she answered with a smile. "I'm still thinking about it. The problem is I have zero experience with TV stuff. I'm just a regular old dog trainer." His dog Daisy nosed through Cora's bag as they chatted, well acquainted with the delights inside after four weeks of working together. Cora cleared her throat and Daisy plopped into a sheepish sit next to the bag. She nodded and mouthed "good girl" to her.

"I gotcha, I don't want to force you into anything that might make you uncomfortable." Wade shrugged his shoulders and paused a beat. "But I really think you should at least try."

Cora laughed at his persistence, enjoying their camaraderie. "They want a résumé. I don't have one! They want a headshot. I don't have one! These are some major barriers to entry, Wade."

"Actually they're not. We can fudge a résumé for you, and Rachel can take your headshot. She's got a great camera and beyond average skills, and we can use one of the backdrops I use for shooting. Done and done. Now what's your excuse?"

"Uhhh . . . the biggest one of all: my skills. Or lack thereof."

"Well, let's figure that out right now. Maybe you're right—maybe you're not cut out for it. I'll film you and that'll decide it." Wade pulled his phone from his back pocket. "Take Daisy and teach me something. I don't care what it is, just pretend like you have an audience and you want to give them a lesson."

"Right now? I feel stupid! This is weird!" Cora's stress blush blossomed on her cheeks. She looked at Daisy, who was contentedly chewing on a bully stick pilfered from Cora's bag. She could handle a family of six watching her work, but the thought of doing it in front of Wade and a camera made her queasy.

"Yup, we're going to kill this beast. I'll know if you're a lost cause within three minutes, and if that's the case I'll find a nice way to break it to you and we'll never speak of it again. Deal?"

"*Bon sang,*" she muttered to herself. "If this is the only way to get you to stop asking me about it, then okay." Deep down, she was the tiniest bit excited to try, to know for sure if she had it in her.

She quickly thought about who she should channel for her first time on camera. Dr. York the Pet Vet, morning news correspondent, lovable geek, and friend to all animals? Skye Peterson, elegant pet stylist to the stars and creator of the Designer Doggy Diaper? Or perhaps Alice Goodwin, the beloved primatologist who radiated her warmth and compassion for animals through the TV screen?

Wade directed Cora to move to the center of the room with

Daisy and pointed his phone at the duo. His wife Rachel's decorating skewed Miami despite the fact that they lived in a quaint Craftsman-style bungalow, and the riotous yellows, teals, and pinks in their family room made for a cheerful setting for her first screen test. "Ready?" He snapped his fingers and pointed at her with a serious expression on his face. "You're on."

"Right now? I should go?"

Wade nodded, and Cora felt herself morph into dog trainer mode even though she felt queasy. She forgot all about channeling someone else, because she couldn't be anyone but herself.

Her voice shook as she began talking, but after a few sentences she felt a sense of ease settle over her as the familiar words came tumbling out. She did this all day every day, and the well-worn grooves of habit, combined with her desire to impart the lesson, far outweighed the strangeness of having a camera pointed at her.

Daisy was a willing accomplice and performed every part of the "stay" training process with telepathic accuracy even though they had barely touched on it during their regular lessons. Normally Daisy was a clumsy, charming doofus during class, tripping over her own paws and drooling stalactites while she waited for her treats. But in front of the camera she was demo-dog perfect, as if in cahoots with Wade to make Cora look good.

I can do this, Cora thought as she wrapped up the three-minute lesson. *It's not that bad!* She finished and then knelt down next to Daisy and scratched behind her ears. Daisy remained in a perfect sit, as if posing for a stock photo of a well-trained dog.

"Okay . . . cut!" Wade exclaimed.

Cora looked down at Daisy because she couldn't bear to look at Wade. "I'm afraid to ask . . . how was I?"

"You're a *natural*! You did what you were supposed to do—you talked through the camera like you were talking to me. You didn't put on an act and you didn't try to change your personality. Granted, there is a performance element to running a show, but they can teach you that stuff."

"Really? A *natural*? I find that sort of hard to believe." Was Wade just trying to make her feel good?

"I'm being honest—I think you should go for it. I wouldn't steer you wrong, Cora."

Cora made a noncommittal noise and stared at Daisy, who was rolling maniacally on the carpet and making huffing sounds, back to her typical goofball personality. Cora shook her head. If a dog could summon the skills to act on camera, than surely she could, too.

Cora's stomach twisted as she inched closer to a decision.

THIRTEEN

Cora checked her phone as she walked out of Wade and Rachel's house, imagining what the real audition might be like. There was a group text from Vanessa to Cora and Winnie that said only "Uh-oh" with a link below the message. Cora clicked it open and saw a video still of a smiling Boris Ershovich.

Do I really want to watch this now? She didn't need more stress but she pushed play anyway. A middle-aged woman appeared on the screen.

"I'm Cheryl Baum for *Washington Post Live* here with Boris Ershovich, who is bringing his popular 'Doggie Dictator' show to the National Theater next week. Boris, thank you for talking with me today."

"It is my *pleasure*," Ershovich responded in his thick Russian accent with his signature magnetism. Cora couldn't deny his good looks. In his mid-forties with a boyish face, clear pale skin, wide-set eyes, and a disarming smile, he had closely cropped brown hair with a racing stripe of gray above his left temple that made him look like a cartoon villain.

"Let's start off with the controversy surrounding your show. You have no shortage of detractors, including trainers and veterinarians, who don't approve of the way you work. How do you respond to that?"

Ershovich laughed. "Well, I say that they're jealous! Look, Cheryl, my methods work. I fix broken dogs, simple as that. My success rate speaks for itself."

"Some of the criticism is fairly intense. There's a website called ChienParfait.com—have you heard of it?"

Cora went numb and paused the clip. This reporter, Cheryl Baum, was her mysterious blog crawler, and she was outing Cora to Boris Ershovich! Her heart pounded, and she felt light-headed. Was this real life? She took a breath and pushed play again, afraid to hear what came next.

"Oh, Cheryl, I don't have time to play on the Internet. I'm a *fixer*, not a surfer." His tone was flirtatious.

The interviewer smiled. "Well, this website is by a local trainer here in DC—an anonymous trainer—and he or she levels some pretty heavy accusations against you, saying that the way you train is inhumane and that you should be kicked off the air. The title of a recent post about you is in French for some reason and translates to, 'Burn in Hell, Boris Ershovich.' I'd say that's someone with a very serious grudge."

"I'd say that's someone who is a *bully*. That is a . . . a . . . what do you call them? A gnome?"

"Troll," the interviewer corrected him.

"Yes, a troll! A common schoolyard bully who hides behind a computer screen."

Cora was nearly hyperventilating. *She* was the bully? Boris Ershovich, whose name almost had the word *shove* in the middle of it, was calling *her* a bully? And why didn't the reporter mention the most important aspect of her blog: her scientific takedown of his methodologies? She was sensationalizing based on a few questionable post titles.

"Let's switch gears. So what can your fans expect to see at your show this weekend?"

"Oh, Cheryl, we have some wonderful stories to tell. Broken dogs get fixed, owners are so happy with me, and it all happens before a live audience. It's going to be an amazing night. The show is sold out, Cheryl, but I'm going to live stream the first fifteen minutes for my fans."

"That's wonderful! You have quite a loyal following. Boris, is there anything you want to say to the dog owners of DC before we finish up? Any words of advice?"

He looked straight into the camera with a serious expression, a master showman. "I always have advice, because you people always make mistakes. Remember, you are the boss of the dog, no matter what. You must *demand* obedience. And finally, don't pet your dogs so much. It makes them spoiled and lazy."

The camera cut back to the reporter. "Boris Ershovich will be performing his sold-out dog training show at the National Theater next Friday. Thank you so much for joining me on *Washington Post Live*!" The clip ended with a shot of Ershovich's punchable face.

Cora's fingers shook so hard that she could barely respond to Vanessa and Winnie. She typed a ghost face emoji and about a thousand exclamation points, unable to put her thoughts into a coherent sentence. Her secret was out, and now her blog was going to be flooded with hundreds of haters.

Winnie texted back immediately. "Don't worry, we got your back, sister."

FOURTEEN

"Sydney, stay, darling. Stay. Stay. Stay." Fran backed away from her dog slowly, chanting the word and holding her hand up, as if giving Sydney a blessing. He watched her move away for a few steps and then followed her.

Cora interrupted her. "Fran, say 'stay' once. If you do it right, he won't need you to repeat it. Set him up to succeed, say it *once* and believe that he can do it. And yes, that sounds totally woo-woo."

"I love it when you get woo-woo. I'm woo-woo. Just look at all of the totems, guards, and gods all over my house," Fran said, pointing to a shelf crowded with statues of Buddha, Durga, Freya, two bright blue foo dogs, and Bastet. "I'm wearing a healing crystal around my neck! I am the very definition of woo-woo."

"Well, maybe all of that spiritual energy will help you guys get this one right. Try it one more time, and then I promise you're done for today."

The pair aced their final attempt. Cora was pleased that Sydney was making progress despite Fran's endearing flightiness.

"Okay, that's a perfect place to end. Nice work! Now let's go over homework."

"Before we do, I want to talk to you about something," Fran said, sounding excited. "You've heard of Santiago Rivera, yes?"

"The Latin drummer? Sure, I know of him, but I don't really know his music."

"Did you know that he got his start in DC? He's doing an invitation-only miniconcert to kick off his tour at Café Fuego, which is part of one of our properties. One of my job perks is I get to attend these types of events, and I would love it if you could come, too, darling!"

"Wow, that would be amazing!"

"Wonderful! And I'm sure *someone* will be very happy that you're going to be there."

"What do you mean?" Cora asked.

"Shit!" Fran covered her mouth. She sighed. "I might as well spill it. Girl power, sisterhood, and all of that, right?" She paused. "You know Eli from my office?"

Cora nodded.

"He thinks you're lovely."

Cora's eyes widened before she could get her reaction in check. The Human Blur liked her? Why hadn't she picked up on it at Beth Ann's?

Fran continued, looking stricken. "*Please* don't let on that I told you!"

"Scout's honor."

Fran leaned toward Cora conspiratorially. "Since we're on the subject . . . what do you think of him?"

"Well, I *haven't* thought of him, really. He seems nice but—"

"Are you seeing someone? I'm sorry, how rude of me not to ask first."

"No, I'm actually single. Painfully single." She pictured Charlie's face but quickly dismissed it.

"Hooray, darling! Allow me to give you some background on him." She paused. "He is a *wonderful* person. He's an incredibly hard worker. He's a team player. He is resourceful—"

"It sounds like you want me to hire him!"

"Whoops, it does. On to the juicy bits, then. He's the most emotionally intelligent man I've ever met. He has three younger sisters so he *gets* women. He's surrounded by women in our office and he navigates our hot flashes with ease. He's been elected the office's unofficial psychiatrist, so everyone goes to him with their troubles. He's bloody hysterical, in a really weird way—you have to learn his sense of humor, so at first some of what he says will sound bizarre. He's a . . . a good egg. I *adore* him. And the two of you together? My heart would explode with joy."

"That's quite the endorsement! I will certainly, uh, keep it in mind." Cora thought about how she enjoyed hanging with Eli while waiting for Beth Ann. Eli was sweet, yes, but could anyone compete with Charlie Gill? Particularly a quirky good egg with a big brother vibe.

Fran studied Cora's face. "If you're into guys like that alpha male Aaron, it's likely Eli isn't your type. But please, just give him a chance. Trust me, darling, little by little he'll win you over if you let him."

FIFTEEN

Charlie was staring at Cora with such intensity that she worried she had something hanging out of her nose.

"Thank you. Seriously, this is *such* a huge help."

Cora had agreed to hold the remainder of Charlie's sessions at 7:00 p.m. because his work schedule no longer allowed for day classes, and her Saturdays were booked for weeks in advance. Having cut her teeth in the always-on-the-job world of tech, she knew the value of long hours, but she forced herself to never take clients after 3:00 p.m. As a business owner, she could afford herself the perk, and it took her a year to feel comfortable doing it. The 3:00 p.m. cutoff was ironclad for most people, but for Charlie . . .

"*Pas de problème!*" she said with a sweep of her hand.

"Madison told me that you speak a little French! I wish I'd kept up with a language. I can order a taco and a beer in Spanish, that's about it."

"I barely have the chance to speak anymore, so I'm getting rusty."

"Well, you can speak French to me anytime. It's such a sexy language."

Red flags. *That was flirty*, Cora thought. *Pretty sure that was flirty. And now I'm here with him at night, alone in his house. And he looks adorable.*

Charlie had changed out of his work clothes into a snug black T-shirt with a drawing of a vintage toy robot on it and jeans. Cora had never seen him without a suit on, so she took the opportunity to study him while he interacted with Oliver. She noticed that the sleeves clung to his biceps. His forearms looked strong, with a few vine-like veins visible. His jeans fit well, and Cora wondered if Madison had helped him pick them. Guys never knew how to buy jeans that fit.

Oliver stood at Cora's feet, looking up at her expectantly and waiting for the lesson to begin with a patience beyond his age.

"Hey, did you eat dinner?" Charlie asked. "I'm starving. I want sushi. You want sushi?"

Cora hated sushi.

"I haven't eaten either. Why not?" She normally wouldn't stay for a meal with a client, particularly alone with a male client who wanted to eat sushi, but she was hungry as well, and Charlie Gill was doing the asking. She changed a lot of her rules for Charlie.

He rifled through a drawer filled to the top with menus, which made it obvious that they ordered takeout frequently. Cora wondered if Madison ever actually cooked in their beautiful kitchen.

"Ah, there it is. Yojisan Sushi. I already know what I want, so why don't you take a look?"

She gingerly took the menu from him and scanned it without a clue as to what any of it meant.

"It's overwhelming, right? Can I order for you? We eat here all the time, and I know what's good. Does that work?"

Cora nodded, grateful that she didn't have to pretend to know what she was doing. She sat down next to Oliver and scratched his chest while Charlie placed the order, contemplating the difference between what was happening with Charlie versus what happened on a real date. Alone at night? Check. A meal on the way? Check. A frisson of sexual tension? Check.

Charlie hung up the phone. "Excellent! It'll be here in about forty-five minutes. Oh crap—I didn't even put it together that the lesson will be almost over by then. Is it okay for you to stay a little bit late? Do you have plans tonight?"

The only plan Cora had was another Bikram session that she was dreading.

"Nope, my calendar is clear, so if you don't mind me cramping your style a bit longer than usual, I'll stay." Cora made a mental note to shoot Maggie a text bailing.

"Speaking of 'stay,' I'm having a hell of a time with it. I can barely get two steps away from Oliver, and then he jumps up and follows me. Can we work on that first?"

Cora walked him through the basics of the behavior again and demonstrated how to do it, while her stomach growled and her mind reeled about sitting down with Charlie to share a meal.

The doorbell interrupted them, and Oliver leaped up, barking like a trained guard dog.

"Can we get Oliver to do the stay now?" Charlie asked above the din.

"Eventually, yes, but we're not even close to being able to use it in real-life scenarios yet. You answer the door, and I'll do some work with him."

Cora clipped the leash on Oliver before Charlie got to the door and stood a few feet away with the young boxer. Oliver swiveled his head back and forth while Charlie chatted genially with the delivery guy, as if trying to decode exactly what was happening with the stranger in the foyer. Cora saw the puppy's mouth go into an O shape, so she tossed a treat for him to chase before he gave voice to the bark in the chamber. It was their first time attempting a real-life training scenario, and even though they were still in the beginning stages of training, Cora was impressed with the dog's commitment to work in the face of such a tempting distraction.

"Soup's on—let's eat!" Charlie announced, holding a bulging bag of food in the air and placing his hand on the small of her back as he passed her. The intimacy of the move surprised Cora and sent a wave of heat to her face.

She followed him to the large round table in the kitchen. The lighting was dim and romantic, and the French doors were open to let in the cool spring air. She stole a glance at the framed photos on the mantel over the fireplace and saw a glamorous smiling Madison in every one of them. Cora felt like she was being watched, which would've been tolerable during the actual lesson. But now, officially postlesson, she felt guilty under Madison's gaze.

Charlie unpacked the bag, placing tray after tray of sushi on the table in front of them. "You said you were hungry!" he said, as if acknowledging the excess of his purchase. Cora nodded and worried about how best to fake her enthusiasm for slimy raw fish and sticky rice. She hoped her hunger would short-circuit her taste buds.

"Where do you want to start? We have Hokkigai, Akagai, Toro nigiri, Gunkan maki, Chuka Idako, and some rainbow rolls."

Cora looked at the horrifying options before her. She saw what looked like two different types of caviar wrapped in black, tiny curled-up bits of octopus, pink slabs of uncooked fish atop rice beds, and something that looked like a red-tipped claw of meat wearing a black belt. She seized on the only name that made sense to her. "How about a rainbow roll?"

"Ah, you're starting slow. I like that! Want some wine to wash it down?"

Was wine a transition to date territory?

"Well, since we're done with the lesson, sure. But normally I don't drink on the job."

"I assure you, you're off the clock now. Take a look at your student." Cora leaned forward to get a glimpse of Oliver, who was on his side and half asleep in the doorway between the kitchen and the hallway. A mentally exhausted dog: her parting gift to every client.

As Charlie searched the cabinet for glasses, Cora sniffed at one of the rainbow rolls. Peeling back the slab of salmon and biting into the edge, the rice tasted fine. She took another bite and got a mouthful of fish and had to stifle her gag reflex. How was she going to fake her way through the meal?

Charlie returned to the table with oversize red wineglasses. "This oughta do the trick," he said as he filled them to the brims. He sat down next to her and looked at her with his typical intensity. "So tell me all about Cora Bellamy. How did you get into dog training?" He took a big swig of his wine and looked into her eyes.

Cora wasn't used to answering questions. She was a steadfast ear for her clients, part confidante, part therapist, but always on the listening end of the conversation. The rare occasions when a client actually asked her a personal question, whether about her weekend plans or what book she was reading, usually ended up with her sputtering an abbreviated reply and gently steering the conversation away from herself. This felt different. She was off duty, and the two of them were hanging out as people, not as helper and helpee.

"I'll give you the highlights: college to corporate America just like Mom and Dad wanted, even though it wasn't what I wanted, good job, great pay, much confusion. Cue quarter-life crisis, quit job, became a dog trainer, and here I am." She shrugged.

"Okay, that was the lamest summary ever. Start over. What exactly did you do?"

"Junior project manager in government contracts reporting for duty, sir." She saluted him.

"Hm. That doesn't feel like a fit to me."

"It wasn't. I did it for as long as I could, until I had a decent nest egg, so I wouldn't have to rely on the bank of Mom and Dad, then I said good-bye high heels, hello sneakers." She waggled her foot at him to prove her point.

"I think I would've enjoyed seeing the high-heel version of you. But the sneaker version is pretty phenomenal, too." He shoved an octopus roll in his mouth and gazed at her.

Don't respond, change the subject, break off eye contact. She repeated it to herself like a mantra, hoping it might give her the strength to resist the X-rated trailer playing in her head.

"I prefer sneakers myself. Comfort wins, you know."

"Speaking of comfort, should we move to the family room? These chairs aren't made for long conversations."

"No, I'm fine!" Cora squeaked out, as an image of a shirtless Charlie draped across her on the couch popped into her head. *Do not move any closer to him. Do not touch him.*

Charlie nodded but didn't hide a furrow. "So why dog training, of all professions?" The creased brow was gone and he was back to staring at her like he was trying to memorize her face.

"Honestly, deep down I've always known this is where I'd end up, despite the corporate detour. Ever since I was little, I've always had this drive to . . ." Cora stopped herself.

"What? Tell me." Charlie sounded like a therapist, and Cora realized that they had officially switched roles.

She was tempted to tell him everything. The mood was intimate and confessional, and Cora knew that Charlie in particular would be sympathetic to what had happened all those years ago. She opened her mouth to tell him about Cooper but swerved at the last minute. "My dog Fritz finally pushed me to take the leap, actually. I saw firsthand how positive training transformed him from out-of-control shelter dog to polite ambassador. I wanted to help people do the same with their own dogs, to find that magic that transforms relationships. So here I am. My life is all about animals. Same with you, but on a much bigger and cooler level, right?" She desperately needed to get his focus off of her, to deflect into more comfortable territory.

He shook his head. "Not cooler. Different. But yeah, I do feel good about what I do. So what's the best part of your job?"

He was out-gaming her again, circling the conversation back to her. "Ummm. I like changing relationships. I like teaching people how to speak dog and teaching dogs how to speak people."

"You're so good at it, Cora." She felt a ripple every time he said her name. She knew he probably picked it up in some seminar about winning over business contacts, but it worked on her.

"Thanks. You guys make it easy."

Charlie grinned at her. "Are we your favorites? C'mon. Admit it. Oliver and I are your all-time favorites." He leaned over and poked at her playfully, like a grade school boy with a crush.

"You guys are up there, I'll admit it. But I have a thing for . . ."

"Lawyers?" he interjected.

"Boxers." She laughed. He made a dejected face. "Okay, and *some* lawyers."

No matter how rusty Cora was at flirting, she knew without a doubt that that's what they were doing.

He reached over and grabbed her wrist. She jumped.

"Sorry! I just noticed the scar on the top of your hand. How did you get it?"

"Take a guess . . . how do you think a dog trainer gets a scar on her hand?"

"Of course. Dog bite. What happened?" He was still holding

her wrist, examining the scar in a clinical fashion, bringing it close to his face.

Cora felt tingly. The room was getting dark, and Charlie Gill wasn't letting go of her.

"Too embarrassing to say. Let's just chalk it up to a rookie mistake. It was *my* fault, not the dog's."

Charlie ran two gentle fingers over the constellation of raised skin. "It must have been a big mistake. Looks like it was brutal." He placed her hand on the table and looked at her. "Sorry it happened."

In that moment, though, Cora wasn't sorry.

In an attempt to shift the energy in the room, she adjusted her chair and sent her wineglass sailing. Shattering on the floor, it woke Oliver from his nap and effectively killed any of the mood that had been building.

"*Merde.* I am *such* a klutz. I'm so sorry!"

"No biggie, they're cheap glasses." Charlie walked to the sink to grab paper towels.

His phone went off on the table, and Cora saw that Madison was Skyping him. She blushed. "Your phone—someone is calling you," she said, as if she hadn't seen the screen.

Charlie rushed over and answered it, leaving the wine pooling on the floor and Oliver doing his best to lick it up. "Hey, Mads!" Cora took the paper towels from him, making sure to stay out of sight, and got to work cleaning up the mess.

"Hiiii, baby!" Madison gushed. "I miss yoooou!"

Charlie cut her off. "Mads, Cora is here, and we just finished Oliver's lesson. We were both starving so we grabbed some sushi, and now we've just had a wine emergency. Can I call you right back?"

There was a pause. "Wine emergency? She's there with you right now? Okay, that's fine." Madison sounded clipped and businesslike now. "How did Oliver do?"

"I'll let Cora tell you." Cora panicked as he turned the phone around and handed it to her where she sat on the floor like Cinderella, surrounded by purple-stained towels and a straining Oliver. Madison looked beautiful, even in the flat unflattering close-up of the phone.

"Hi, Madison, how are you?" she asked, not expecting an answer. Cora gestured to the mess on the floor. "I just dorked out and spilled my drink everywhere! Um, Oliver is doing really great! He's super smart and super easy to train. He misses you, though!"

"Isn't that sweet? How can you tell?" Madison smiled but her eyes narrowed.

"Oh, well, a dog trainer just knows these things!" she trilled as the blush crept up her neck. Cora resented that Madison wouldn't take her well-intentioned embellishment at face value.

"I can't wait to see how *perfect* you're making our dog. When I come back he's going to be a *perfect* little gentleman. Right?"

"He'll be a gentleman, you have my word." *My word,* she thought ruefully. *Here I am thinking smutty thoughts about your boyfriend and I'm talking about my "word."*

"I expect nothing less," Madison replied, sounding cloyingly sweet but cutting at the same time.

Cora nodded, hoping that the awkward showdown was coming to an end. She rubbed an itch on her cheek and a few grains of rice fell off. *Wonderful*, she thought. *I had food on my face the whole time.*

Charlie took the phone back. "Babe, I'll call you in a little bit. Love you!"

"I love you too, baby! Muuwhah!"

Cora saw Charlie silently pucker his lips at the screen then hang up.

"Sorry about that," he said to Cora. "We usually talk at the same time every night, and I just lost track of time." He looked at her plate. "How are you liking those rainbow rolls? Pretty amazing, right? Stop cleaning and take some of this Hokkigai, too, it's ridiculous." He held the container with the belted fish claws out to her.

Cora made her way back to the table reluctantly. "Oh, I'm good right now, thanks," she said, pointing to a half-eaten roll on her plate to prove her point.

"You're a slow eater! I'm going to eat all of these myself if you don't hurry up."

"Just keep going, I'm totally fine." She hoped that he would polish off all of the trays and not notice that she was barely eating anything. The sushi wasn't all that was trashing her appetite, though. It was Charlie Gill. His unwavering gaze, his fingers on her skin, the smell of his summertime aftershave every time he leaned close to her. And then there was the very real possibility of forgetting her honor code and doing something she knew she'd regret.

"So how did you and Madison meet?" Breaking yet another rule by asking an uninvited personal question, but the red wine combined with her empty stomach emboldened her.

"Me and Madison? It's kind of embarrassing. I saw her walking down the street and I chased her down. I literally pulled my car over, jumped out, and ran down the sidewalk to meet her. Such a creeper thing to do." He shook his head, feigning embarrassment at it.

"No, it's so . . . sweet. You were overcome by her beauty." Cora felt queasy. No one had ever chased her down.

"Exactly! I mean, she looked like this blinding vision of blondness. The sun was shining on her . . . she looked like . . . like an angel." He stared off, clearly reliving the moment.

She couldn't help herself. "So what happened when you got to her? Did you know what you wanted to say?"

"I sounded like such a dork!" She doubted that anything that came out of Charlie's mouth sounded dorky. "I just introduced myself and asked if I could take her out for some coffee. And to my surprise, she said yes."

Of course she said yes, Cora thought. *Look at you.*

"So how long ago was that?" she asked him.

"Uh . . . we've been living together for three years now, so it was five years ago. And now that you know the math, don't ask me the inevitable question, please." He smiled a wan smile.

"Huh?" she faked, even though she knew exactly what he meant.

"The *m* word."

"Right. I would never ask that. That's personal." She took a huge swig of wine and looked over at Oliver, hoping to telepathically wake him so that he might save her from the conversation with some puppy shenanigans.

Charlie looked at the roll he was about to eat and said, "Well, between you and me, it's sort of on the radar screen."

She felt like he'd punched her. He hadn't been flirting with her, he was just being kind to her, in the same way that he'd been kind to the sushi delivery guy, and everyone else that he met.

"Well, that's got to be exciting," she managed to say.

"I guess it is. I mean, I have my doubts about it, of course. It seems so . . . predetermined. You meet, date for an appropriate amount of time, and then get hitched to the old ball and chain. I'm not there yet, but isn't that how it works?" He looked at her questioningly.

"What comes next is whatever you *want* to come next," she said firmly, hoping that it would end the conversation. She needed to leave, to get away from Charlie and his mixed-up signals. At least now she could will herself to shift her focus from dissecting a possible flirtation to training his dog—what she was actually being paid to do.

Charlie didn't catch her subtext. "Yup." He sighed. "We shall see." He looked down at the trays strewn before him. "Eat more, Cora. I feel like a pig!"

"Nope, I'm good. I have to head out anyway." She made an exaggerated show of checking the time on her phone. "What do I owe you for dinner?" Her tone was as clipped as Madison's had been.

"You have to go already?" He sounded disappointed. "But you barely ate anything! Stay, hang out with us!"

"I've had more than enough, trust me. Seriously, what can I throw in?" She dug into her bag for her wallet as Oliver jumped on her. *Now he wakes up!* She kept her head down so Charlie Gill wouldn't see the splotches on her chest and neck.

"Please, not a thing. You get dinner next time, okay? My pleasure to have you here. And Oliver loved it, too."

"Yes, so nice, thank you for dinner. So I'll see you next week?" He nodded. "Good luck with homework, and holler if you have any questions." She sounded professional and disinterested, which was exactly how she planned to make herself sound for the remainder of their sessions together. Charlie Gill was a client and nothing more, no matter how many compliments he paid her or how tingly he made her feel when his hand brushed her back.

Besides, in a few weeks, she'd never see him again.

"Thanks again, Cora. This was great." He smiled at her and leaned forward to squeeze her shoulder. "You seriously are the best."

He loves his girlfriend, he loves his girlfriend, he loves his girlfriend, she reminded herself as the warmth of his touch radiated through her body.

SIXTEEN

"Why are you so grumpy?" Maggie asked Cora accusingly.

"What makes you think I'm grumpy?"

"Because you're acting like a total bitch."

Cora had been storming around the kitchen, complaining loudly about the empty milk jug in the fridge and tossing utensils back into the drawer. Fritz kept his distance in the hallway, confused by Cora's sour mood. She was ready to spit venom at Maggie, but she took one look at her friend and teared up.

"What's wrong? Oh my God, what's wrong, honey?" Maggie walked over and put her arms around Cora. The floodgates opened, and Cora began to sob.

"It's nothing. It's stupid! It's so stupid and I feel stupid." She surrendered to the tears.

"Tell me! Is it Aaron?"

"No, screw Aaron," she spat.

"What is it? Tell me."

"There's this guy, a client, and he's really perfect but he has a perfect girlfriend who is bitchy, and I couldn't help it and I really started to like him." She hiccuped a sniffle and continued. "I was pretty sure he was flirting with me but it turns out he's going to propose to her soon! I just feel dumb, Mags. I've been acting all stupid around him, and I can't stop thinking about him. I was sure he was flirting! He called me the total package, Maggie! Isn't that flirting? And I'm horny. I haven't been on a date with anyone in forever and I don't know what guys are thinking anymore!"

Maggie chuckled. "I was on a date last night and I have no clue what guys are thinking either. Well, I know *one* thing they're always thinking."

"You know what I mean, don't joke!" She wiped her eyes with the dish towel.

"I'm sorry. How long has this been going on?"

"A few weeks."

"Why didn't you tell me? I don't mean to make this about me, but I'm a little insulted you didn't fill me in." She paused. "Ohhh, wait a sec—it's all making sense now. This is mascara guy, right?"

Cora nodded.

"Is he your nighttime client? Is that who you were with last night?"

She nodded again. "Takeout sushi dinner after our lesson. With wine. Oh, and I forgot to mention that his perfect gorgeous girlfriend is out of town."

"Wait a sec, you're drinking wine and hanging out with him while his girlfriend is away?" She shuddered. "That's sort of gross. He sounds like a douche. Why can't you be attracted to a nice guy for a change?"

"He *is* a nice guy. He's almost too good to be true, minus

the girlfriend. He practices animal law. And he's adorable." Cora looked glum. "No, more than adorable. Smoking hot."

"Sorry, but having you stay for dinner while his girlfriend's not home is a douche move, even if you do have a professional relationship. Think about it. Would you want your boyfriend to have his gorgeous, funny, amazing personal trainer, or stylist, or barista hanging out with him while you're out of town?"

Okay, Maggie was right, but Cora tried to play it off. "If I knew what it was like to have a boyfriend I might have an opinion."

"Stop it. You're being stupid."

Cora welled up again.

"Oh, honey, I'm sorry! You're really sensitive right now. Are you ragging?"

"Maybe, I don't know. I'm just sad and lonely and I feel stupid and ugly and unlovable."

Maggie hugged her again. "I love you, girl."

"Unless I become a lesbian, you don't count."

Maggie put both her hands on Cora's shoulders. "What are you doing today? Clear your calendar, I have an idea!"

"What?" Cora eyed her warily.

"Girl date, girl date, it's time for a girl date!" Maggie sang as she danced around the kitchen. She stopped in front of Cora and posed dramatically. "Shopping montage!"

Cora shook her head. "I'm not in the mood today."

"No, you're coming to work with me, and we're going to do a *Pretty Woman* shopping montage, minus the prostitution and actual spending. Darnell and I are in the evening gown department today, so we can rock out the frocks on you, baby! Picture it; you, me, D, Lhuillier, Mischka, Balmain . . . c'mon, it'll be fun! We'll get a gorgeous new profile photo of you for Facebook!" Darnell was Maggie's beloved "work husband."

"Not with these swollen eyes." She thought for a moment. "I probably should get out of the house, though."

"Yes! You're coming! Go get ready, I'm leaving in thirty minutes."

Cora stayed in her leggings, flip-flops, and the zip front hoodie she'd slept in. She didn't care what she looked like. She texted her two morning clients during the Metro ride and begged off—business owner's privilege—but decided to keep Beth Ann on her schedule at two because the situation seemed so dire for little Chanel. Cora didn't want to give Beth Ann any opportunity to back out of training, and even though she wasn't sure how she was going to help the pitiful dog, she was convinced that she'd find a way.

They got to the store right as Darnell was unlocking the main gate into Saks, looking dapper in a fitted suit with a subdued Burberry plaid. The lapels and trouser seams were trimmed with thick black cording, and the back of the blazer had a giant black skull with rhinestone eyes.

"Look what ze *chat* dragged in," he said with an exaggerated French accent, eyeing Cora from head to toe in mock judgment.

"Careful, D, she's on the edge today," Maggie warned.

"Hi, Darnell," Cora said and smiled thinly. He saw the sadness in her face and reached out to give her a hug.

"My poor little dog lady, queen of the lonely hearts. So single it hurts, am I right? Maybe if you put some effort into your look, you'll find a new man." He picked a few dog hairs off her shoulder.

Cora jumped away from him as if he'd slapped her.

"Seriously, Darnell?" Maggie scolded.

"What? I'm kidding! Cora is perfect just the way she is."

"Nice save," Cora said glumly.

"She's here for montage madness, but I'm not sure you're in-vited anymore, D. Muzzle yourself, okay? Cora had a bad night so we need to cheer her up with some couture," Maggie said as they walked through the empty store, ignoring the bitchy reps at the makeup counters.

"Oh, your wish is my command, baby! I got nothing else to do. Our department is going to be Whitney Houston all day."

His cheer was infectious, so Cora moved past his hurtful com-ments and looked at him questioningly.

"*D-e-a-d* like Whitney in the bathtub."

"Too soon, D," Maggie said, shaking her head.

The gown salon was an explosion of sumptuous fabrics and sparkle. Some of the dresses were so ornate, laden with layers of tulle and heavy beading, that they hung on their own racks, look-ing like the first attendee to a fairy-tale ball. The clothing was such a departure from Cora's daily life of button-down shirts, jeans, drool, and fur that she couldn't help but be enchanted by the over-the-top femininity of it all.

"Can you guys get in trouble for letting me try this stuff on? I sort of feel like a criminal. And I sure don't look like I belong here."

"You're not going to *steal* anything, you're going to try things on and see if you happen to fall in love with a piece. Because you have that special event coming up, right?" Maggie winked. "Oh, and look, you're in our appointment book!" Maggie scribbled something in the leather-bound book on the service desk.

"I do always say that you find the dress first and the event will follow," Darnell added solemnly.

"Right. So maybe if I buy this"—Cora checked the price tag of a beaded black gown hanging near her—"five-thousand-five-hundred-eighty-dollar Givenchy gown I'll get invited to a state dinner?"

"You *never know*!" Darnell answered.

"So should I just grab stuff? How does this work?"

"Darnell is going to get you all set up, sweetheart. Now let me take a look at you." He circled Cora, pretending that he'd never seen her before. "You look like a . . . six. But in couture you might be an eight. Those bitches."

"I haven't worn a dress in so long that I have no clue what size I am. I'm in your capable hands."

"Perfect! Maglomaniac, please see this gorgeous young debutante to a fitting room."

Maggie escorted Cora to a large room with mirrors on every wall. "Get nekkid, girlie. We'll be in with some options in a second."

Cora stared at herself up close in the full-coverage mirror. She hadn't felt this down since just after the breakup, and she wasn't sure why. She doubted that the fancy dresses would do much to cheer her up, especially when she looked so blotchy and puffy from crying.

Darnell tapped on the door as Cora slid her leggings off. She peeked out the door and saw that both he and Maggie had a stack of dresses in their arms.

"Time to start mainlining some serious sparkle," Darnell said. "It's impossible to feel sad in glitter. We're gonna start with floor-length stuff then move on to cocktail. I want to see you in this

Donna Karan first, then the Léger, then the Stella just to switch things up. Slay us, baby."

"Wait a sec," she said, running her hand down a nightgown-thin peach silk dress midway through the stack. "I'm not trying this one. If it's this wrinkled on a hanger, it's going to be a nightmare on my body."

"That's nineties Calvin Klein realness, I'll have you know. Kate Moss waif shit. I order you to try it," Darnell answered. "And besides, if it looks good on you, you can always keep it looking tight with that steamer your girl stole from our employer."

"Darnell! They were throwing it out!" Maggie exclaimed and widened her eyes at him. "It was *in the trash*, totally broken. I didn't steal it!"

"Uh-huh, okay. Whatever you say."

They walked away bickering like a married couple.

The Donna Karan dress was a simple strapless column of black sequins, with some forgiving ruching at the waistline. Cora stepped into it and was surprised by the weight of the dress. She contorted herself to pull the zipper all the way up, and when she turned to look in the mirror she was shocked.

The dress transformed her, accentuating every curve and hiding any perceived flaws. She looked stunning, even with red-rimmed eyes and unruly hair. The sequins rippled like moonlight on water when she walked. The high slit in back wasn't just to give the dress added sex appeal—it was so formfitting that without it Cora would have been forced to take baby steps. Even she couldn't deny that she looked amazing in it.

She walked out to the main room. "Guys? What do you think?"

Darnell turned around and screamed.

"Is that good?" Cora laughed.

"Yes. That's good."

Maggie stood a few steps away with her hand over her mouth. "Holy shit, I forgot that you have a *body*! Look at your glorious tits! How are they so goddamned perky in a strapless dress?"

"Yeah, I'm not going to argue with you. I look pretty awesome in this. And you know I never say that." She spun around slowly so they could take her in.

"I don't think I've ever heard you say that you look good in anything! Cora, you look perfect."

Darnell appraised the dress from a distance, like an art critic getting ready to weigh in on a sculpture. "Yes, this one is good, *really* good, but now that I see what you're workin' with"—he gestured to her body—"there's no doubt that the Léger will be even better. Go put that one on."

Standing in front of the triptych mirror in the middle of the department, Cora shifted her weight from one hip to the other, miming party laughter and turning so that she could see how she looked from the back.

"Yes, your ass looks good, too," Maggie chastised. "Go change!"

Cora went back to the dressing room, slipped off the dress and peeked at the tag. $2,995.00, unthinkable. She took the gold Léger dress off the hanger and checked the price before putting it on. $1,990. *Better,* she thought, even though she rarely spent over $50 on any article of clothing.

The Léger didn't look promising, reminding Cora of vintage shapewear, with seams that accentuated the bustline and hips.

Even tighter than the Karan, this one had the added challenge of Léger's signature bandage-like horizontal strips laced with spandex. Cora eased the shimmering fabric up her body with her back to the mirror. It felt like a good, snug pair of leggings. She pulled the thin straps onto her shoulders, smoothed the twin vertical seams down the front of the dress, and turned to look at herself.

Holy shit. Her jaw dropped.

Darnell had been right, the Léger was better in every way. While the black dress flattered her, the shimmering gold of the Léger made her skin look incandescent. The bandages managed to both slim her and accentuate her curves at the same time. The subtle mermaid swoop at the bottom of the gown gave the skintight gown a modicum of class. She felt like a goddess.

Cora walked out to the sales floor and posed seductively with her hand resting on a jutted-out hip. "How ya like me now?" she drawled.

Maggie whooped like a cowboy. "Holy shit! Holy *shit*! You must own that dress and wear it every day! I didn't think the Karan could be topped *but look at you in Léger*!" She turned to Darnell to get his opinion and stopped. "Oh my God, Darnell, are you *crying*?"

"A little." He sniffled dramatically. "She looks so perfect in that dress, and I'm crying because I knew she would." He pounded the desk. "I was born to do this."

Cora laughed. "You were! You're a dress savant. Now can we get back to me and how good I look?"

"Usually Léger is too *Real Housewives of New Jersey*, but you make it look elegant. I'm so proud of our scruffy little dog trainer!"

He tilted his head, appraising her again. "I need to do something really quick, come here." Darnell ducked behind the counter, grabbed a makeup bag, and ran a few brushes over Cora's eyelids, brows, and cheeks. She looked in the mirror and was once again stunned by what she saw. In a few strokes he had changed the landscape of her face.

"Now, can I ring you up, baby? Because when a dress looks like this, it's meant to be. You have an event in your future, I feel it! So buy the dress already," Darnell insisted. "I'll be your date to whatever it is, even if it's some weird dogs and cats party."

"I'd give you my employee discount . . . ," Maggie offered.

"Plus it's going to go on end-of-season sale soon. Markdowns galore," Darnell added.

"Guys, I have no reason to buy something like this. I'm not fancy. And I'd have a really hard time spending so much on a dress."

Maggie snorted. "You know you could totally afford it. You work nonstop, and you never go out. Buy the dress, audition for that damn show, and then save it for when you're up for an Emmy."

Cora rolled her eyes and shook her head.

Darnell started to visibly deflate.

"I promise, if something la-di-da comes up in my world, I will come back and buy this dress. Scout's honor." She held up three fingers.

"Deal," Maggie answered.

"Hating you," Darnell said with a pout.

Cora grabbed Maggie's phone from the counter and looked at the time. "I have to go, I have a client this afternoon—the one whose dog I'm worried about. Time for me to change back into a pumpkin."

SEVENTEEN

Cora made it to Beth Ann's building with six minutes to spare. Even though Beth Ann had given permission for her to go straight up, she paused in the lobby to see if Eli might be around. The only other person in the cavernous space was the doorman, who didn't look up from his phone as Cora raced to the elevator. Once again Cora heard Chanel's barking the minute she stepped into the hall, which led her to believe that her client might be late again, or worse yet, a no-show.

She knocked and triggered a more intense barrage of sound from behind the door, a combination of shrieking howls and mad scratching. She waited, convinced that she was being stood up, until she heard the doorknob rattle.

"Did we have a lesson scheduled for today?" Beth Ann looked like she had just gotten out of bed.

Cora was dumbfounded. "Yes, uh, we do. Every Friday at two for the next three weeks. You picked the day and time, remember?"

Beth Ann rubbed her eyes and looked down at Chanel, who was running into the hallway to jump on Cora, then back into the apartment over and over again. "I'm sorry, I totally forgot." She was wearing an oversize sweatshirt with the neck cut out so that her shoulder was exposed and overlong pajama bottoms that were dirty at the bottom from being stepped on. Her hair was piled on top of her head in a greasy bun, and her face was splotchy and pale. She wouldn't look Cora in the eyes.

"Are you sick? Do you need to reschedule?"

"No, no, it's fine. We can do it now, come in." Beth Ann turned and shuffled into her apartment, beckoning Cora to follow.

"You know what? I want to take Chanel on a quick walk before we get started. It looks like you're just waking up, so she probably has to potty. I've got a leash, don't worry about finding yours." Beth Ann nodded and walked away, and Cora reached into her bag to grab it as well as a pair of nail clippers. She had wanted to show Beth Ann how to begin the desensitization process for nail clipping, but she wasn't even sure if they were going to have a real lesson. Cora couldn't bear the thought of the dog walking on stiletto claws for another day.

Cora leashed Chanel up on the tiles right in front of the door. As predicted, the little dog squatted and let out a stream of urine the moment Cora touched her to clip on the leash.

"We'll be back," she shouted into the dark apartment, not expecting to hear an answer.

Chanel walked to the elevator briskly and Cora used their time alone to assess the unfortunate little dog. Beth Ann was an unfit pet parent, but Cora wasn't sure what impact the neglect had had on Chanel. Some dogs that grow up in a deprived home environment are so nervous about life outside the front door that they completely shut down when presented with anything new, while others seem unflappable and well adjusted no matter how dire their circumstances.

Cora knelt and petted Chanel during the elevator ride down to the lobby. Though she loved dogs of all sizes and breeds, there was no sugarcoating the fact that the little dog was an odd-looking creature. The dirty patchy fur, stained eyes, talon nails, and snaggle tooth made her seem like an unloved street dog, even though she was living in an expensive high-rise with a young woman who seemed to have unlimited shopping funds.

Cora lifted her hand to her nose and sniffed. Chanel smelled awful.

The little dog high-stepped through the lobby like she did it every day. She didn't seem scared or nervous, which made Cora feel slightly better about her circumstances. Maybe she did get walked every so often?

"Excuse me," the guard called out. "Is that your dog? Because you're going to need a visitor's pass if you've got a dog with you."

"No, this is Beth Ann Devlin's dog. She's in number one-one-one-five."

"Miss Devlin has a *dog*?" He frowned and typed something on the tablet in front of him. "Huh, I guess it says here that she does. I had no idea."

"Are you at this desk a lot?"

"Yup, all day every day."

"And you've never seen her with this dog?"

"Nope, never."

"Oh, *wow*. Okay, thank you." Cora continued toward the large double doors and looked down at Chanel. "How in the world am I going to make this better?"

Chanel dragged Cora to the closest grassy patch and immediately emptied what was left in her bladder. The little dog obviously wanted to be clean, but Beth Ann didn't give her the opportunity to potty where she was supposed to. After she finished her business, which also included a compact pile of poo, Chanel stood with her face turned up to the sun, eyes closed and panting, as if drinking in the world. Neither of them wanted to go back inside.

Cora felt powerless to help. She'd cobbled together a dog trainer code of ethics when she began her career, stealing "First, do no harm" from the Hippocratic Oath. It guided every interaction she had with her canine clients and prevented her from doing anything even close to what Ershovich did on his show. The second part of her code was "Help the helpless." For the first time since she'd started Top Dog, she felt like she was failing. Chanel had the bare minimum of what she needed to survive—food, water, and shelter, which meant that animal control couldn't be summoned—but she lacked what dogs require to thrive. How was she going to get through to Beth Ann?

Cora sat down on a low retaining wall and patted next to her, and Chanel immediately jumped up and sat with her body resting against Cora's leg. Of course, there was a right way and a wrong way to attempt a nail trim with an unfamiliar dog, but Cora had no choice. She needed to get this done in a hurry.

"Now, Chanel, this might feel uncomfortable for you, but I promise it won't hurt. Trust me, I do this all the time on dogs much bigger and grumpier than you." She pulled the clippers from her back pocket and grasped the dog's tiny paw in her hand. "We're going to do this sooo fast, okay?" Chanel looked up at her with what looked like a smile of acceptance.

Cora cut the first nail quickly, and Chanel didn't move. "Yay, wasn't that easy? Look what you get. A treat!" Cora offered the dog a small piece of freeze-dried chicken, which she gulped down. "Let's keep going!" Chanel wagged her tail in agreement.

Chanel didn't protest once as Cora clipped all her nails, accepting the novel handling with the grace of a veteran show dog that was used to getting poked and prodded by strangers. Cora couldn't believe how tolerant she was, despite being thrown in the deep end of the grooming pool. Nail trims were a serious business, with some dogs requiring a trip to the vet and mild sedation to get the job done. Chanel acted like they were just two girlfriends hanging out at the spa.

"I can't believe how good you are!" Cora laughed at the homely little dog spinning in happy circles on the retaining wall next to her. "You are the best dog ever!"

A voice called out, "Holy crap, is that Chanel?" Cora looked up to see Eli loping toward them.

"Fancy meeting you here," Cora responded. "Yes, this is your neighborhood menace. Come face your foe!" Even though she'd anticipated feeling awkward around him since Fran had told her about his crush, she was happy to see his friendly face. She needed it to bolster her for the next round with Beth Ann.

Chanel hopped off the wall as Eli got closer, turning herself in a joyful circle, wagging her tail so fast that it looked like a hummingbird's wings.

Eli knelt down so that Chanel could approach him at her own pace. Cora was impressed he didn't rush over and try to pet her. "Awww, she's so . . . weird-looking," he said as he surveyed her. "Like a dirty little space alien. With a goofy toof."

"I don't know how I'm going to deal with this situation," Cora said, speaking more candidly about her client than she meant to. "Something's not right with Beth Ann today. She forgot I was coming and she was sleeping when I got here. Does she work?"

Eli scratched behind Chanel's ears as he answered. "She had a job for a while but I rarely see her coming or going anymore. I think she might be a trust fund baby. I know her parents live in Houston, and she came out here to take a job on the Hill."

"She doesn't strike me as a 'working on the Hill' type."

"Yeah, me neither. Maybe that's why she's not."

Cora considered this new information. At one point Beth Ann had the wherewithal to leave her familiar life in Texas and move to a new world all by herself. What had happened?

"I like this little weirdo." Eli looked down and spoke directly to Chanel as he petted her. "I like you even though your barking is making me nuts!"

Cora watched Eli interacting with Chanel, and it was clear that he was a dog person. He had a way with Chanel that the little dog couldn't seem to get enough of. He sat down on the ground and she immediately crawled into his lap and rolled onto her back for more belly rubs.

"I don't mean to pry, but why are you home at two on a Friday?" Cora asked. "Is everything okay?"

"Oh, it's just my typical 'big brother to the rescue' gig. My sister is moving this weekend and she's totally helpless, so I took the afternoon off to assist. You know, lifting heavy things, holding doors, project managing. It's kind of my lot in life." He shrugged and looked down at his phone. "I should get going."

Cora sighed. "I'm dreading going back in, but we've been out here for ten minutes already."

"I'll escort you guys. Like a warden taking the prisoners to death row." He stood up and gestured dramatically toward the door.

Eli studied Cora as she walked his way. "Hey, this"—he waved his fingers near his cheeks—"looks really good. Your face, I mean. You look . . . like, fancy. Sorry, am I allowed to say that? Was that rude?"

Cora had forgotten that she was still wearing Darnell's handiwork. She blushed. "Oh, thanks. I never wear makeup, but my friends did a little makeover on me this morning."

"Well, it looks nice. I mean, you *always* look nice, the few times I've seen you. Like a . . . Disney princess or something. Really, like, natural." He was fumbling, gesturing with his hands to try to convey what words couldn't.

"Seriously? A Disney princess? Which one?" It was the most creative compliment she'd ever received.

"Umm, I think that one with the really long hair." He snapped his fingers trying to recall the name.

"Rapunzel. *How* do you know the Disney princesses?"

He shrugged again. "Three sisters. I put in my time as both Prince Eric and the Beast."

Chanel put on the brakes the moment they got to the double doors, as if she couldn't bear to go back inside.

"She is *not* having it." Cora took a step forward and tried to encourage Chanel to follow by making kissy noises, but she refused to move.

Eli gently picked up the trembling dog and spoke softly to her. "You poor thing. I'm sorry things are so rough for you. Maybe you can come visit me sometime? I live right down the hall, so come knock on my door anytime." Chanel climbed up Eli's chest and nuzzled her face in his neck. "Wow, she stinks."

They got off the elevator and stood close so Cora could untangle Chanel from Eli. He looked sweet cradling the bedraggled dog who was already in love with him.

"Ow, ow, little dog! She's digging her claws into my shoulder!"

"She doesn't want you to let go! Oh my God, this is *killing* me!" Cora whispered, just in case Beth Ann was standing near her door and could hear them. When she took Chanel from Eli's arms, the dog air-swam in an attempt to get back to him. "She really likes you!"

"I really like her, too. I might have to steal her."

"Shhhh!" Cora widened her eyes and jutted her head toward Beth Ann's door.

He grimaced and nodded. "Okay, I'm going to go now!" He spoke loudly and overenunciated, as if trying to reach the people in the cheap seats.

"Nice talking to you, see you later," Cora answered with a similar fake cadence. They smiled at each other, whispered "Bye," and went their separate ways.

Cora knocked on Beth Ann's door and opened it at the same time. "Knock, knock! We're back." She followed the sound of the

TV and found Beth Ann standing in the center of the pitch-black room looking down at her iPad. Chanel didn't go over to greet her, instead choosing to sit next to Cora.

Beth Ann didn't look up. "Oh, hey. I'm just ordering some stuff I need from Bergdorf's. I'll be done in a sec."

"Sure, um. I'll just unpack my things so we can get started."

"Actually," Beth answered, still looking down at her device, "I need to talk to you about training."

Cora's stomach dropped. What had changed in the past fifteen minutes? Was she getting fired? "Okay. What's up?"

"I don't want to use treats to train Chanel. She's going to get too fat. If you can do it without treats, we can keep going, but if not, maybe we should just stop now."

Cora had heard the complaint from a few clients over the years but had always managed to convince them of the need for treats during the early stages of training. Beth Ann had seemed fine using them during the few minutes they had worked together at their abbreviated first session.

"Um. What if we use really tiny pieces? You don't have to use treats for every repetition for the rest of Chanel's life, just during the foundation steps."

"Nope. No treats," she answered dully.

Cora felt her flush rising but she didn't want to anger Beth Ann and lose the opportunity to try to help Chanel. "Does she like to play? Is she toy driven? Maybe we could use balls or tug toys so that we're not using as many treats?"

Beth Ann finally pried herself away from her tablet and stared at Cora. "How would I know if she's 'toy driven'? That's your job."

Another piece of the puzzle fell into place; Beth Ann had never played with Chanel. Cora knew to tread lightly. Normally she couldn't tolerate a client as unpredictable as Beth Ann, but she was determined to make life better for Chanel.

"You know what? Maybe it's best if I head out today, and then we can regroup and really get started at our next session? I get the feeling that you're not a hundred percent good to go right now, so let's just call it a day and then we can try again next week. I'll bring a bunch of different toy options, and we can try some play training together."

"Um-hm." Beth Ann was once again immersed in her device, scrolling rapidly.

"Great. I'll text you the day before to confirm. Oh, and I wanted to let you know that I trimmed her nails."

"Okay?" Beth Ann shrugged her shoulders and shook her head as if she had no idea why Cora was telling her.

"Well, she was awesome about it. I mean, it was easy, so you should have no problem keeping up with it. I can show you how next time."

She shrugged again. "Whatever."

"Okay, I'll see you next week. Holler if you have any questions." Beth Ann didn't answer, so Cora picked up her bag and walked to the door. Chanel walked right next to her, as if the two of them were leaving together.

Cora leaned down to pet Chanel and quietly comfort her. "*Ma puce.* I'll be back next week, okay?"

She opened the door, and the little dog darted out and headed for the elevator. When Cora caught up with her, Chanel put her head down and cowered, as if admitting defeat. It broke her heart to see the little dog's spark go out.

"I'm sorry, I'm so sorry," she whispered as she picked the dog up and walked her back to Beth Ann's door. "Your life is going to change, I promise."

EIGHTEEN

Cora and Maggie, each outfitted in sweats and equipped with full glasses of wine and nervous stomachs, sat in front of Cora's computer on the kitchen table. Winnie and Vanessa had canceled on the alcohol-fueled Doggie Dictator live stream hate-watch, both opting out just a few hours before they were due to meet at Cora's.

"It's starting, it's starting," Cora said as she pointed to the screen. Fritz was curled up on top of her feet beneath the table.

"This is going to be a shitshow," Maggie said. "I can't believe you're making me watch it. This could be you instead of him, you know."

"If I were on a show, it wouldn't be like this," Cora said, staring at the screen.

Ershovich's theme song came on, pulsing with jarring chords that were meant to evoke a feeling of danger and suspense, as if he were training lions and not man's best friend.

"This music gives me PTSD," Cora said.

The camera scanned the crowd, flashing by the smiling up-turned faces that craned to see the man of the hour.

"Look at that lady's hair—that looks like Winnie from the back," Maggie said, pointing to the screen.

"Isn't this the theater where Lincoln was shot?" Cora asked. "Maybe it is Winnie and she has a plan?"

"No, that was Ford's Theater, and don't even joke about it."

Ershovich, in a tight black button-down shirt and slim-fitting black pants, strode out with his hands in the air, drinking in the crowd's adulation.

"I hate that he's sort of hot," Maggie said, taking a slug of wine without removing her eyes from the screen.

Cora nodded. "It would be so much easier to take him down if he looked like a toad."

The crowd quieted and Boris began speaking. "Ladies and gentlemen, welcome to *The Doggie Dictator*!" The applause swelled until Boris quieted them again. "Tonight I have some miracle transformations to share with you. I'm going to show you a dog that was so vicious, so out of control, that her entire family was afraid of her."

The audience collectively sucked in their breath.

Ershovich nodded his head in agreement. "This dog was a menace, and in truth should have been put down. But after I worked with her . . . well, why don't we all see what I was able to do?" He gestured to the jumbo screen behind him as it began playing the setup footage.

The story unfolded like every episode. Interviews with the attractive family intercut with clips of the dog looking scary and displaying the "dangerous" behavior. The dog, Sadie, was an amiable-looking mixed-breed brindle rescue dog that was perfectly behaved until she was approached while eating. The clip showed several interactions where the parents and teenage children walked toward her food bowl, which caused her to freeze, growl, then bare her teeth.

"Oh, this is textbook resource guarding," Cora said. "Very predictable buildup, very clear signaling. No small kids in the house to trip up the training process. Give this family to me, *I'll* show them how to deal with it."

"He thinks this dog should be put to sleep? That's insane."

The clip cut to Boris explaining that Sadie thought that she was head of the household, and her reason for guarding was because she hadn't submitted to her owners. Cora hissed at the screen.

"Your dog has zero respect for authority," he said to Sadie's people sternly. "It's really no wonder that she acts like this. All shelter dogs are broken in some way, many irreparably." He gestured to Sadie with a barely concealed look of disgust on his face. "And she looks like she has pit in her. Of *course* she's aggressive."

Maggie turned to look at Cora, braced for her predictable outburst.

Cora jumped out of her chair, startling Fritz. "What did he just say? Is he serious? Rescue dogs are *broken*? And pits are inherently aggressive?"

Adrenaline coursed through her body, making her hands tremble. Getting people to adopt rescue dogs was tough enough, and now shelters would have to refute people spewing Ershovich's lies. Given his reach, the comment would be a crippling blow for rescue organizations, particularly those that worked with pits.

The clip ended and cut back to Boris on the stage. "Want to know how I fixed her?"

The crowd roared, and the camera swooped over their heads, capturing the excitement. Someone held up a predictable hand-made BORIS IS FOR US sign.

"Stay with me, we'll be right back after the break," Boris said, bowing with his hands clasped in front of him, as if he were a holy man entering a temple.

His theme music swelled, and the camera panned back to shots of the ecstatic audience. An overweight woman in a flo-ral top flashed a sign that said TRAIN MY DOG, PLEASE! Men pumped their fists at the camera, making tough guy faces. The camera paused as a woman and her friend stood up to reveal a two-part sign.

Cora blanched. "Oh . . . my . . . God . . ."

"It's it's it's," Maggie stuttered.

Vanessa's sparkly heart-covered sign said BORIS WILL U . . . She smiled and danced for the camera in a jaw-dropping hot pink minidress, keeping it engaged as Winnie stood up next to her and unfurled her sign.

STOP ABUSING DOGS?!

The camera hovered on them as if the camera operator couldn't believe what he was seeing and had to reread it to make sure. Va-nessa threw down her sign and pointed to Winnie, who stood holding her sign over her head with an angry expression on her face. Still the camera remained on them. Vanessa gave the finger and mouthed "Fuck you!" right into the camera and the feed went dark.

Maggie downed the rest of her wine in a single gulp. "Holy shit, C! Your girls are gangsters!"

"It's *unbelievable*! The best thing I've ever seen in my life! They're not going to make it onto the show, but someone's going to leak it, I guarantee it." Cora grabbed her phone and pulled up Twitter.

Sure enough, it was already gaining traction. People were supporting the anti-Ershovich message.

Maggie left the room to get another bottle of wine. Cora massaged Fritz's shoulders and stared off into space, trying to make sense of the electric surge that was coursing through her. She'd felt powerless to stand up to Ershovich's bullshit for long enough. Now she had an amazing opportunity, an e-mail that had appeared in her inbox for a reason. A long shot by any estimation, but a chance just the same. A way to help the helpless in the biggest, loudest, most public way possible.

People seemed ready to hear an alternative, and she was finally ready to answer.

Cora leaned down and whispered in Fritz's ear, "*Il doit être arrêté.* It's time to overthrow the dictator." Then she sent a text to Wade.

NINETEEN

Wade mobilized the moment Cora said she was ready, setting up the audition photo session in his home studio for the following day, before she could change her mind. Though Wade and Rachel were eager to help package her for her submission, getting a professional-looking photo of Cora and Fritz was proving to be more difficult than anticipated.

"Okay, act like this isn't painful," Rachel joked. She rested her expensive-looking camera on her hip and twisted her long black hair into a bun with the other hand.

"Is my face that awful?" Cora asked. She knew that her smile usually looked strained in photos.

"I'm kidding! But you do look *veddy* serious, and I think it's affecting Fritz. He seems a little stressed."

Cora looked down at her dog, who was draped across her lap. "Oh, I think it's your camera. Most dogs freak out at traditional cameras because it's weird to dogs when people hide their faces behind that thing. Plus, that high-pitched whine from your flash is probably a little scary for him."

"Is *that* why Daisy runs away every time I try to get a good photo of her? Makes sense." Rachel scrolled through the images. "In every shot so far, either you look a little off or Fritz looks a little off. See?" She handed Cora her camera and showed her how to flip through the first photos.

Cora scanned the images. Maggie had picked the Liberty floral button-down, casual blazer, and boyfriend jeans, so she knew her outfit was on point, but there was no ignoring her dazed expression in every photo. "Yikes, you're right. I need to lighten up a bit, huh?" Cora had wide eyes and a frozen fake smile in each photo, and Fritz was either looking up at Cora for direction or at the camera with his ears back. He was yawning in many of the photos, a universal signal for canine stress. They both looked uncomfortable.

"What should we do?" Rachel asked.

"I've got an idea," Wade piped up from his desk in the corner. "Let's get Daisy in the shot, too. Would Fritz be okay with that?"

"Would *you* be okay with that?" Rachel asked Cora.

"That might be cute! Two big dogs and me? I'll look like the hound master."

"Well, if that's the vibe you're going for, let me get our neighbor's French bulldog, Lucy, in the picture, too. Want to give it a try?"

"Sure, it'll be absolutely ridiculous. Let's have them all play in the yard for a few minutes before we try to get them to settle down for a photo, though."

Wade ran to his neighbor's house to fetch Lucy, then met Rachel, Cora, and the dogs in their backyard. Daisy and Lucy had been friends since the Cohens brought Daisy home as a roly-poly puppy, and they still romped together despite their size difference.

After fifteen minutes of hard-core play, the people hustled the panting dogs into the editing room. Cora put Fritz in a down-stay on the backdrop, then lined Daisy up a few feet away and put her in a down-stay as well.

"Check out my good dog!" Wade exclaimed as Daisy held her stay. "See, we *are* practicing!"

Cora didn't want to push her luck trying to get a trifecta of stays, so she picked up the brindle Frenchie and gingerly walked between the two resting dogs. She sat between them cross-legged with Lucy standing on her lap.

"Aww, I like how this looks," Rachel exclaimed. "Here we go!"

The quick playdate in the yard took the edge off the dogs' energy levels, so they posed without protest, each with a wide panting grin. Rachel snapped photo after photo while Cora laughed and petted the dogs surrounding her.

"I can't get them to look at me at the same time. One of them is always looking away," Rachel said as she flipped through the photos on her camera. "So close, though!"

"Make a funny noise," Cora suggested. "Like a little squeak or bark. That usually works to get them to look and give a head tilt."

Rachel made a crying sound like a lost puppy, and all three dogs froze and looked at her with curious expressions on their faces. She tried a kitten-like "meow" and each dog cocked its head in a universal "huh?" look.

"There it is! The money shot!" Rachel exclaimed as she snapped away. "This is great." She continued making strange sounds, each one eliciting a new and adorable expression on the canine models' faces, and finally Cora could relax and enjoy the process.

"I think we've got it," Rachel said, resting her camera on her shoulder after about ten minutes of shooting, when the dogs had tired of modeling.

Fritz fell onto his side, and Daisy plopped down facing him, placing her front paws on top of his. Lucy was already on her back between them, indelicately splayed with all four paws pointing in opposite directions.

"Wait!" Rachel said quietly as Cora started to stand. "I see one more shot. Lie down in between them and look up at me." She grabbed a step stool and moved it closer so that she was looking down on the resting dogs.

Cora tiptoed among the dogs and positioned herself on the floor amid the sleeping scrum. She pulled Lucy next to her so that the fat little dozing dog was on her back nestled into Cora's side. Daisy sighed and adjusted herself so that the top of her head rested against Cora's cheek, and Cora reached back and snaked her arm around the dog's shoulder. Fritz, suddenly possessive, placed his big square head on Cora's chest and reached his paw across her body, as if to hug her. Cora took his paw in her other hand.

The effect was a canine version of Yoko and John's iconic *Rolling Stone* cover, with the three dogs flanking her at every angle. Cora closed her eyes and surrendered to the sleepy sweetness surrounding her while Rachel snapped away above them.

"Perfection," Rachel murmured. "Okay, I promise now we're *truly* done."

Cora sat up and the dogs barely stirred. She gently stroked Lucy's pink belly. "I can't thank you enough for doing this. May I peek?"

Rachel handed her the camera, and Cora was stunned by the final images of the day. The initial photos of them sitting at attention looked professional and adorable, but the last few shots were something else entirely. They actually radiated the love Cora felt for all dogs.

"You are an artist, Rachel. These are amazing."

"Aw, you're gonna make me cry! It's easy to take great photos when you have subjects like you guys. That was pretty magical."

Wade interrupted, "All right, all right, enough of the sobfest. We've got more work to do. Cora, come here." He beckoned her over to his computer. "Check this out." He pushed a button and suddenly Cora's face filled the screen—her impromptu on-camera training session with Daisy.

"Oh my God, turn it off!" she screamed, hiding her eyes.

"Deal with it. If you're serious about doing this you're going to have to learn to critique yourself."

Cora peeked from behind her hands and saw that Wade had filmed some additional footage of Daisy, so the shots of her talking to the camera were supplemented with close-ups of Daisy's attentive face. He also added music and graphics, so the casual three minutes of footage they had filmed off-the-cuff now looked like a professional training piece. The clip ended with a screen showing Cora's full name, e-mail address, and phone number.

She was dumbfounded. "That's amazing—you made me look like I know what I'm doing. Why . . . why are you doing all of this?

Why are you guys helping me so much? Can I pay you? Can I give you free dog training for life?"

Wade smiled. "Oh, we're definitely taking you up on the free dog training. But it's no big deal to do this stuff. I edited that footage while you guys were taking the photos. This kind of project is fun for me . . . I deal with boring stuff in my real job. Dogs are easy! Plus I had a mentor who did something similar for me way back when. I'm paying it forward."

"And you gave me a reason to pick up my good camera again," Rachel added. "Now that the twins are in preschool maybe I'll get back to my photography. I used to be so creative, but now there's barely enough time for me to brush my teeth. *You* did *me* a favor!"

"I'm just so honored by all of this. Really . . . thank you."

"We're not done yet. Let's pick your favorite photo. Wade gave me strict orders that you're not to leave until you've submitted your stuff."

Cora was incredulous. "You mean you want me to send it right—"

"Now," Wade interrupted. "You're already late submitting, let's get this train moving. The clip is done. The photos are done. We're sending it off. Today."

Rachel popped the memory card into her oversize computer and the photos filled the screen. They quickly narrowed their choices down to two favorites, one of the images of the dogs sitting next to Cora, each with a tilted head and happy expression, and one of the final images of the day with the dogs dozing around her.

"They're both so different. How can we choose?" Cora asked.

"I have a favorite. Wade, what about you?" He walked over to the screen and stood next to Rachel.

"I have a favorite, too. No question."

Cora stared at the images. One looked professional and typical— she had seen similar shots on other trainers' websites. The other looked like art.

"It might be risky, but I like the sleepy one. I love it because it's not all about me . . . it's about . . . relationship."

"Me, too!" Rachel and Wade said simultaneously. Wade offered Cora a high-five.

"This photo alone should at least get you an audition."

"Is the mutual admiration society done with the meeting? Let's get this bad boy submitted," Wade said, ever the taskmaster. "Log in to your e-mail on my computer."

Cora sat down at his desk. "I'm so nervous!"

She looked at Rachel and Wade, and they nodded encouragingly at her. Fritz made his way over to where she sat and rested his head on her knee, offering his support as well.

"Wish me luck, everybody."

She held her breath, closed her eyes, and pushed send.

TWENTY

F ritz walked slowly through Rock Creek Park, seeking out the shady stretches and panting, as if he'd just run a few miles. Springtime in DC was unpredictable, with typical temperate days intermixed with sweltering hints of the summer to come. The sun was warmer than Cora expected, and she worried that she and Fritz might have overdone it during their Sunday meditation stroll. Sometimes his gait showed his age, and even though her vet told her that he was in great shape for a senior, Cora still worried about him constantly.

Cora tried to be fully present during their Sunday walks, but when she found a shady patch and sat down next to Fritz, she couldn't resist checking her phone just once. An e-mail from the Rescue League highlighting the at-risk dogs in the shelter in need of foster homes tugged at her heartstrings.

She hadn't fostered a dog since she and Aaron broke up. She missed it, though, and guessed that Fritz did as well. He was always a gracious host to the dogs passing through their home, welcoming the new dogs with the finesse of an ambassador and

helping build their confidence through gentle play and companionship. She looked over at him and asked, "Want to save a life,
Fritzy?"

Cora scrolled through the dogs' photos in the e-mail. Every
single one looked adorable, and her heart broke that she couldn't
take them all in. She wrote post after post on ChienParfait about
how wonderful shelter dogs were, and that they weren't broken
or damaged. Now she felt like she had to work overtime to undo
the Ershovich damage. She wrote about how easy fostering was,
and how rewarding. She followed up with her fosters once they
were in their forever homes and told their new stories of happi-
ness, easy living, and friendship, always including heart-tugging
before-and-after photos. But she was blogging into the abyss; each
post received only a few hits.

She kept scrolling through the e-mail until a face stopped her
in her tracks. The dog had short light blond fur with a subtle white
mask, a liver-colored nose, and a light brown spot on the top of her
head nestled in her impressive worry wrinkles. Her origami ears
were pointy with the tips folded down, as if they never quite made
it to a full point during her puppy growth spurt. Her muzzle was
puffy, which made her look like she had a little shar-pei in her. Her
head was tilted to the side in the picture, as if the photographer
had just asked her a question she couldn't answer. There was something in her face that Cora couldn't resist.

The dog's description was all too familiar. "Josie is an owner
surrender. She's an adorable young pocket pit mix, weighing in at
only forty-three pounds. She's a snugglebug and she loves everyone she meets, including other dogs, children, and cats. She knows

how to sit, and she takes treats very gently. Josie isn't doing well in the shelter environment. The shelter is almost at capacity, and we're in desperate need of foster homes. Please consider helping Josie."

Fritz nuzzled Cora's hand, as if giving his approval. "Should we?" she asked him. Finding a foster was almost like falling in love at first sight, and Cora was powerless when it happened. She dashed off a quick text to her friend Abby, who volunteered at the League, to get the behind-the-scenes scoop, and discovered that Josie would be a perfect fit.

Cora texted Maggie, knowing what her answer would be but asking anyway as a courtesy. Maggie was always a doting Auntie to Cora's temporary lodgers.

Cora put her phone down and rubbed Fritz's shoulders. She hoped that a part-time new buddy would put the pep back in his step. He had slowed down suddenly since their last foster, and she hoped that bringing a dog like Josie in would liven him up again.

She leaned over and kissed him. "Off we go, bud. Let's walk." He stood up and shook his body off, and they headed back to the main path. They spotted a dog in the distance, and Fritz's tail immediately started wagging in anticipation. Cora nodded. "Yup, I think Josie is just what you need, boy."

TWENTY-ONE

Cora had only been in the Feretti household for ten minutes and already things were going to hell.

"What do you mean by 'they need more exercise'?" Simone Feretti asked, sounding incredulous and defensive at the same time.

Cora watched the two sleek German shorthaired pointers chase each other through the spacious living room, trying to figure out a way to gently express her concerns without further angering her new client.

"I'm sure you know that these dogs are bred to hunt and retrieve for hours," she began. "If they don't get a ton of brain and body exercise every day, you end up with . . . this." Cora gestured to the canine scrum at her feet, which was grappling close to an end table crowded with candlesticks. The dogs' dark brown heads and chocolate chip–spotted coats blended seamlessly into the Feretti décor, their streamlined elegance a fine complement to the calming tans and creams in the room. Their temperament, however, was anything but.

Simone's forehead remained an expressionless expanse, though it was clear that she was furious with what she was seeing. The kicked-up edges of the Oriental rugs and jostled throw pillows were more than she could take. Her sleek blond bob trembled as she watched her dogs wreak havoc in her picture-perfect life.

"Hunter, OFF!" Simone shouted. "Blade, *stoy! Stoy!*"

Cora cringed when Simone invoked Ershovich's seething Russian correction. The bastard was everywhere.

"When are you going to take them outside and start training them?" Simone asked. "They're destroying my house." A thin, twisty vein began to bulge in the center of her forehead.

"Actually, you and I are going to train them together, as a team," Cora replied as color flooded her cheeks. She tried to envision how a woman with a flotilla of household staff would interpret the word *team*. "It's important that Blade and Hunter develop that bond with you. And we'll be working inside for the whole hour today."

Simone leaned back in her chair and crossed her arms. The woman's lack of emotion was throwing Cora off her game. There was nothing for her to grab onto to make a connection with Simone, no scrap of pleasantry that she could spin into camaraderie. Cora's success depended on building relationships with both the dogs and the people, and Simone wasn't going to allow that to happen.

"This should keep them busy while we talk," Cora said as she handed each dog a bone from her bag. She circled back to her initial point, hoping that Simone might fill in the blanks about their unusual household dynamic. "So these guys are canine athletes and they really need to work—"

"I *know* they need to work. I know that," Simone interrupted, smoothing the hem of her Chanel blazer. "My husband hunts with them in the fall. They're hunting dogs, and they live like hunting dogs. They have the entire backyard to play. We have a very large fenced property. They run around like lunatics out there all day long. In fact, this is the first time they've been inside in days."

Cora's eyes widened involuntarily, and she struggled to collect herself. "Um, I'm not a big fan of making dogs live outside . . . they really just want to be close to their people. Pack animals, you know? I didn't realize that they're living in the backyard . . ." How had she missed that during their initial phone call? Even though the dogs' outdoor accommodations were probably as sumptuous as the Feretti home, Cora knew that dogs living isolated from their people were treated like livestock rather than like beloved pets.

Simone's face hardened and she clenched her hands so tightly that her slender fingers turned white.

"They're not *living* outside. They are *hunting dogs*." She enunciated the words, as if that would make it clearer to Cora. "They have a custom-built climate-controlled doghouse and run in the yard. As you can see, these dogs are maniacs when they're inside, that's why we keep them out back. The problem is they've been barking, and now our neighbors are complaining about the noise. I bought electric collars to curb the barking until you've finished training them. I'd like you to fit them on the dogs."

Only if you let me try one on you first, Cora thought.

"Electric collars are actually shock collars, and I never train with pain," Cora replied in measured tones, aware that she had to tread lightly if she hoped to save the dogs. "Shock collars are dangerous tools that can cause serious trauma, including fallout from—"

Simone raised her hand in the air to silence Cora. "Will you train these dogs the way I want or not?"

Blade and Hunter had abandoned their bones and were wrestling in between where Cora and Simone sat, their playful growls adding to the tension in the room. Cora felt a flush rising in her cheeks. She wanted to tell Simone without any sugarcoating that the way she was treating her dogs was cruel. That their less-than-desirable behavior was a direct result of their banishment to the yard. That she should have purchased lawn ornaments instead of animals with needs. Based on her read of Simone, Cora knew that no matter how she tried to spin it, the message would sound judgmental, rather than helpful.

So the two women sat in silence, staring at Blade and Hunter as they tussled. Cora admitted to herself that she wasn't going to be able to work with Simone, but she didn't know how best to convey the news to the tightly wound woman sitting across from her. Agonizingly, she was convinced that she could help Blade and Hunter transition from lawless yard dogs to well-mannered companions. The dogs she could handle, it was the humans that were going to be a problem.

Cora took a deep breath. "I'm thinking that I might not be the right trainer for you."

"Yes, I think that you're right," Simone replied, arms crossed and eyes unblinking.

"Okay. Good. That's good, I'm—I'm glad we agree," Cora stuttered and smoothed her hand over the flyaway curls near her forehead. The hot red embarrassment splotches spread from her cheeks to her neck. "There's no charge for today, of course. I'll just pack up and be on my way. But I'd like to forward you some information about the dangers of shock collars and refer you to a few other positive trainers in the area—"

Simone silenced Cora with her hand again. "Thank you, but that'll be unnecessary." Her tone was glacial. "I'm going to put the dogs outside before they do more damage."

Simone turned and reached for Hunter. He ducked away, knocking into the delicate pedestal table near the couch and tipping over a crystal vase filled with dogwood blossoms. The unexpected crash-splash sent both dogs running from the room.

"Felisa! Felisa, the dogs are loose!" Simone screamed as she ran out of the room after them. Cora raced behind her and knocked into the petite Hispanic woman who had let her into the house, nearly sending her to the ground. The dogs rounded a corner and disappeared into the kitchen, with all three women close behind them.

"They're trapped in here now—shut the other door, Felisa!" Simone moved toward Blade, who was pacing in a corner of the professionally outfitted kitchen. She looked like she wanted to tackle him. The closer she got, the faster he paced. Felisa stood in a corner and chanted "Oh, oh, oh," as if she wasn't sure quite what to do.

"Wait, can I make a suggestion?" Cora interrupted. "I've got some treats in my back pocket, and I bet if we all just stand still and I toss the treats in front of me, the dogs will come over and we can get them without a struggle."

Simone continued moving toward Blade as if she hadn't heard Cora, arms outstretched. The dog panted and ran back and forth with his rear end tucked. Hunter stood quietly in the desk nook, watching the drama unfold. Everyone—dogs and humans—held their breath as Simone paused and then leaped at Blade.

She miscalculated how fast he was, which wasn't surprising, given how little daily contact she had with the dog. Blade swished by Simone's legs as she lunged for him, knocking her knees out from under her. Clearly embarrassed, Simone righted herself and turned to glare at Cora.

"This is *unacceptable*. Get them." It was a command, not a request. She crossed her arms and moved to the back of the cavernous kitchen.

Cora nodded, her face hot from the tension and Simone's unwavering stare.

"Hey guys! Hey pups!" She knelt down and threw a few treats in front of her. Hunter, unscathed by the chase, came willingly from beneath the desk and collected the treats on the floor.

"What a sweet boy, *mon petit loup*," Cora whispered to him. The dog flinched when he saw her outstretched hand but returned his focus to the scattered treats. Cora wondered if his hand-shyness was a result of a lack of human interaction, or something more sinister, like Ershovich's direction to "be the boss no matter the cost." Cora could understand why Simone might gravitate to Ershovich's advice, since she seemed to want canine robots instead of dogs with spirit and personality. The Doggie Dictator trained the dog out of every dog he worked with, and the world applauded him for it. Cora gently grasped Hunter's collar. "Okay, okaaaay, you're fine now."

She turned to Simone and shrugged. "One down . . ."

Felisa rushed over to take the dog away without even being asked, whispering calmly to him in rapid Spanish.

Cora reached into her pocket and scattered a few more treats on the ground. Blade assessed her nonthreatening body language and approached her slowly, then began hoovering the treats near her feet.

"There's a boy," Cora cooed. "Nice work, *chouchou*." She ran her hand along his smooth fur and then took hold of his collar. Blade trembled as Simone walked over to grab him. She handed the dog off to Felisa and turned back to Cora.

"Felisa will see you out." Simone walked out of the room without another word.

Cora waited in the kitchen for Felisa to return, unsure if it would be rude to go back to the family room unchaperoned. She was sweating, and her stomach hurt. She'd had her share of challenging clients, but none could compare to what had just happened. Even Beth Ann was more neglectful than cruel! She was angry at herself for letting the session get so out of hand, and depressed that she wouldn't be able to help the dogs. It felt like Cooper all over again, but in a much grander setting.

Felisa came back in the kitchen through the back door, shaking her head. "Those *perros*."

"I wish I could help," Cora said, shrugging her shoulders, hoping her body language could convey her powerlessness.

"They want to come in. Sometimes, I go outside and . . ." She pantomimed petting.

"I bet they like that."

Cora followed Felisa back into the family room and packed her bag. She glanced out the large picture window and saw Blade and Hunter standing in the middle of the yard, staring in as fat raindrops began to fall.

TWENTY-TWO

Cora's new foster, Josie, sat in the cramped backseat of Cora's Volvo calmly looking out the window, as if she made this trip every day. Cora never knew what kind of passenger she'd get when she brought home a foster, and she'd dealt with everything from terrified droolers to maniacal barkers over the years. Josie's face in the rearview mirror looked relaxed, and she surveyed the world outside the window with interest but not obsession. Her tail moved in wide circular wags. Josie's serenity was a good sign. Fritz peered back from the front seat every so often to confirm that the pretty blonde was indeed still with them. He had bonded to her almost immediately during their meet and greet at the shelter.

Everything changed the minute the car stopped in front of Cora's building. The cessation of movement jarred Josie into consciousness, much like a baby wakes when Mom stops rocking. She whined loudly and scratched at the windows, and Fritz looked at Cora with an expression that said, "*Who* is that?"

Cora struggled to unload Josie from the car. She wasn't sure if the suddenly nervous dog would dart because of the unfamiliar environment, so she took her time, triple wrapping the leash around her hand while Fritz watched from the sidewalk.

A middle-aged woman walked toward them, staring down at her phone. She didn't look up until she was almost on top of the trio, and when she saw Fritz blocking her path and Josie panting a few steps away she stopped short and shrieked.

"Don't worry," Cora assured the woman. "They're super friendly." Fritz took a step toward the stranger and wagged his entire hind end, as if to prove his ambassador skills.

"Get it away from me!" the woman yelled. She remained frozen with her hands out in front of her. Fritz sat down a few paces away from her, seemingly amused by the woman's misplaced distress. Josie remained glued by Cora.

"Fritz, *flanchet.*" *Flanchet* was the one French word Cora used with Fritz, a bastardization of the word *flank*, and he knew it was serious business when he heard it. He immediately came to her side, pressed his shoulder against her leg and looked directly up at Cora's face, as if nothing existed but her. Cora was so used to people freaking out when they encountered him that she worked on the cue until it was flawless. Fritz wasn't a *chien parfait*, but when he did *flanchet* he certainly looked like one.

The woman shuddered and speed-walked away. Cora felt sure that Ershovich's anti-pit influence was seeping into public consciousness.

She walked them to the top-secret grassy pee patch hidden in an alley up the block and waited until Josie stopped sniffing and calmed down enough to go. Fritz then led the way to their apartment and Josie ice-skated along behind them on the tips of her nails. She seemed disconnected from both Cora and Fritz.

Even though Cora preached proper foster dog acclimation protocols to her clients and on her blog, she didn't practice them. She knew she was supposed to employ baby gates, enforced separation, and careful delineation of resources until the dogs were comfortable with each other. But she flouted the rules because she knew Fritz could handle whatever rolled his way, and so could she. Cora unclipped their leashes once safely inside and watched the Fritz house tour begin. He walked directly in front of Josie on his way to the kitchen and took a drink from his bowl. He peeked around the corner to where she stood anchored by the door and then took another drink. "This is where our water is located," he seemed to say.

He passed by Josie again, walked over to his toy basket and gave her a look that said, "When you're ready to play, this is where the fun stuff lives." Cora made a mental note to watch for toy guarding behavior.

Finally he walked over to one of his many beds and stood in it, glancing her way. "This is pretty comfy, we can sleep here if you feel like it."

"You're such a good host, Fritzie," Cora said admiringly. She squatted down next to Josie, who remained glued to her side, and gave her a few shoulder rubs. "It's going to be okay, don't worry. You'll get the hang of this place." Cora walked to the couch, hoping the nervous dog would follow her.

"C'mon over. Come sit by us," Cora said to Josie, patting the dog bed in front of the couch, where she'd settled to check her e-mail. Josie walked toward them slowly, with her head lowered. "Good girl! There you go! Come rest."

Josie climbed in the bed and turned in four tight circles on the cushion, the genetically encoded ritual of tamping down the earth emerging from deep within her doggy DNA. She curled in a tight ball and sighed. Cora put her hand on Josie's back, and the dog barely stirred. "Take all the time you need, sweetie."

Cora texted Maggie a photo of sleeping Josie and then checked her e-mail. She sifted through the new client inquiries, junk mail from various dog supply outlets, and saw an unfamiliar address with a subject line that stopped her in her tracks.

"Your submission."

She opened the e-mail, but held her phone to her chest and took deep breaths before she read it.

Hi Cora, Thank you so much for your wonderful submission for *Everyday Dogs*! We would love to schedule time for a quick interview and video test. Please give me a call and we can talk about dates. Regards—Mia Nguyen

Cora's fingers tingled. It was happening! She had done it—she had passed the first hurdle, and they wanted to meet her! She forwarded the e-mail to Wade and then stared off into space. She was elated and terrified at the same time.

The sound of a key in the front door interrupted her racing thoughts, waking Josie from her REM sleep and sending her skidding toward the source, barking a fierce warning. Fritz watched her run to the door with a bemused expression on his face.

"Well, hello there! Is that any way to greet your new auntie?" Maggie was well versed enough in dogspeak to know that Josie's barky greeting was all bluster. "You are *so* pretty! Look at you!" The barking quieted, and Cora could hear Maggie murmuring to Josie.

The pair walked into the family room. "Oh my God, this is the cutest dog *ever*! Not counting you, Fritz." She reached down to pet Josie. "She's like a tiny little supermodel! How's she doing so far?" Josie looked up at Maggie with a lovesick expression on her face. No creature was immune to her charms.

"It's only been a few hours, but she's doing okay. A little on edge, which is to be expected. She and Fritz really like each other."

Maggie stopped and stared at Cora. "What? What's going on? Something's weird. Why are you looking at me like that?"

"I just got an e-mail . . ."

Maggie closed her eyes and crossed her fingers. "Please be what I think it is."

". . . from Bolex Media."

"Ahhhh, I told you!" She opened her eyes and whooped. "I told you they'd like you! Tell me everything!" Josie looked up at Maggie with her ears back, unsure if her booming voice meant war or peace.

"There's not much to tell. They want me to call to set up a time to meet. Interview and 'video test,' whatever that means."

"This is so freaking exciting! Why aren't you more excited? This is *huge*! They want to check you out, see how you take direction, make sure you're not a psychopath . . . I can help you prep! Auditions are my jam, baby. Are you freaking out?"

"You don't even know," Cora replied.

"Please, I totally know. You look like you're wearing Kabuki makeup."

Cora nodded and grimaced.

"You're going to be fine! They liked you enough to ask you to meet, so just go with it. You were meant for this. Trust me."

"'Meant for this'? You really think so?"

"What's your main goal in life, Cora Bellamy?"

"To help as many dogs as I can."

"Well, this could help a *ton* of dogs. Just remember that when you start to freak out."

"You're right. Maybe that's my mantra. 'This could help a ton of dogs.' If I remember it's about them and not me, I can get through this."

"Preach!" Maggie sat down next to Josie, who plopped into her lap. She ran her hand gently down the dog's back, and Josie leaned back against her so her head rested against Maggie's chest. "This dog is a winner. Whoever winds up with her is going to be very lucky. Right, cutie-face?"

Josie just sighed and snuggled in closer.

TWENTY-THREE

"How long has it been since you've had sex?" Maggie asked without lowering her voice. They were sitting outside The Wafflery, polishing off the remainder of their brunch. A table of fit yoga moms looked their way and laughed.

"I'm sure you can figure it out," Cora replied as she downed her mimosa, squinting at Maggie over the rim. "Count back."

"Okay, so you and Aaron broke up like . . . a year and a half ago?" Cora nodded. "And you qsaid things were pretty shitty toward the end, so . . ." She paused dramatically. "You haven't had sex with anyone in two years? Not even a one-night stand with some rando?"

"I came pretty close with that one guy right after Aaron and I broke up, but then I started crying and it totally killed the mood. Kind of unbelievable that it's been so long, isn't it?"

"It's a crime against humanity, darling!" Maggie whispered dramatically in a heavy British accent. "Are you going *mad*?"

"Nope, I'm past that point and settling into spinsterhood. Can we talk about getting some cats?"

Maggie rolled her eyes and ate the last bite of her challah

French toast. "Whatever. I'm going to make it my duty to get you some booty. Know this, woman. I am going to get you laid!"

"I'm ready." Cora laughed and picked up her phone to check the time and saw that she'd missed a text. "Wow, I think it's already working . . . Charlie Gill just texted me. Is this the start of your 'get Cora laid' promise?"

"Mr. I-have-a-girlfriend-but-don't-act-like-it? Please. I thought we were past this douche."

"Would you please stop saying that word?" Cora read the text out loud. " 'Sorry to get in touch on a Sunday, but can you call me today if you get a chance?' "

"He wants you to *call* him? Seriously? Do you guys usually text each other?"

"Sometimes. He sends me cute photos of Oliver. He asks training questions, we chat a little. He's never this cryptic."

"Call him, I wanna hear what he has to say."

Cora hadn't seen Charlie since their sushi session. Time had eased the sting of their conversation, and Cora used selective memory to block out Charlie's marriage talk. She couldn't stop thinking of the way his fingers felt as they brushed the top of her hand. He *had been* flirting, she was sure of it. She'd replayed the night thousands of times in her head, and every time she came to the same conclusion: Charlie was attracted to her, too.

"Do it. I want to eavesdrop," Maggie demanded.

Luckily, the yoga moms had left so they were alone on the patio. Cora sighed and dialed Charlie. The phone rang and rang, and Cora started to script the message she was going to leave when Charlie picked up, catching her off guard.

"Hey Cora, thanks for calling me!"

"No problem. What's up? Is everything okay?"

"Everything is great! Oliver is doing so awesome with his lessons, I can't wait for you to see him. Anyway, I have kind of a weird question for you."

Cora grimaced and looked at Maggie. "Okaaaay."

"So every year the ALPF has this big fund-raising gala—"

"Oh, you need my services donated for the raffle. I get asked to do stuff like this all the time. Sure, no problem, I'd be happy to contribute."

Charlie paused. "Well, that's nice, but that's not what I was going to ask. Every year I go all-out and buy a table for eight people and invite a bunch of my friends with the understanding that since I paid for the table, they have to bid on tons of auction stuff to support the cause. So this year I bought the big table, and six of my friends are in, but Madison's not going to be back in time, so I'm one down. I would hate for the seat to go to waste, so would you want to go? It's a really fun night for a cause I know you believe in. Oh, and the guest speaker this year?" He paused. "World-famous primatologist Alice Goodwin. Who doesn't love Alice Goodwin?"

Cora's heart thudded. She tried to hide her grin from Maggie. "I *adore* Alice Goodwin, I've always wanted to see her!" Maggie furrowed her brow and tilted her head at Cora to signal her confusion. Cora turned away from her. "So Madison can't make it?" Maggie dragged her chair over so that she could see Cora's face and stared at her.

"Yeah, we thought she'd be back in time, but it's not going to happen. We're both so bummed. The gala is on the twenty-third.

Want to check your calendar and let me know when I see you for our next lesson?"

"As long as it's . . . cool that I go. I mean, I don't want to step on Madison's toes or anything. Like, if she manages to change her plans, I'll bow out, of course."

"There's like zero chance that she'll make it. I'll let her know that you're going to be sitting in for her." Cora's stomach lurched as she pictured Madison getting the news. "Oh, and I don't know if this will encourage or dissuade you, but it's a formal event."

"Well, that definitely adds a wrinkle. I don't own a gown." Maggie heard the word *gown* and slapped both hands on the table in front of Cora.

"I guess there's some shopping in your future then! Check your schedule and let me know if you can come, okay?"

"I will. And thanks again for thinking of me." Cora hung up and stared at Maggie, incredulous. "He wants me to go to the ALPF gala. That thing is major, like the Academy Awards for animal people. I could make so many connections there."

"Huh? Wha?" Maggie shook her head and acted like she couldn't process what she was hearing. "Like a *date*? What the hell is going on with that guy?"

"No, no, not just the two of us. It's not a *date* date. He got a table, a bunch of his friends are going. Madison won't be back in time, and he has an extra seat."

"So he's asking *you* to go. You, the cute single chick, not his friend Larry from accounting. That's weird, Cora."

"I don't think it's like that," Cora said, even though a tiny part of her was hoping that it actually was. "Alice Goodwin is going to be there, and he thought I'd like to hear her speak. You know I love her."

"I can see right through you. Yeah, Alice is awesome, but that's *not* the reason you want to go." Maggie shook her head. "I don't think you should."

"What's with the high-and-mighty stuff all of a sudden?" Cora snapped angrily. "You're always down to have an adventure and break some rules. Why can't I do something a little reckless for a change?"

"Normally I'd say go for it, the hell with his bitchy girlfriend, go ahead and steal him away. But this feels different, Cora." She leaned forward and reached for her friend. "You're still in a tender place. This is the first time I've heard you talk about any guy since Aaron, and I'm worried. He's really giving you mixed signals, and that's not cool. I just don't want you to get hurt again."

"What if I just want to have fun and see what happens? It's not like we're going to be there alone. I'll be like the weird fourth cousin at a wedding that everyone ignores. And I'm not going because of Charlie, I'm going because of *Alice*," Cora fibbed.

"What do you want to happen? Have you even thought about that? Would you be okay with a one-night stand?"

"I haven't thought about it."

"Liar. You've got sex on the brain, I can tell."

It was true. "Okay, okay. I'll admit that even though he has a girlfriend, and even though you think he's the *d*-word, I'm still attracted to him. There, I said it. And I'm pretty sure it's mutual. I don't know, maybe he thought everything was great with Madison until . . . until he got to know me. It feels like we have a connection."

"So you want a relationship with him? Not just a fuck-and-run?"

Cora choked on her coffee. "Maybe?"

"So your goal is to break them up?" Serious conversations with Maggie often devolved into interrogations.

"No! I wouldn't do that. I just want to . . . make myself available to him, I guess. Let him decide what he wants. Is that bad?"

"Bad? It's disgusting. It sounds like you should be one of those dumb bitches on *The Bachelor* or something. You're better than that, Cora."

"Sorry I'm insulting your feminist sensibilities. Listen, I'm not going to throw myself at him, but if we have a moment, I'm not going to stop it."

Maggie shrugged. "Whatever. I said my piece. Do whatever you want. I just want to go on record that I think it's a mistake, and he's a douche." She paused. "But at least you have reason to buy that goddamned Léger now."

"Holy crap, Darnell was *right*! I found the dress, and now here's the event."

"He'll be thrilled. He was so convinced that it was going to happen that he hid it behind some awful mother-of-the-bride dresses."

Cora grinned despite herself at Darnell's omniscience.

The gala would simply be a chance to get dressed up and surround herself with like-minded animal lovers, supporting a cause they all believed in, and maybe make some professional connections. The fact that Charlie would be at her side was inconsequential. At least that's what she told herself, hoping that everyone—Charlie, Maggie, Madison—would believe it, too.

TWENTY-FOUR

"I hope you don't mind, I have some people coming over tonight," Maggie said while she stroked Josie languidly, the two sprawled on the couch like twin odalisques. Cora couldn't help but be a little jealous that Josie was Maggie's shadow. Fritz was sacked out on Cora's bed, overtired from keeping Josie entertained all day.

"Of course not. Anyone I know?"

"Darnell, a few other people," she replied vaguely.

"Cool. Is it okay if I hang with you guys? I've got no plans tonight."

"Duh, of course, dummy."

The doorbell rang. "By 'tonight' do you mean 'right now'?" Cora asked, making her way to the door as Josie barked out a warning beside her. Cora stood in front of the door and asked Josie to "hush," placing a treat in her fist in front of Josie's nose and waiting until she had stopped barking before she tossed it away. Josie chased the treat down the hallway and Cora opened the door.

"Hello, pretty," Darnell said. "This must be Miss Josie." He reached down to scratch her beneath her chin. "How's the hunt going for her new home?"

"It's not," Maggie shouted from the other room.

"I think someone has fallen for her," Cora whispered, pointing down the hall.

"Is keeping her an option?" he whispered back, still petting Josie.

"She claims she's not ready for a dog, but who knows what that means. I could probably work it out with our landlord, but that would mean no more fosters."

"Stop *whispering*!" Maggie shouted again.

Darnell started toward the family room and called to Cora over his shoulder. "Your Léger is still in hiding, and now it's on sale. When are you coming to buy it for that fairy-tale gig you got coming up?"

"Soon," she answered vaguely, trying not to think about what might happen when Charlie saw her body weaponized in that dress. She whistled for Fritz, who trotted out of her bedroom with sleepy eyes. "I can't believe you didn't wake up! Uncle D is here! Go see him!"

Darnell dropped to the floor and allowed Josie and Fritz to snuffle and lick him, laughing the whole time. It was hard to tell who was doing the most kissing, Darnell or the dogs.

"You love those dogs more than me," Maggie pouted.

"Never, my darling," he said, getting up and planting a kiss on her cheek. "You're my work wife for life."

"Speaking of work, I still haven't gotten my nom and I'm getting pretty stressed about it," Maggie said.

"Aw, baby, it's coming. Don't worry." Darnell had already been nominated for the Saks Excellence program, which would fast-track him to a promotion as a buyer.

The doorbell rang, and Josie sounded off anew. Cora followed her to the door, worked the "hush" routine again and opened the door. She was shocked to see Winnie and Vanessa standing there.

"This is your intervention!" Vanessa exclaimed, holding a bottle of wine above her head.

"What? Why are you guys here? Did Maggie . . . ?"

The duo pushed past her and cooed over Josie, greeting her gently and allowing her to sniff them one at a time.

"Maggie asked us over for your intervention. Your audition intervention," Winnie said, as if it would make sense to her.

"What does that even mean? I don't understand."

Vanessa stood up. "We thought it might be helpful to do a practice run to get you ready for the audition, so the Hounds are here to help you with the dog part of it, and Maggie is going to do the acting part of it."

"And I'm your swagger coach!" Darnell called out.

Cora couldn't say a word, overcome by love for her friends.

"And who better to help you than the newly crowned queens of social media?" Vanessa asked. Winnie and Vanessa had become minor Internet celebrities after their Ershovich protest, christened "Hot Pink and Woodstock" by the likes of Buzzfeed and *The Huffington Post*. Winnie's training business had tripled, and Vanessa was finally taking clients on her own to meet the demand. Their stunt had also reignited the conversation about Ershovich's methodology, leading to debates on morning news shows featuring telegenic vets and trainers on both sides of the equation. Cora studied the experts as they weighed in with their arguments. They were all a mix of flawless logic, perfect brows, and flat ironed hair. She didn't have a chance.

"You guys . . ." Cora struggled to put her gratitude into words.

"Come on, slackers, let's get to work," Maggie ordered.

The group gathered in the crowded family room, Josie and Fritz sitting at attention side by side while the rest scattered on the floor and couch. Someone's phone went off.

"I almost forgot—tonight is the finale of *America's Hottest Landscaper*!" Vanessa exclaimed as she turned off the ringtone.

"You set an alarm for that crap?" Winnie asked.

"I know, I know, I hate myself. It's *so* bad. Sorry, Cora, but I can't help it."

Cora hadn't watched it in weeks, but she couldn't avoid the online gossip about the show. The final three contestants were Carly the hot girl, James the underdog, and Aaron, of course. How he didn't get kicked off after that slur was a mystery to her.

"Let's try to cram some practice in before we turn it on. It is okay if we watch, right?" Maggie said, turning to Cora.

"Sure, whatever."

"Are we ready to do this? I'm going to critique you and make suggestions as we go along."

Cora looked around the room sheepishly. "This feels really weird and embarrassing, you guys."

"You're gonna be great, don't worry. Okay, stand in front of the TV. Boozehounds, you ready?"

Winnie went first. "Cora, answer quickly and with the first

thing that comes to mind. I'm starting with a softball; what dog influenced you the most?"

"Oh God, you call that a softball?" Maggie asked. "You guys clearly don't know the Cooper story."

Cora hated talking about it and had only ever told her family and Maggie before. A sanitized, happy-ending way of telling the story didn't exist—there was no happy ending for Cooper—so she kept it locked inside. Cooper was always with her, though, whether she chose to think about him or not.

She'd been twelve when she'd seen the pathetic dog chained to a doghouse when she was riding her bike to a friend's. Even then, Cora's love of animals was strong enough to make her get off her bike and approach the strange dog in an unfamiliar part of town. He was black and tan with ears that lay plastered to his head and a thin body hunched from a lifetime of tirades and beatings. He gave a few halfhearted barks as Cora approached, but she knew, instinctively, that the dog wanted her to get closer.

The moment she touched him, he curled into a ball on her feet and wagged the tip of his tail. They fell in love with each other in that instant. Cora tried to visit Cooper every day, stealing handfuls of food for him from her family's stash and lavishing him with enough love to carry him over until her next visit. She never saw the dog's owner, but she often noticed the blinds moving as she sat with him.

Cooper was the sweetest dog Cora had ever known. He blossomed each time he saw her, gradually transforming from a shy, untrusting shell of a dog to her devoted friend. His affections were always guarded, though, as if he had been so broken by the people in his life that he was afraid to make a misstep with Cora.

Cora pleaded with her parents to help Cooper, but there were no antichaining laws in effect at that time, and because he had shelter and a food bowl, the authorities were powerless. The plywood doghouse did nothing to protect Cooper from the rain, wind, or sweltering sun, though. Cora hated that she could feel his ribs when she petted him, and how he paced back and forth so much that he wore a deep path in the dirt, and the way he howled mournfully when she pedaled off after each visit.

She spent six months visiting him, and then one day he was gone. Cora ran to his doghouse, hoping he was curled up and sleeping inside, but he wasn't there. She noticed broken beer bottles strewn in the dirt yard near the doghouse.

Someone opened a window and yelled at her, "Cooper is gone. Stop coming here."

Cora was afraid of the shadowy figure but she needed answers. "Where is he? What happened?"

"What happened was that he was stupid. Now don't come back here, kid." The window slammed shut.

Cora detoured on the way back to her bike so she could investigate the area near the doghouse. Cooper's dirt trail was packed with something dark. She ran to look at the collar still attached to his dog chain and saw that it was dried blood. She pedaled home crying, destroyed by what might have happened to her friend. The image of his empty chain never stopped haunting her, and it eventually propelled her into dog training, so that on her watch no other dogs would end up like Cooper.

Cora quickly explained Cooper's story, and the mood in the room changed from jovial to heartbroken.

Winnie spoke up. "We all have a story like that in our past, right? That's why we do what we do."

"Use that passion to fuel your answer, C," Maggie said. "Go for it."

Cora nodded. "Um, my biggest canine influence has to be, uh . . ." She paused. "It's, um, a dog from my past named Cooper. He had a tragic life, so I pledged to him that I would help every dog I could. It's, uh, a way to honor him, I guess."

"Okay, okay, that was good!" Maggie said encouragingly. "But you have to watch the *uh*s and *um*s. Try to end with a confident summary; 'I train in honor of the first dog I loved, Cooper.' And smile. Fake it, baby."

Vanessa raised her hand like a schoolgirl. "What would you say is the biggest challenge when helping people train their dogs?"

Cora smiled at Vanessa. "The biggest challenge for me is helping people understand that some training problems take time to address, like teaching a dog who has been pulling on its leash for years to stop dragging you down the street. I don't carry a magic wand in my bag."

"What do you hate about dog training?" Winnie asked.

"Driving. DC traffic is awful, and it really makes scheduling my clients tough."

Darnell chuckled. "I see what you did there, boo. It's like when people say their biggest weakness is they work too hard. What you really want to say is that some people are assholes, am I right?"

"I'm lucky, most of my clients are wonderful."

"You're really playing up the goody-goody thing. I like that." He nodded at Cora approvingly.

"I'm sorry, that sounds like a cop-out," Vanessa said with a concerned expression on her face. "Give us something real. What's the toughest part of your job?"

Cora paused and chewed on the inside of her cheek, her mind drifting to Chanel and Blade and Hunter. "The toughest part is when I can't help the dog. Sometimes, no matter how hard I try, it's beyond my control. I hate that."

The Hounds nodded and whispered between themselves.

"I need to jump in here for a second," Maggie said. "Look at your body language, C. You are twisted up like a hypochondriac's tissue. Can you . . . unfurl a little?" She demonstrated by shaking her shoulders and arms.

Cora imitated her.

"Now please stand straight. Shoulders back, show off what your mama gave you. Watch your feet, you look a little pigeon-toed. If you don't know what to do with your hands, do the newscaster thing; hold your hands together at belly button height, but don't keep them there the whole time. Gesture naturally if you can. And *please* don't cross your arms, you look super pissed when you do that."

"Am I doing okay, guys? Because this feels really awkward."

Everyone spoke at the same time, offering encouragement and praise.

Maggie stood up and clapped her hands to quiet the room. "Let's not torture her any more. You're all done, and you were fantastic. We love you, Cora."

"Thanks for doing this, you guys. I feel a little less nervous now."

"We're counting on you!" Vanessa cheered. "We've got five minutes before *AHL* is on. I'm opening the wine and getting ready."

"You do realize that you're sort of a traitor to Cora for watching this show, right?" Darnell asked Vanessa as she walked to the kitchen.

"I'm not rooting for that jackass," Vanessa answered. "I want James to win."

The finale consisted of a single challenge on the property of the sprawling French country mansion where the contestants had been living, involving three large sculpture garden installations and heavy equipment. The players were being judged by a panel of experts including a botanical garden director, an editor from *Modern Gardening* magazine, and the president of a tractor company who was undoubtedly relishing the product placement on the show.

"I hope Aaron loses," Cora said after they'd all settled in. Seeing him rounding the final lap in the lead was more uncomfortable than she had anticipated, but it made her feel small to want him to lose.

"We all do, baby. I'm a traitor to my sexual orientation because I want Carly to win, not Mr. Abs," Darnell replied.

"Well, the fact that he's a raging homophobe might discourage your support as well," Maggie added. Darnell made a noncommittal noise.

The challenge required the finalists to bring to life their plans for modernist sculpture gardens by moving large boulders with a miniexcavator. The contestants had to tread gently over the sod they had painstakingly laid in the previous episode, taking care not to turn the wheel roughly or pause in one spot for too long and risk damaging it.

Brittany, the host, spoke gravely into the camera. "The sculpture garden challenge is a timed event, so our finalists have to execute their plans while keeping an eye on the clock. James, you're up first. Good luck."

James shed his black tank top before he climbed into his excavator, exposing his sinewy chest and the dark Asian-style tattoos on both of his arms. He had been a quiet but fierce competitor during the series, and a fan favorite to steal the win from extroverts Carly and Aaron.

Sadly, his installation looked like Stonehenge if it had been assembled by a kindergartener. Aaron sat close to Carly on the sidelines, whispering to her and laughing as James sweated through the challenge. The judges didn't hide their disapproval.

Brittany stepped in front of the camera again, speaking with the reverence of a choir director. "Carly, are you ready to take your turn with the sculpture garden challenge?"

She nodded her head and blew a kiss toward the camera, bounding to her customized pink excavator like she knew she had already won.

Carly opted for ease over style, selecting four large round polished rocks that she merely needed to transport to her assigned plot and place in size order, a design that subliminally referenced her unmissable implants. She worked quickly, pushing the excavator to its top speed. It jostled over the uneven terrain, bumping her around in her seat and causing her oversize breasts to ricochet in her tiny sports bra.

The camera cut to Aaron. "Mmmm, girl. Make your ponytail bounce!"

"Oh my God, did he really say that?" Maggie asked.

"I don't get it, why does he care about her ponytail?" Darnell asked.

"Duh, it's a gross way of saying he wants to see her boobs bounce. Cora, I'm sorry but he is *such* a tool."

"I know, I know. I'm mortified," she replied, unable to stop staring at the TV. He seemed so at ease on camera. She hoped that skill lurked somewhere in her, too.

Vanessa looked up from her phone. "Ugh, 'make your ponytail bounce' is already trending on Twitter."

Carly finished the challenge, and the two male judges golf clapped for her while the lone female judge looked down at her clipboard and made notes. Her time beat James's, so unless his design was deemed superior, he was out of the competition.

"Aaron, are you ready to go?" Brittany asked solemnly.

"Yee haw, you bet I am!" he shouted, pumping his fist.

"Wait a sec, when did he pick up that accent? Isn't he from suburban Fairfax or something?" Winnie asked.

"He is. I have no idea when he converted to good-old-boy-ism," Cora answered, still mesmerized by what was unfolding on the show. Aaron seemed familiar and foreign to her at the same time. She remembered the way he walked, his laugh, his broad hands and his quick smile, but she had never seen this practiced cockiness to his mannerisms, as if he had studied other successful reality show contestants for tips on how to act on camera.

Not to be outdone by James, Aaron stripped off his tight T-shirt and casually flexed his bicep as he climbed into the excavator. He whipped through his installation even faster than Carly, assembling a large flat rock atop two twelve-foot-tall supporting rocks like a cubist table. He finished with the delicate placement of a huge round boulder on top of the table, and the judges clapped.

"One second, y'all, not quite done," he said, holding up a finger. He moved the excavator to the display and tapped the round rock with the claw on the front of the machine. The rock split open and a cascade of small polished river rocks streamed out like water, spilling over the edge of the table and pooling artfully in the grass below.

The camera cut to the judges who stood side by side with their mouths hanging open, then back to Aaron, who beamed from the cab of the excavator.

"Oh crap, that was really good," Winnie stage-whispered.

"Can we turn it off? I don't want to see him win," Cora said.

"Shhh, it's not a sure thing yet. Let's just see what happens, these shows are unpredictable," Vanessa answered, leaning forward but keeping one hand on Fritz.

The judges deliberated while flashbacks of the show played, highlighting the contestants' highs and lows throughout the series. The reel focused on Aaron's choreographed hug with Andy during the "forgiveness" episode, where he acted as if he had gone through a master class about gay rights. When the show went back to the live shot, the previously eliminated contestants had gathered behind James, Carly, and Aaron. Brittany stepped forward with an envelope in her hand.

"It's the moment we've all been waiting for. It's time to announce the winner of *America's . . . Hottest . . . Landscaper.*" She paused to let it sink in. "Our champion will receive a check for a hundred thousand dollars, their very own customized miniexcavator worth over ten thousand dollars, courtesy of Crenshaw Tools, a lifetime supply of GrowRite natural fertilizer, and a monthly column in *Modern Gardening* magazine."

The camera cut to the finalists, who all managed to hide their excitement behind stoic smiling faces.

"Ladies and gentlemen, the winner of *America's Hottest Landscaper* is . . ." The pause seemed to go on indefinitely.

"SAY IT!" Vanessa screamed at the TV. "Just say it already!"

"Carly Gannon!"

The room was silent for a moment.

"And justice prevails!" Maggie shouted, dancing around the room. She high-fived each of them as she pranced by. Cora clapped her hands and rocked back and forth maniacally.

"It's over! *He's* over!" she exclaimed.

"Look at Aaron—he's *pissed*!" Vanessa said gleefully. Aaron barely hid his scowl as he hugged Carly.

"That is what you call a plot twist, my friends. The king is dead, long live the queen!" Darnell said triumphantly.

TWENTY-FIVE

Cora's phone rang at five after ten the next morning. She was still reveling in Aaron's loss and fighting off the killer hangover from their celebration the night before. Cora had lucked out and scheduled her first client for noon, but Maggie couldn't get out of her regular shift at Saks, so she was already at work and Cora was surprised to see her picture come up on the phone's display.

"Ca-can you come pick me up?" Maggie cried into the phone. "I don't want to ride the Meh-Meh-Metro like this." She hiccuped.

"Maggie, what's wrong? Are you okay? What happened?"

"I got *fired*!" she wailed.

"What? How is that possible?"

"The steamer! They think I stole the stuh-*steamer*!"

"The broken one? They were throwing it out. Did you tell them it was broken and Gym Jake fixed it?"

"I told them everything, Cora, they won't *listen to me*! They escorted me out like a criminal!" Her wails got louder. "Please just come get me. I'm in the parking lot."

Cora glanced at the time. "I'm on my way right now."

Fritz and Josie barely stirred as she ran by them, both exhausted by their early morning wrestling match. "Aunt Maggie is going to need a lot of love when we get home," she told them.

Making it to the mall in record time, Cora found Maggie sitting under a tree in the far corner of the parking lot. Her face was covered in a spiderweb of mascara streaks.

"Darnell told them about the steamer," Maggie spat at Cora as she climbed in the car. "*He's* the reason I got fired."

"Why does it even matter? They were throwing it out, right?"

Maggie shook her head and looked out the window. She clearly wasn't ready to talk about it. She rarely cried, so Cora tried to give her space as she processed what had happened.

They rode home in silence, with Maggie occasionally hiccuping a leftover sob. Maggie's progression from tears to fury was a quick and predictable one. Cora actually felt bad that Darnell was on the receiving end of this much rage.

"Can I ask how it happened?"

The words came out in angry bursts. "The guys from corporate were in. Darnell made some crack about how I shouldn't be up for the Excellence program because I stole a steamer. Corporate heard 'steal,' and I was out on my ass." She clenched her fists. "I want to kill that fucker."

"Are you *serious*?" It sounded like just one of Darnell's badly timed jokes. "Why would he do that?"

"He did it because he didn't like the competition. He's used to being number one, and for the first time in a long time he wasn't going to be because my numbers are *insane* this quarter. I can't believe he's jealous of me!"

Cora knew that wasn't the case. Darnell was Maggie's devoted friend, and there was no way he would ever do anything to sabotage her. More likely, he had just reacted to the discomfort of the moment with a wisecrack.

"Was he . . . kidding? You know how he makes those stupid jokes all the time. Was he trying to be funny and show off?"

"It doesn't matter, Cora! He said what he said, and now I don't have a job!"

Cora thought better of trying to debate Maggie. She felt awful for her friend.

"There goes my three-year plan," Maggie muttered. "All that work, all that low-level folding and stocking and groveling, and I've got shit to show for it. I was working toward something, Cora! I was on the executive track. I paid my dues on the floor and I was about to move up, big-time. I was so goddamned good at my job."

Cora reached over and squeezed Maggie's hand. "I know you were. They do, too. I'm so sorry, Mags."

Maggie stormed down the hallway in front of Cora and furiously wrenched the front door open, as if it too had conspired to get her fired. She took two steps in, tripped, and landed hard on her knees, then let out a wail that summoned the dogs from the couch.

Fritz and Josie ran to where Maggie knelt, crying with her face in her hands, and immediately began licking and pawing at her. Cora stood in the doorway and let them work their magic, knowing that nothing she could say or do would be as effective as the ministrations from the dogs. Maggie rolled on to her side on the ground, and Josie spooned into position against her, leaning back to lick the tears dropping from her chin. Fritz stood behind Maggie with one paw resting protectively on her shoulder. His ears were pinned back, and his tongue flicked around his mouth lizard-like as if tasting the air, telegraphing the stress he was feeling. He glanced back at Cora for direction.

"It's okay," she mouthed to him. She made her eyes soft and sad and nodded toward Maggie on the floor so that he would know to stay with her. She walked to them wordlessly and sat at Maggie's feet, and the three of them let their friend cry until her tears stopped.

TWENTY-SIX

"**M**y name is Cora Bellamy. I am Cora Bellamy. Hey, I'm Cora Bellamy! *Je m'appelle Cora bel Ami.*"

She stood in front of the mirror on the inside of her closet door, introducing herself to an imaginary audience with a variety of inflections and facial expressions, hoping to hit on one that felt natural, but the more she repeated her name the stranger it sounded.

Cora leaned in close and studied her face in the mirror. Her skin was blemish free, and it was doubtful anything would sprout overnight. Her dark brows looked tidy, her undereye bags were minimal, and with enough makeup, she hoped that she could pull together a camera-ready look for the audition.

She crossed her arms and turned around to stare at the two brand-new outfits carefully placed on her bed and wasn't surprised to find Fritz nestled in between them. One was a pale pink featherweight sweater paired with slim-fitting black pants, the other a bold black-and-white chevron-print blouse and dark jeans, topped off with a dramatic pink statement necklace. Usually Maggie would've been at her side during such an important shopping trip, helping to select a look that Cora never would've considered, but she couldn't rouse Maggie from the couch.

"Mags, can you come in here for a sec?" Cora hoped that she could refocus her, if only for a moment. She desperately wanted her friend's cheerleading as she prepped for the audition.

Maggie wandered in with Josie in tow. She looked disheveled, swollen, and shell-shocked, as if she still couldn't believe what had happened, even after a week. Cora knew there was an ounce of drama queen in her over-the-top response to her firing, but she allowed her friend to revel in it.

Josie hadn't left Maggie's side as she worked through the stages of anger, a life preserver or an anchor, depending on Maggie's mood. Only Josie could offer her the comfort she needed. Cora christened the dog "Clara Barkton" because of her impressive nursing skills.

"Hey, can you help me decide between these two outfits for tomorrow? You're the pro, so what should I wear?"

Maggie squinted her eyes at the options. "Uhhh. Either. I'm sure you look perfect in both of them." She shrugged her shoulders and reached down to pet Josie.

"So, you have no artistic preference? Like, from a stage presence perspective?"

"They're both good. Either one. And remember, it's not about what you wear, it's about *you*." Maggie sounded exasperated.

Cora couldn't believe what she was hearing. Maggie had built a successful career based on the power of the right outfit, so her saying that it didn't matter was like a zealot renouncing religion.

"Okay, what would you wear then?"

Maggie shrugged her shoulders again. "Chevron, I guess."

A little wounded by her friend's lack of enthusiasm, Cora frowned.

"You don't want my help anyway, Cora. What do I know? I'm just a fucking unemployed loser that watches Netflix all day with a homeless dog." She looked down at Josie and scratched her head.

"Speaking of Josie, can we talk about what's going on for a sec? What are we doing, Maggie? Abby has sent a few people my way who saw her photo on the League's website, and I keep putting them off. It's not fair to her or you, or the people who might want to adopt her. We need to make the call." Cora sounded snippier than she meant to.

"That's cool, I get it." Maggie sat down on the floor next to Josie, and the dog immediately leaned into her, as if magnetized. "Yeah, let's find her a home. It's time, right? Want to meet your new mommy? Huh? We'll find you a nice house with a yard in the suburbs." Josie looked at Maggie intently, wagged her tail, and placed a gentle paw on her leg as Maggie scratched the wrinkly part of her forehead. Maggie slowly lowered her head and began to cry.

"What's wrong?" Cora asked.

"I don't want to," she sobbed. "I can't let someone else have her. She's *my dog*!" Her crying intensified, and Josie began pawing at Maggie and licking her face furiously, trying to comfort her.

Cora ran to where Maggie sat and knelt down next to her. Fritz sprawled on the ground in front of them in an attempt to divert their attention, as if he knew that no one could feel sad while petting his belly.

"Of course she is! Everybody knew she was your dog but you!

Don't worry, we'll keep her. It's okay, it's okay." Cora rubbed Maggie's back. "She's your dog."

Maggie looked at Josie and sniffled. "You're *my* dog, Josie! You're mine and you're not going anywhere!" She leaned over and hugged Josie, who tolerated the intrusion with grace.

"I'll text Abby and let her know," Cora said.

"Wait," Maggie said, untangling from Josie. "Having two dogs means you can't foster anymore. Now I feel terrible for all of those other dogs you won't be able to help . . ." Her bottom lip trembled.

"We'll figure something out. Maybe we can talk about moving? I feel like we're outgrowing this place anyway."

"I'll be moving back home if I don't find a job soon," she replied glumly.

"Mags, you haven't even tried," Cora said gently. "You've barely left the apartment except to walk the dogs."

"I know, I know. It's time. I'm done mourning."

"Have you thought about what you might want to do next? Retail again?"

"No way! Retail fucked me. I'm done. I'll figure something out. Maybe I'll be a high-class escort."

"The money's supposed to be great." Cora shrugged, and they both laughed.

"I'm sorry I've been so awful lately."

"Everyone is allowed to have a bad spell."

Maggie smiled through her tears. "I really am proud of you, C. Don't worry, you're going to be amazing tomorrow."

"I'm ready," she said, and for the first time she knew that it was true.

TWENTY-SEVEN

"You must be Cora! I'm Mia Nguyen." The young woman offered her hand and smiled. Mia was impeccably dressed in the arty girl uniform: a perfectly shrunken striped T-shirt, a long slim black skirt, and funky wedge sandals. Cora coveted her precision-cut angled bob.

"I am, so nice to meet you!" Cora answered, mustering a voice that she hoped didn't betray her nerves. The two women had been trading e-mails for days, trying to nail down the exact time and location for Cora's audition. They had settled on a Monday afternoon in an overflow room of a doggy day care center in northwest DC. Cora didn't know much about the day care facility, but she knew the head trainer on staff, Brooke Keating, had a fame whore-y reputation for putting her famous clients' testimonials and photos all over her website. Based on the photos, Brooke was only one degree of separation away from the President and the First Dog.

"I just need you to fill this out before we get started," Mia said, handing Cora a clipboard. Her hand shook as she reached for the pen. "We're just finishing up with someone else, so I'll let you take care of that and I'll be back in a minute. Vaughn, our executive producer, can't wait to meet you!"

"Great, okay, thanks!" Cora replied, sounding overeager and nerdy. She took a seat on one of the folding chairs ringing the room and got to work filling out her contact information and dog training background, which she had already provided to them in triplicate.

Her phone pinged and she dug it out of her bag quickly. *Nothing like texts coming in during the audition to throw me off my game,* she thought as she silenced it. There was a good luck text from Wade and Rachel, and a random text from Charlie, a selfie of him holding an upside-down sleeping Ollie. "We miss u," it said, followed by a frowning emoji. She missed seeing him, too, but she wasn't about to admit it. "Too cute!" Cora texted back, hoping that it walked the line between dismissive and interested, and shoved her phone back in her purse. This wasn't the time to think about Charlie Gill.

She took a peek around the room as she filled out the form. It was painted a cheerful yellow with a cartoony dog-themed mural and the unmistakable smell of industrial cleaner just barely masking urine. The walls were surprisingly thin, given what the room was used for, enabling her to hear tantalizing bits of what was happening in the other room. She rushed to complete the form so that she could focus her energies on eavesdropping.

"Brooke, that was great!" Cora heard a male voice exclaim. "Can you get Honey to do it again?"

Cora heard Brooke's muffled reply from across the room, and then heard her repeating an upbeat cue a few times in a row.

"Yeah, awesome stuff," the voice exclaimed, and Cora heard clapping. "Okay, I think we're good here. Thank you *so much* for coming today, you were really perfect. Ryan, get the mic, and, Mia, can you show her out? Honey, you come over here to me. C'mere girl." Cora heard the dog's nails on the floor as it ran over to the man. She tried to guess the breed just based on the sound of its paws.

The door opened, and Cora righted herself. Brooke was "really perfect"? Hearing the feedback made Cora even more nervous.

Mia walked out with Brooke. "We loved what you did, thank you so much! Is the number on the form the best way to reach you?" Brooke nodded modestly. "Great, we'll be in touch soon!" Mia ducked back in the room and shut the door to keep the mystery dog from following them out, leaving Cora and Brooke alone. Brooke walked to her bag on the other side of the room, completely ignoring Cora.

"Hello there?" Cora called out. "I think we've met before, but I'm Cora Bellamy from Top Dog?"

Brooke zipped her bag shut and turned to face Cora. "Oh, right, we met at that conference thingy." Brooke had put extra effort into her look, with her coppery hair ironed flat and more makeup than usual on her handsome face. She was pretty in a slightly inbred British aristocracy kind of way.

"How did it go in there?" Cora asked, grimacing.

"Vaughn and Mia are great," she replied, emphasizing their names, as if they were old friends. "It's *intense*, though. Like, the hardest thing I've ever done. But I'm really happy with my audition." She shrugged like she couldn't help her awesomeness.

"Oh, that's great," Cora said, feeling the butterflies migrate from her belly to her throat.

"Good luck," Brooke said flatly. "Oh, and you're going to love Honey. She's a total ringer, I've worked with her before."

Cora felt like she'd been punched in the gut. Just how connected *was* Brooke? And why were they continuing to audition people if Brooke already had it wrapped up?

"Thanks. Oh—what kind of dog is Honey?"

"Doberman. Smart as hell." As she left the room, Brooke adjusted a light switch on the wall to drive home the fact that she belonged there and Cora was the interloper.

Cora felt her fingers go numb. She looked down at the scar on the top of her hand and rubbed it, as if trying to make it disappear. The bite had occurred in the infancy of her training career, when she reached for a bone her Doberman client was guarding. The dog reacted by nailing her on the hand and forearm in rapid succession. The embarrassment over her misstep—because it was her stupid mistake—was almost as painful as the bite itself. She had trained Dobes over the years and had learned to conquer her nerves and enjoy them, but she was a little superstitious about the breed, and having to audition with one seemed like fate trying to tell her something.

"Cora, all set?" Mia asked as she came in the room.

"Yup, yes indeedy," she replied brightly. Her nerves were turning her into a flight attendant.

She stood on shaky legs and followed Mia into the audition room, essentially a larger version of the room she had just been in but with a pile of agility equipment stacked in the corner. A dark-haired man approached Cora with his hand out.

"I'm Vaughn, so nice to meet you, Cora! Loved your photo with all of those sleeping dogs!" He had the air of the most raucous guy on the rugby team. His hair was slightly long with a frat boy wave in it, and he swept his palm across his forehead frequently to move it out of his eyes.

"Thank you! My client took it, she's basically an artist mixed with a magician." Cora felt instantly at ease in the room despite the circumstances. Brooke was right, Mia and Vaughn *were* great.

"You should see some of the submission photos we got. Sheesh! One woman was bending over petting her dog, and it was basically a clear shot down the front of her blouse to her push-up bra."

"So what am I doing here then?" Cora asked with a gleam in her eye. "Clearly you found your trainer!"

Vaughn and Mia guffawed, and Cora was pleased that her stupid joke had landed. Maybe Brooke didn't have this in the bag!

"So let's get your mic on and get started. Our intern Ryan usually takes care of it, but he took Honey out for a quick potty break."

Vaughn told Cora how to feed the mic wire down her blouse, and looked away when she had to fish it out of her bra. He attached and reattached the mic on the inside edge of her shirt a few times, stepping back and tilting his head to see if it was visible.

"Fantastic, good to go. Almost as good as when Ryan does it."

Mia stared at Cora. She spoke to Vaughn quietly. "After all of that work, do you think her shirt is going to read funny?"

"The stripes! How did I miss that? We were so busy talking about cleavage that it slipped my mind."

"It's totally my fault. I think I forgot to tell her about wardrobe the last time I talked to her. I'm sorry," Mia said to Vaughn, as if Cora wasn't in the room.

"Is my shirt bad? What's wrong?" Cora asked, her heart pounding.

"I think we'll be okay, it's just that black-and-white stripes can make the camera go a little crazy sometimes," Mia answered.

Cora was shocked that Maggie hadn't thought of it. Her friend was *really* off her game.

"Don't let it throw you, we'll make it work," Mia said, reading Cora's worried expression.

The door on the opposite side of the room opened and Honey the Doberman walked in, trailed by a skinny knit-capped hipster guy Cora assumed was Ryan the intern. He dropped the leash, and Honey made a dash for her.

"Are you my student?" Cora asked the dog as she danced at her feet. "You are *very* beautiful. Yes you are!" She leaned down to pet her and looked up at Vaughn. "Is she yours?"

"I wish! Do you know Gwen Almquist? The local NBC meteorologist?" Cora nodded. "Honey is her dog. Gwen and I go way back, so she's doing me a favor by letting us borrow her."

Cora knelt next to Honey. "So you're a weather dog! What's the forecast for tonight?" The dog was surprisingly calm, and she leaned her body against Cora companionably as she stroked her sleek fur.

"Why don't we get started? Cora, can you test the mic? Just say 'one two three' a few times."

"One-two-three-one-two-three," Cora intoned seriously. Vaughn looked back at Ryan, who had slipped on a pair of headphones. He gave a silent thumbs-up.

"Good! Off we go! Cora, could you sit in that chair right there?" He pointed to a lone chair in the center of the room. Mia wordlessly walked over, grabbed Honey's leash, and led her back behind where Vaughn was sitting with his camera. He adjusted a few buttons on the camera and looked up. "We're just going to start off with a couple of quick questions before you work with Honey. Cool?"

"Cool," Cora replied, wiping her sweaty palms on her jeans and taking a deep breath. She knew that after facing down the Boozehounds' barrage of questions she could take anything. She was amazed at how calm she suddenly felt.

"So please state your name and your dog's name, if you currently have a dog."

Cora smiled. "My name is Cora Bellamy and my dog's name is Fritz."

"What do you like best about Fritz?" Vaughn was looking at the small monitor on the back of the camera, so Cora had no choice but to look directly into its unblinking eye.

"What *don't* I like?" She laughed. "Seriously, I'm in love with my dog. It's sick." She felt herself lapsing into French but corrected herself before the words came out. "I kiss him on the mouth, like, all the time. But if I had to pick one thing I'd say it was . . . his sensitivity. I pity the next man I date, because no one gets me like Fritz!" Cora knew she was rambling and thought of Maggie yelling at her to be pithy.

Both Vaughn and Mia were smiling.

"What kind of dog is he?"

"He's a pit bull."

Vaughn's eyebrows went up. "Okay, you're our first pit person. Lots of drama with them these days, right?"

Cora knew what he was implying but didn't touch on the Ershovich controversy. She willed herself to deliver a calm soundbite. "Everyone has opinions about pits. The sad fact is that most are based on misinformation. My Fritz is a mythbuster and an ambassador. He's helping to spread the word about how special these dogs are."

"Way to be, Fritz. Can you tell us about your favorite client?"

"Ooh, that's a tough one." Cora paused and looked down. She was drawing a blank, not because she didn't have any favorites, but because she had so many. "Ummm . . ." She felt her cheeks turning pink. "Uh." She squirmed in her seat and smiled nervously.

"Okay, how about someone—"

"Wait, I just thought of who it is!" Cora interrupted him. "Sorry! I do have an ultimate favorite!" Vaughn nodded and Cora continued. "His name was Orville and his dog's name was Skye. He was older than my usual client, by a lot. I think he was in his early seventies. I was worried that he wouldn't like the way I train, because I'm force-free, and most of my older clients are used to the traditional choke chain kind of stuff that people did a long time ago. Well, not only did he like my training technique but he also amazed me with the stuff he taught Skye on his own. Every week he surprised me with a new trick. He *loved* training her with positive methods, and I loved watching them."

"That's pretty amazing. You love your job, huh?"

"I do. I'm lucky." Cora shrugged her shoulders and smiled.

"How do you feel about Boris Ershovich?"

She couldn't dodge the question this time. Cora paused to gather her thoughts. She knew she should start by mentioning the few good things Ershovich taught people, like the need to exercise their dogs more and brush up on their dogs' manners, then gently move on to the things that troubled her, and outline, scientifically, why they were unsound and dangerous practices. Reason and rationality would be her allies as she listed her problems with his philosophy.

But instead . . .

"I hate him. I absolutely hate him. He's a menace. He is single-handedly sending dog training back to the dark ages. He's a monster that abuses dogs in the name of training, and I wish he would fall off a cliff and disappear forever."

"Whoa, there. Tell us how you really feel!" Vaughn said, raising an eyebrow.

Cora put her hand over her mouth and looked at Mia, who was staring at the monitor with a shocked expression on her face.

"I'm sorry, that was really inappropriate! I have very strong feelings about him, obviously. Can I start over?" She didn't wait for them to answer. "I feel that Boris Ershovich uses techniques that have a strong history in traditional dog training but don't accurately reflect what we now know about the ways dogs learn. I appreciate his advice to exercise dogs more, but I think that the bulk of what he does is dangerous. His show flashes a disclaimer at the beginning telling viewers not to try his techniques at home. That says something. I *want* people to train the way I train." She hoped her revised answer negated her passionate one.

Vaughn nodded. "Hm, makes sense."

Mia scribbled something on her notepad.

"Do you have any experience on TV? Like, any interviews with local media? Stuff like that?" Vaughn asked.

"None. I hope that doesn't disqualify me."

"Not at all! You're what they call a 'fresh face'! That can be a good thing." Vaughn smiled at her. "So now I want you to do some work with Honey. I'm going to feed you a few lines and I want you to say them back to me. Honey's going to be next to you on leash, so try to interact with her as well when you say the lines. Makes sense?"

"Yup." Cora's nerves were kicking in. She stood and ran her hands down the front of her pants in an effort to dislodge a wedgie.

Mia walked Honey over to Cora and took the chair away. Cora looked down at the dog and nodded, as if sealing a secret pact with her.

"I want you to introduce yourself and then say, 'Honey's people have a big challenge; she jumps on everyone that comes over! I'm here to show them how they can change her behavior and make her the ultimate hostess! Are you ready to get to work, Honey?' Then you can look down and pet her or something. Got it?"

Cora mumbled the words to herself and nodded. Memorization wasn't her strong point.

Vaughn paused and looked down at the camera. "Okay, go for it."

"Hi, I'm Cora and this is Honey, and she jumps on guests! It's time to show her people how to make her a good hostess. Are you ready, Honey?" She reached rapidly toward Honey to pet her and the dog leaped away, startled by her abruptness. It was as if every bit of Cora's dogsense had disappeared in an instant.

"Great!" Vaughn said. "Loved it, really good. Can you try it one more time for me, as a safety? Oh, and this time don't forget to say '*I'm here* to show them' blah blah blah. We need to establish you as the expert."

"Yup, sorry about that. I'll do it again, no problem. Can you repeat it for me one more time though?" Cora felt the blush simmering in her hairline. She was blowing it.

Vaughn said the intro again with the exact inflection and cadence as the first time he said it. He sounded like an actor.

"Ready? Go!"

"Hi, I'm Cora, and this is my friend Honey. Honey's people have a tough challenge; she jumps on everyone! I'm here to show them how they can change her behavior and make her the ultimate hostess! Let's get to work, Honey!" She opted to kneel next to Honey when she finished the second take, and the dog stepped closer and licked her face. Cora laughed.

"Right on, that was great! Did you like that one, Mia?" Vaughn turned to her.

"Yup, awesome. Let's keep going."

Cora felt like they were rushing her through the process. Where was her applause?

"Now I want you to free form some instruction with Honey. Have you ever taught agility?"

Cora felt her stomach drop. She had never done any dog sport instruction. This audition was over.

"No, not really, but I guess the foundation steps for agility are universal. What do you want me to do?"

Ryan had taken off his headphones and was wheeling a large A-frame, a five-foot-tall triangular structure striped with a blue and yellow granular rubbery substance for traction, to the center of the room. Agility dogs were taught to run up one side and down the other, making sure to touch the yellow contact points at the base of the structure with at least one paw during ascent and descent.

"Why don't you just play around with Honey and the A-frame? Show us how you would teach her to go up it. And just so you know, she hasn't done this obstacle yet, so it'll be new for her. We're using different equipment with everyone. Brooke had her do the . . . what is that table thingy called?"

"Pause table," Mia offered.

A pause table was just what it sounded like: a low broad table, like a coffee table with the legs lowered, where the dog was required to take a five-second break between the high-speed obstacles. It was unbelievably simple to get a dog to climb on top the first time, and Cora tried not to feel bitter that Brooke had had such an easy obstacle.

Cora walked over to the intimidating A-frame. It was the first time she'd ever been near one. She unclipped Honey's leash, and the dog did a quick lap around the room.

"Honey? Come over here, girl!" Her voice lapsed into her typical happy dogspeak pitch, and Honey zoomed back to her. She hoped they couldn't see the sweat stains forming under her arms.

"Sit," she said. Honey immediately assumed the position, and Cora reached into her back pocket to grab a treat. "I hope you don't mind, I brought my own treats," Cora said slightly apologetically.

"No, that's great! It's another glimpse into the way you work," Vaughn answered. "Now ignore us and keep going. Feel free to talk to the audience through the camera, but don't talk to us."

She nodded. Honey stood next to her, waiting for another treat. Cora felt something shift within her and she snapped into dog trainer mode. She forgot about the strange eyes on her, the mic pack protruding from her back pocket, and the unforgiving gaze of the camera. She began talking as if giving casual instructions to one of her clients, and pictured Fran smiling and encouraging her.

"The A-frame looks like a daunting obstacle because of the height, but if you break the process down into pieces, it makes it much easier for the dog," Cora bluffed. If she had a choice, she would first teach the dog to walk on the A-frame when it was flat on the ground first, instead of attempting to do it when it was five feet high, but she didn't have that option, so she pressed on.

"I'm going to use a small tasty treat to lure Honey through the initial steps of the process." Cora stressed the "initial steps" aspect because she knew there was no way Honey was going to go up and over the obstacle right out of the gate. She hoped Mia and Vaughn were dog-savvy enough to realize it.

"I'm going to place the treat right in front of Honey's nose and use her natural inclination to follow it to move her body to the base of the A-frame." She demonstrated the luring motion, and Honey followed along as if she already knew the script.

"When she's right at the bottom, I'm going to mark her position by saying 'good!' and then give her the treat." Cora handed over the treat, and Honey danced in place.

"Now I'm going to lure her up the ramp just a tiny bit, so that she has to put her front paws on it in order to reach the treat." Honey stepped up the A-frame to where Cora was holding the treat. She said "good" to mark the dog's progress and gave her the treat again.

"This is a very smart dog," Cora said as she smiled at her student. "The next step is to try and get those back feet off the ground and onto the ramp, which can be a little scary for a first-timer." Cora brought the treat so that it hovered about halfway up the A-frame, and Honey gamely raced toward it to try to reach the treat. Cora misjudged the dog's speed and drive and was shocked when Honey jumped up to grab the treat and fell off the edge of the A-frame with a dramatic crash. She landed ungracefully next to it.

"Oh, Honey! Oh no, are you okay?" Cora dropped to her knees and petted Honey for a moment and then looked at the camera. She was surprised that Mia and Vaughn remained silent. Honey shook off the fall and looked at Cora expectantly. "That was a bit of a scare for both of us, but Honey's a trouper and she's ready to keep going! Let's give it one more try and end on a high note!" Cora's voice trembled when she said the word *try*. She led Honey to the same point on the A-frame and rewarded her when she managed to climb up without incident.

"I think that's a great place to end today's lesson. Honey, good job!" Cora looked at Mia and Vaughn again and shrugged her shoulders questioningly.

"Awesome, we loved it! You rolled with Honey's little accident and made it work. Good stuff," Vaughn answered.

Mia scribbled in her notebook and then looked at Vaughn. "I think we got everything we need, and that means we're done for the day! Cora, you're our final audition."

"How many did you have?" She petted Honey, who stood close to her in the hopes of getting another piece of freeze-dried chicken.

She counted on her fingers as she quietly rattled off names. "You're number five."

"Wow, there's a lot of interest in this show."

"There's definitely interest on the casting side, now we just have to make sure that World of Animals likes what we have to offer."

"Do you mind if I ask how the process works?"

"Not at all. So the first step is finding our top three candidates for host, and we hope to be done with that in the next two weeks or so. Then we show their auditions to our contact at WOA, Dalton Feretti. He's the VP of development, and we basically need his blessing for everything if we want this show to make it to air."

Cora nodded absentmindedly, rehashing her performance in her mind as Mia talked. The name jarred her back to consciousness.

"What, um, what was that VP's name again?"

"Dalton Feretti. He is *the man* at WOA when it comes to new programming. We're lucky to have him on our side. Don't tell anyone, but he and Vaughn were college buddies way back when," Mia explained.

Vaughn victory-punched the air as he broke down the camera.

Cora thought about her lack of poker face and hoped that neither of them had noticed her expression. Dalton Feretti, Dalton

Feretti. She committed the name to memory so that she could confirm her fears when she left the building.

"Thanks, Cora," Vaughn called to her. "You were awesome! Give Fritz a pet from us."

"Yes, thank you again for coming. We really loved what you did. You have a unique way with dogs, I can tell," Mia said as she walked Cora to the door.

Cora took note of her word choice. *Is "unique" good?* she wondered. *Where was my "really perfect"?*

"I've got all your contact info, so we'll let you know if we need anything else from you. Thanks again," Mia said.

"I really enjoyed it. Thank you for the opportunity. I'll keep my fingers crossed!" She smiled in a hopefully genuine way.

Cora dashed to her car and pulled out her phone to see a missed call from her mom, probably to ask how the audition went. She typed "Dalton and Simone Feretti" into the search bar and pushed enter, her heart pounding as the results loaded. Immediately switching to the images section, she scrolled through the photographs until she found a tiny blurry thumbnail of a man and woman standing side by side. It was from *Washingtonian Magazine*'s "Best of Washington" party, and the caption next to the image read, "World of Animals exec Dalton Feretti with wife . . ." and cut off. Cora hit "visit page" and held her breath as she scrolled down to find the photo. She didn't even read the caption before enlarging the photo on her screen.

There, standing next to a shiny-faced man with a manicured goatee, was the perfectly preserved face of Simone Feretti.

TWENTY-EIGHT

Cora received a text from Beth Ann exactly six minutes before their third session was about to begin, just as she entered the lobby. "L8, b there in 5," it read. Cora was encouraged that Beth Ann was out of her apartment, given how closed off she had seemed during their last lesson. Her attempt at politeness was an added bonus.

Cora settled on a bench, ready to rehash her audition for the millionth time and stress about the Feretti connection. Even if her audition had been flawless, which it wasn't, the Feretti connection had stopping power. She checked for Eli, hoping he was around to distract her with tales of surly front desk clerks and questionable housekeeping.

"Here I am, here I am!" Beth Ann yelled from across the lobby. Her face was bright red and shiny with sweat. She was wearing a sleeveless pink tank and multicolored leggings with a splattered neon paint design, a choice so coordinated that it made her look like she'd just stepped out of a fitness magazine.

"Hey, only ten minutes late—not bad," Cora said with a smile.

She had mentally prepared to go into full cheerleader mode to keep Beth Ann engaged and happy during the lesson, but it seemed that Beth Ann's post-run endorphins were doing the heavy lifting for her. "Great day out there, huh?"

"Amazing! The best! I haven't run in months and I feel like I'm finally getting back on track. Know what I mean?"

Cora nodded. They walked to the elevator together, and she scanned the lobby for Eli. "Such a good feeling. So how's Chanel these days? Have you been getting her out much?" She probed gently, not wanting to upset Beth Ann.

"Oh no, I think she's afraid of being outside. She acts like she doesn't want to leave the apartment."

Cora's heart sank. Beth Ann was experiencing a renaissance, but Chanel wasn't a beneficiary. "Well, let's see what happens today. I can show you some tricks if she acts nervous. I have a feeling that she'll be happy to get out on such a beautiful day, though."

"Yay, sounds good!"

Chanel met them at the door with her usual routine of leaping and excitement peeing. She seemed to focus all of her greeting energy on Cora. "Can we get her right outside?" Cora asked.

"No, I have to take off these sweaty clothes first. I feel like a slob. I'll just take her to the balcony real quick. I wasn't gone for that long so she might not have to potty. I can change super fast, I'll be two seconds."

The lesson was already descending into the predictable pattern that Cora felt powerless to change. She threaded through the boxes that seemed to have multiplied and joined Chanel on the balcony while Beth Ann went into her bedroom. The little dog jumped at her with a desperation that hurt Cora's heart. She was wild-eyed and couldn't stop panting, like she was trying to convey that everything was wrong, *everything*, and she needed out of this life immediately.

"I know, *lapin*, I know," Cora murmured to her. "I'm trying. I have an idea, I think you're going to like it." She sat on a rusted metal café chair and pulled Chanel onto her lap, mulling over the unorthodox suggestion she was about to make. The dog's panting slowed, and Chanel leaned into Cora's chest. The pair stared off into the distance, each comforted by the other's warmth.

Cora looked at her phone. Nearly ten minutes had passed with no sign of Beth Ann. She popped her head into the apartment and heard running water, and it dawned on her that Beth Ann was in the shower. Cora paced in circles on the tiny balcony with Chanel at her heels, trying to figure out how to convey her frustration with how their lessons were going without hijacking Beth Ann's runner's high. She looked at Chanel. "I could steal you. Just pick you up and leave. Would she even care?"

Five minutes later Beth Ann slid open the door. A wave of perfume rolled out and engulfed the balcony in vanilla. She was in too-short jean shorts and a Don't Mess With Texas T-shirt. "I'm ready to work now!" She reached toward her dog. "Chanel, baby, are you ready, too?" Chanel backed away.

Cora cleared her throat. "We don't have much time left. Beth Ann, we're three weeks into training and we haven't taught Chanel anything, not even 'sit.' Are you sure you want to do this? I really want to work with the two of you but I'm not sure that *you* want to."

"Oh, please don't. Please don't quit." Beth Ann's lower lip trembled.

"I promise you, I don't want to quit," Cora replied in the same soft voice she used with nervous foster dogs. "But you sort of need to, uh, get with the program. We only have an hour to work through a ton of stuff, and somehow the time just disappears every week."

"I know, I know," Beth Ann said, her eyes filling with tears. "Where does the time go? Where is time going, like, *really* going? I don't get it. I mean, I try to manage my time and be responsible and get things done and then . . ." She trailed off and began weeping.

Cora could console the tearful overworked mom who was frustrated with her puppy's nonstop accidents by showing her shortcuts for potty training. She could offer a shoulder to cry on and a few tears of her own when talking about putting down the family dog. But Beth Ann's tears were something animalistic that Cora didn't recognize. She reached out to rub Beth Ann's back and noticed Chanel trembling under the café chair, as if she was familiar with the storm clouds.

"I'm sorry I upset you. That wasn't my intention—"

"It's not *you*, it's, it's, it's . . . *everything*!" Beth Ann choked the words out between sobs. "Nothing makes sense to me anymore. Nothing." She buried her face in her hands and cried harder. Cora rubbed her back and tried to find the right thing to say. She thought of Eli just a few steps down the hall as Beth Ann's wails intensified. Maybe he could help her play therapist?

"Is there someone you can talk to?" Cora asked. No other supportive questions or calming platitudes that might quell Beth Ann's torrent sprang to mind.

Beth Ann shook her head.

"Listen, I have an idea," Cora said gently. "I'm thinking it might help make your life a little easier. How would you feel if Chanel stayed with me for a bit? I could finish her potty training and get her used to being outside. Give her daily lessons. It would be fun for her, like sleepaway camp."

Beth Ann's watery eyes widened. "You . . . you want to take my *dog*? You want to take my only friend away from me?" Her voice was nearly a shriek.

"No, no, not *take* her, just hang with her for a week or so. Then you could focus on finding time and stuff," Cora sputtered, shocked by the turn the conversation had taken.

"Never," Beth Ann said, staring at Cora with scary intensity. "Never. Chanel stays with me."

"Of course, that's totally fine," Cora backpedaled. "It was just a thought. No problem."

The three of them stood on the balcony in silence, unsure of how to proceed.

"I'm sorry," Beth Ann said softly, once again back to the sad girl persona. "This is really uncool of me." She rubbed her face with the back of her hand and smiled through her tears. "I'm okay. Seriously, I'm okay. Let's get to work."

"Are you sure? Do you want to just watch me do some training this week, and we can pick up next week?" Cora wondered if Chanel would be her first ever student to complete her program without learning a single thing.

"Nope, I'm all set." Her crying faded to a few hiccups, as if a switch had flipped.

Cora realized she had yet another challenge to overcome. "Great. I brought a few toys we can try out to see if Chanel is play-motivated, since you don't want to use treats . . ."

"Oh, we can totally use treats. I was just feeling fat last time. I was projecting."

Cora dug her nails into her palms. The Beth Ann roller coaster was unlike anything she'd ever experienced. She desperately wanted to help Chanel but she didn't feel equipped to handle the human side of the relationship.

"Excellent, that's great. So let's go back to what we tried during the first lesson. Chanel, are you ready to have fun?" The little dog wagged her tail but stayed under the chair. Chanel threw a glance at Beth Ann and backed up.

"I think my dog doesn't like me," Beth Ann said ruefully. It was the first time she had accurately read her dog's body language.

"Aw, she likes you! She's just . . . concerned. She could tell you were sad. Dogs really pick up on people's energy." Cora's lies were becoming more and more convincing. Chanel was definitely a sensitive little soul who could read Beth Ann's distress, but it made her stay far away from her troubled owner.

"Thanks for sticking with me, Cora. I know I'm tough."

"It's going to be fine, we'll get through some good stuff today," Cora replied, focusing on dog training and avoiding the real issue.

She watched Beth Ann shuffle into the dark apartment with her shoulders slumped in defeat. For the first time since she had met the pair, Cora felt just as bad for Beth Ann as she did for Chanel.

TWENTY-NINE

Oliver came charging at Cora with a single-minded determination that made her worry about her knees. She'd been painfully slammed by other overexuberant dogs many times, and while Oliver was just a gangly boxer baby, a direct hit would still be painful. The sky was getting dark and they were nearing the end of their lesson, but she knew that she had to channel his youthful energy level into a more controlled approach during his recalls.

"I'm going to show you how to teach an automatic sit at the end of the recall. It's super easy, and it'll keep him from bouncing off of you every time you call him," Cora shouted to Charlie across the yard. So far the lesson had been completely professional, even though she kept hoping he'd find a reason to touch her.

"Yeah, I'm worried about the family jewels every time I do a re-call!" He gestured vaguely below his waistline, and Cora couldn't help but think about his package. *So much for professional,* she chided herself.

Cora ignored the comment. She called, "Here!" and Oliver

raced toward her. She showed Charlie how to do the luring movement, and Oliver skidded into a sloppy sit almost on top of her.

"Not bad—he'll get better every time. You try it."

Charlie tried it and nailed the move. He grinned at Cora.

"Perfect—love it," she shouted to him before she could keep
the L-word from escaping her lips yet again.

"So awesome," Charlie crowed as Oliver performed a show
dog–worthy sit in front of him.

Charlie reached down to pet his dog as they walked to Cora.
"Hey, I have a weird training question for you before you pack up.
Not on your basic curriculum."

"I think I've heard it all, so you can't surprise me."

"Okay. I like having Oliver sleep in bed with me, and I know
you said it's fine as long as he doesn't guard the bed or anything,
which he doesn't. The problem is that he thinks that he can't get
up on the bed on his own, and I know he's totally capable of jumping up! I bring him up initially, and it's great for a few hours but
then he gets off and goes to his own bed because he's hot, then
a few hours later he wants to come back up and he whines and
scratches the edge of the bed and wakes me up. How do I teach
him that he can make it up on his own?"

Cora knew what Charlie needed help with as soon as he said
the word *bed*. Of course he wanted a warm body near his while
Madison was gone. Images of a shirtless Charlie in bed flashed
through her head. "Oh, that's pretty easy. So the first thing you do
is to get Oliver used to—"

"Could you come up to my room and show me? Do you mind?"

"Ha!" Cora choked out a nervous laugh, unsure how to answer

without sounding like she was more than happy to go to his bedroom. "No, no, I don't mind! Sure, let's do it. Let's try it, I mean."

"Excellent, follow me." Charlie and Oliver led the way through the house, up the narrow staircase to a room at the far end of the second floor. Cora tried to peer into the other rooms they passed to suss out what might happen inside of them.

"Here it is," Charlie said as he swung open the door. Oliver ran in and banked off the bed as if he desperately wanted to jump up on it but couldn't summon the springs to make it happen. Cora paused and took in the dramatic, masculine room. It looked like Madison had ceded control of the decorating decisions in the bedroom so that Charlie could get out from under the shabby chic that dominated the rest of the house. The deep foggy blue-gray walls were stacked with oversize vintage architecture prints. The two matching black lacquer nightstands flanking the bed were each crowded with an assortment of books and magazines. Cora identified Madison's by the pot of Jo Malone hand lotion sitting next to the pile. A large, black, Greek key–patterned rug anchored the show-stopping king-sized bed. The bed was the unmistakable focal point of the room, with a tall black leather headboard and nailhead trim. Cora saw the dent in the pillow on Charlie's side of the bed and imagined his head resting against it.

"See what I mean?" Charlie pointed to Oliver, who was standing on his hind legs and scraping at the top of the bed with his paws.

"Ooh, he's going to snag your beautiful linens!" Cora exclaimed, eyeing the expensive-looking white duvet. She made a kissy noise to get him to come to her.

"Can you help? Please? I'm exhausted from his up-and-down all night. Just look at my bags." He moved closer to her as she slid a half step away from him.

"Looks fine to me," Cora answered with a nervous smile because maintaining eye contact with Charlie for more than a few seconds was impossible. "Let's get started."

She walked over to a low blue-patterned ottoman. "I want to cheat this behavior instead of doing it the by-the-book way, so do you mind if I let Oliver use this?"

"Everything in our house is his, of course you can."

Cora pushed the ottoman so it bordered the end of the bed. She took a treat from her pocket and put it on the middle of the ottoman where Oliver could see it. He immediately jumped up and ate it. Cora said "up" as he leaped. She took a second treat and placed it on the end of the bed and again said "up" as Oliver made the leap.

"That works. I can just leave the ottoman there until he gets a little bigger," Charlie suggested.

"Sure, you can do that, or we can show this lazy boy that he actually *can* jump all the way up."

Cora repeated the ottoman-to-bed process with Oliver a few more times, and then took the cushion off the ottoman and put it on the floor where the ottoman had stood. She put the treat on the end of the bed this time, and Oliver leaped up without a problem, even though the cushion gave him only an additional four inches of height.

"Mind games," Charlie exclaimed.

"Yeah, sometimes dogs develop weird superstitions, and for

whatever reason Oliver thinks that he's not capable of jumping up without help. Now for the real test." After a few successes that way, Cora removed the cushion from the floor and again put a treat on the end of the bed. Oliver looked at Cora, then at the bed, and then back to Cora. He sat down.

"Looks like he needs some added inducement. Charlie, would you mind getting in bed?"

"I never say no when a woman tells me to get in bed!" He climbed in while Cora blushed and focused on Oliver.

Charlie patted the bed beside him and said, "Up, Ollie boy! Up, up, up, up!" Oliver looked at Cora and didn't move.

"Awww, he wants you to be up here too. C'mon, get in, Cora!"

He was right. Cora knew that if she got in bed as well, human-loving Oliver wouldn't be able to resist jumping up.

"Well, this is pretty unorthodox, but you *do* need to get your sleep." She perched herself on the opposite side of the bed. The moment she drew her feet up off the ground Oliver sprang into the air, seemed to hover there for a moment, and landed squarely in the middle of the bed.

"Yeah, buddy! There he is, there's my jumper!" Charlie laughed and petted his dog, who hopped in circles as if he couldn't believe what he'd just accomplished. Cora joined in, laughing at Oliver's silliness, which only made him more animated. He sprinted from one side of the bed to the other, pausing in front of Charlie then Cora then back to Charlie, seeming to say, "I did this all by myself! Look at me!"

Oliver flopped on his back and pawed the air, his energy flagging after the mental workout. "Someone wants a belly rub," Cora said. She edged her way to Oliver and scratched his undercarriage. Charlie leaned in and rubbed Oliver's belly as well.

"You're getting double teamed, Oliver. Lucky guy." He chuckled.

Cora grimaced and imagined what they looked like spread out on the bed together. The scenario was so far past professionalism that she gave in completely. She pulled her legs all the way up on the bed and put her head down next to Oliver, making sure it was far away from Madison's pillow. "I'm exhausted. I could go to sleep right here."

"Be my guest, we wouldn't mind." Charlie moved in closer to Oliver. "I'm pretty tired, too." He put his head down so that he was facing Cora. Oliver relaxed in the space between them. Cora closed her eyes for a few moments, and when she opened them Charlie was staring at her. She didn't look away.

"Bet you've never had a lesson like this," Charlie said softly.

"Never. But that's what I love about my job. Different every day." Cora was trembling inside but she managed to keep her voice steady as she spoke.

"Is it weird that we did bed training?"

"Not at all. You had a legitimate training concern, and we addressed it. And now we're taking a break." She was amazed that she could explain away the divide they were crossing so coolly.

"Is it weird that we're still in bed?"

"I don't feel weird. Do you, Oliver?" Cora tickled Oliver's belly playfully. Charlie reached over and rubbed Oliver's stomach, and their hands touched. Charlie slid his hand on top of Cora's and left it there, resting on top of dozing Oliver.

In that moment, looking into Charlie's eyes, Cora didn't care about anything else. She didn't care about doing the right thing, or Madison, or how unprofessional she was acting.

She leaned over and kissed Charlie Gill.

He met her lips as if he'd been waiting for them. Movie kiss perfect. He stroked her cheek softly as their lips met, until Cora's hunger for him made it obvious that he could abandon any tender pretext. She heard him groan quietly as their kisses turned primal.

Oliver sighed and pushed against Charlie with his front paws, as if registering an editorial comment about what was happening right above his head, which halted the moment. Cora was mortified by what she'd done. How could she have let her libido drown out her common sense?

"I'm sorry, I'm so sorry." She moved quickly to the edge of the bed, and Charlie grabbed her arm.

"Cora, it's okay." He stared at her. "If you hadn't done it, I would've."

"This doesn't make any sense. I'm sorry, I have to get out of here. Madison—"

"I don't want you to go."

The room was dim, illuminated only by the light from the hallway. There was no question what would happen next if she didn't leave. After ages of self-imposed celibacy, she was aching to strip off her clothes and lose her new-ginity to Charlie. She wanted nothing more than to kiss him and not stop. Instead, she hung her head.

"This isn't who I am. I can't, Charlie. You're not thinking straight. You're just lonely."

"I've been attracted to you since the first time I saw you. C'mon, I know you could tell."

Cora shook her head and looked at the door. She knew how easy it would be for him to woo away her shaky resolve if she met his eyes. She wanted to get up and leave but she was anchored to the bed.

"I don't know anything anymore. I just know this isn't right."

Charlie moved across the bed until he was right next to her. "Are you saying you don't want me to do this?" He leaned over and kissed her, and she melted into him. He straddled her and deftly lowered her flat on the bed. His hands were everywhere, grazing her breasts, skimming the tops of her thighs, dipping between her legs, and pulling impatiently at the buttons on her shirt.

A muffled metallic sound pierced the silence. Charlie sat up and grabbed at his back pocket.

"It's Madison, right on time." He jumped off Cora and struggled to turn on a lamp, and Cora ran to a dark corner of the room, tucking in her shirt. "Hey, babe! What's up?"

He answered the phone with a stunning nonchalance given what had just been happening seconds earlier.

Cora was shocked.

He listened for a minute. "No, I didn't see that! Seriously? No, I have no record that you tried to Skype me!" Charlie made a silly face at Cora. "Actually, can I call you back in a sec?"

Cora made her way to the door, but Charlie quietly snapped his fingers at her. "Stay!" he mouthed, and she froze in place. He turned his attention back to what Madison was saying. "Oh, okay. Sure, we can talk now." He shrugged at Cora, and she mimed pointing at a watch. She had to get out of the room, quickly. There was no way she was going to listen to him lie his way through a conversation with Madison.

She walked through the dark house while echoes of his voice rolled off the walls behind her. Unable to find any light switches, she made her way to the kitchen in the pitch-black. She packed up her training bag slowly, hoping that Charlie would finish the call and come down to make sense of what had just happened between them. Her only escort was a subdued Oliver, who placed a companionable paw on top of her foot as she finished packing her supplies.

Cora paused at the bottom of the stairs and heard Charlie laughing. She couldn't make out the words but the conversation was clearly nowhere near over, and he wasn't breaking it to Madison gently. Anger bubbled inside of her.

She berated herself during the drive home. *You're nothing to him. But that kiss! Maybe he's struggling with his feelings. But he said he wants to marry her.* The flip-flopping made her even angrier. *Don't be so naïve!*

She kept checking her phone, wondering if he was going to reach out to her, or if she'd have to pretend that his latest breach never happened, just like she did after sushi night. She was almost home when the text finally came through. "SO sry! Mad only had a few minutes to talk. I feel terrible. U hate me?"

Cora waited until she had parked her car to respond. "Do wht you have to do, it's fine."

He sent a smiling emoji back to her, then another text. "U still good to come to the gala?"

She sat in the car with the phone in her hand, imagining the different scenarios that might play out if she went. Even after everything that had happened, she still wanted to get dressed up and eat a fancy dinner with Charlie and his friends. She wanted to drink too much wine and fall into his arms and blame whatever happened on the alcohol. No one had ever kissed her like that before, not even Aaron.

"Sure." The one-word answer was loaded, and they both knew it.

"Great!" A pause followed by another text. "And maybe we can finish what we started tonight?"

Cora replied immediately. "Nope. Can't do that to Madison. Sorry." The text sounded confident. She wondered if he could tell she was lying. Three long minutes passed before he replied.

"She won't know."

His response made her feel cheap. While she had been convinced that they were working toward something real, keeping their relationship a secret solidified Cora's role as a sidepiece and nothing more. Cora typed and erased her thoughts several times, and she knew he could see the reply bubbles percolating on the screen. She settled on, "I'll contact u for gala deets as date gets closer. Thx."

She was angry at herself for not bowing out, but the attraction between them was messing with her head and convincing her to make stupid choices. *You can still beat this*, she thought. *Just go to the gala, don't drink, listen to Alice, focus on meeting new people, and it'll be fine. Keep your distance from him. Simple.*

Charlie replied with a thumbs-up emoji. Then a heart.

It wasn't going to be simple.

THIRTY

"Hello? Hello? Is this Miss Cora the dog trainer?" an unfamiliar female voice with a slight twang asked.

Cora was just leaving her final client of the day and hadn't planned on picking up her phone, but the 713 area code called and hung up three times in a row without leaving a message.

"Yes, this is Cora, how may I help you?"

"Hello, this is Beth Ann Devlin's mother, Pamela. May I talk to you for a moment, please?"

Cora immediately knew that something was up and became flustered by the possibilities. "Oh, hi, Mrs. Devlin. Is everything okay?"

"No, actually it's not at all. And I'm sorry to involve you, but I don't know who to turn to about this . . . . Beth Ann . . ." Pamela's voice cracked. "Beth Ann had a pretty bad breakdown a few days ago, and we only just found out about it. Her daddy and I flew in from Texas as fast as we could. She's not in good shape." Cora heard Pamela take a shaky breath.

"Oh, Mrs. Devlin, I'm so sorry! Is she all right?" Cora's heart pounded. What could she have done differently at their last session? Had Beth Ann hurt herself?

"She's okay, she's just in a bad place . . . mentally." Pamela Devlin audibly struggled to admit it out loud. "We're getting ready to take her back home to River Oaks tomorrow, but we have to get a few things in order before we leave. Beth Ann thought you might be able to help with little Chanel."

Could both Beth Ann and Chanel be about to be saved?

"We would take her ourselves, but I'm deathly allergic to dogs. I'm breaking out in hives as we speak," Pamela continued.

"Of course, no problem, I'd be happy to take—" Cora stopped herself, remembering Josie. The week-long camp she'd proposed to Beth Ann would've been fine, but an extended stay with no end in sight was impossible. "Oh no. My roommate just adopted our foster dog and I can't have three dogs at my place. Give me a second to think." Cora racked her brain, trying to come up with a suitable alternative. She hesitated to get in touch with any of her rescue friends because she felt a special connection to Chanel. She desperately wanted to help the little dog herself, but she knew she couldn't swing it with two other dogs in the house. Then it hit her.

"Mrs. Devlin, I think I have a solution that will work. Can you give me a few minutes to check with someone?"

"Of course, sweetheart. We're not leaving until the morning. Just give me a call when you figure it out."

"This is sort of an awkward question but . . . are you looking to find a permanent home for Chanel? Or does Beth Ann want her back at some point once she's . . . feeling better?"

"Honey, I don't *know*," Pamela's Texas twang slipped out. "I don't know anything right now. I'm thinking that Beth Ann is better off with us at home, and Lord knows I can't have a dog in the house. So let's call it permanent."

"That's fine then. I'll call you when I know something."

"Thanks, sweetheart. We're at the Hay-Adams Hotel, and you have my cell number. Chanel is going to stay at Beth Ann's apartment tonight, and we'll be back in the morning to say good-bye to her and make the necessary arrangements with y'all."

"Wait, you're leaving Chanel there alone tonight?"

"Well yes, honey. My hives, I told you about these awful hives I'm getting."

Cora had to think fast. "Oh, well, I bet Chanel is really scared about everything that's going on. Is there any way that I could come and pick her up later today?"

"That would be fine, thank you. I'll leave a key with the front desk, you can just let yourself in and out." Pamela seemed eager to get off the phone, as if she'd already washed her hands of the responsibility of finding a home for Chanel.

"Mrs. Devlin, please send Beth Ann my best and . . . and tell her . . . I'm thinking of her," Cora stumbled trying to find the right words.

"That's so nice, sweetheart. She spoke very highly of you. She considers you a friend. I do hope y'all will keep in touch." Cora was stunned and saddened by the revelation. What had Beth Ann told her mother about the three short hours they'd spent together?

"Of course. Take care, Mrs. Devlin."

Cora hung up and immediately texted Fran. "Hi there, can u pls give me Eli's #?"

Fran texted, "Be still my heart! Do you need to tell me something?"

"Haha. No, I have a canine emergency and I think he can help." Fran texted his number and included a few heart emojis.

Cora tried constructing a concise text detailing what had just happened down the hall from him, but she couldn't find a suitable way to express everything. She entered his number, hoping he'd pick up.

"This is Eli," he said, sounding like he was still at the office.

"Eli, hey, it's Cora Bellamy, the dog trainer?"

"Cora, hi! What a surprise! What's going on?"

She outlined what she knew about Beth Ann's breakdown, hoping that he would put the pieces together so she didn't have to ask him outright.

"That's so sad! I feel terrible I wasn't more plugged in when I saw her around. So how can I help?" He wasn't making the leap.

"Eli, this is a huge imposition, and I feel totally awkward asking you, but you really seemed to connect with Chanel . . ."

"Oh my God—Chanel! I'm so stupid. Yes, of course I can watch her for a night or two. It's the least I can do."

Cora didn't want to push for a lifetime commitment right out of the gate. "That would be great! A night or two would be a big help. Can you start . . . tonight?"

Eli tripped over his words. "Tonight? Um, I sort of have plans but I'm sure I can postpone it. Anything for Chanel, right?"

She paused, wondering what sort of plans Eli might have. A date? "They left her key at the front desk. I can run over in a few hours and help you get her set up."

"Fantastic. I literally have nothing dog-related in my apartment. I can go out and get stuff tomorrow, but can you bring me, like, dog food and bowls? Or can we grab stuff from Beth Ann's apartment?"

"Have you ever been in her apartment? I'll bring supplies for you, don't worry."

Eli sighed. "This situation sucks for Beth Ann, but I'm excited to help Chanel."

"I bet she'll be ecstatic to hang with you. She really seemed to like you," Cora said, hoping that her subliminal suggestions were working. "I'll text you when I get to your building."

Cora hung up, took a breath, and mentally compiled the supplies she'd need for Eli and Chanel. Cora was thrilled that the little dog was going to finally be free of the dungeon apartment, but she felt awful about the price Beth Ann had to pay. But Eli was a dream foster parent: kind, loving, patient, and willing to step up to help without a second thought—a perfect solution!

THIRTY-ONE

"Can I just leave my ID with you while I go up? Remember, I was here a few weeks ago and I walked her dog through the lobby? I swear, I'm just here to get Chanel. Eli Crawford is going to watch her." She tilted the bag of supplies so the guard could see inside. "See? I brought a bunch of stuff for him." Cora couldn't believe that Pamela Devlin had forgotten to leave word at the front desk that the key was for her. The security guard Cora had passed three times had no recollection of ever seeing her and refused to hand it over. Pamela wasn't answering her phone so she texted Eli.

Eli was in the lobby minutes after she texted him. "Yo, Teddy, why are you hassling this young lady? Does she look like a criminal to you?" He wore a green hoodie with a craft beer logo on the chest and jeans. She'd never seen him out of work clothes, and she had to admit that he looked kind of cute, in an approachable way.

"What up, Eli? I'm just doing my job, and yes, she seems like the shady type to me." The security guard finally cracked a smile.

Eli joined Cora at the desk and gave her a wink. "We need to help out a little space alien in distress, and we heard that you have the key to the galaxy. How do we go about securing it?"

"I'll give *you* the key no problem, as long as you accompany this character." Cora smiled and rolled her eyes but remained quiet.

"You have my word that I won't let her out of my sight." Eli shifted gears. "So did you hear what happened with Beth Ann?"

"Hear what happened? I saw it, man. Rough stuff," Teddy answered.

Eli leaned in conspiratorially and pushed his glasses up. "Tell us. How bad was it?"

"Well, her mom and dad came rushing in here yesterday like her apartment was on fire or something. An hour later, they come down with Beth Ann, and that poor girl was a mess. Crying like someone died and shaking, all wrapped up in a blanket like a baby. Bare feet, all dirty and nasty. I felt so bad for her. She was always real nice. A little strange sometimes, but just a real nice girl."

"Yeah, she was," Eli said glumly. "I mean, she *is*. And now she'll get the help she needs."

"Definitely. And Chanel, too," Cora said, hoping to remind them of her reason for being there.

"Right! Chanel. May we have the key?" Eli asked.

"I'm breaking some rules doing this, but you're my dude, Eli. I trust you." Teddy handed over the key, and Cora gave him her widest smile. He pointed at Cora. "Watch this one. She looks like trouble."

"Oh, I won't take my eyes off her, trust me," Eli said as they headed across the lobby to the elevator.

"Thank you so much for doing this," Cora said once the doors closed behind them. "I totally would've taken Chanel, but my roommate, Maggie, just adopted our foster dog, and three dogs would be a one-way ticket to eviction-ville."

"You foster! That's so awesome. I always wanted to try that."

"Well, you sort of are right now." Cora decided to work the back door approach with Eli. "Chanel can hang with you for a bit while I try to find her a forever home. I'll be quick, I promise."

"Yeah, okay. Makes sense."

"That is, unless you fall in love with her."

He looked directly into Cora's eyes and paused. "That could happen."

The elevator chimed their floor. They stepped into the hallway and instead of keening wails, Cora heard nothing. She looked at Eli with wide eyes.

"Yeah, I know," he replied, reading her thoughts. "It's eerie. Chanel has been completely silent all day. I hope she's okay."

Cora fumbled with the lock on the doorknob and still heard nothing from inside the apartment. "I'm sort of freaking out that it's so quiet in there. And I can't open this damn . . . door . . ." Cora grew frustrated and jiggled the knob helplessly.

"Please, let me do it." Eli slid the key in the lock effortlessly and then turned the knob. "After you."

Cora flipped the light switch by the door and was shocked that the piles had multiplied in the week since she'd last been there. The apartment smelled of spoiled food, urine, and unwashed dog. Cora could only imagine how horrified Beth Ann's parents must have been to discover their daughter living in such squalor.

"Oh wow, this is really bad. Worse than I imagined," Eli said, stepping in gingerly.

"I know, it's awful. I'm mad at myself that I didn't do more to help her."

"Don't blame yourself, Cora. You're her dog trainer, not her therapist."

"Yeah, but I saw how it was in here, and how unbalanced Beth Ann seemed, and I couldn't change it."

Eli turned to face her. "Okay, so what could you have done? Report Beth Ann to Animal Control? Get her committed? It's not like you had a ton of options."

"I know, but maybe if I'd been, like . . . a friend, or something. Maybe she would've reached out to me before things got too bad?"

"From what I know about Beth Ann, being her friend wouldn't be easy. She's a little kooky. Obviously." He gestured to the filthy apartment.

Cora frowned. "I just feel like I should've helped her more."

"Well, now you can help Chanel," Eli said with finality. "Where is our stinky little friend?"

The pair worked their way through the rooms, weaving through the boxes and dirty plates, calling out to Chanel.

"This is unlike her, she always comes running to the door when I show up. How are we going to find her in this mess?"

"She's right here," Eli called out.

Cora walked to where he was standing. Chanel was wedged beneath the couch with her back foot sticking out. "She really knows how to disappear, huh?" He knelt down. "Hey, little alien.

Will you come out?" He touched her paw, and it disappeared beneath the couch. "Crap. Now what? Want me to lift the couch?"

"No, no, let's wait a bit. She'll come out in her own time. I don't want to traumatize her any more. Do you mind?"

"Of course not. My next twenty-four hours are dedicated to her. I even took tomorrow off."

"Are you serious? That's amazing, Eli, thank you."

He sat down on a barstool next to her. "She's had a rough life so far, and I want to do what I can to make it better."

Cora watched him out of the corner of her eye. Eli seemed truly worried about Chanel, and Cora was touched that he was so invested in the pathetic dog. His gaze remained fixed on the bottom of the couch, as if willing Chanel to appear. "Why is she hiding? She likes both of us."

"Yeah, but who knows what's been going on in here for the past few days. Chanel seemed sensitive to Beth Ann's moods, so if she was raging around the apartment it might have really freaked her out."

They sat together in silence, each contemplating what might have transpired, and the journey ahead.

"Can I change her name? No self-respecting straight dude can hang with a toy poodle named Chanel."

Cora laughed in agreement. "Of course! It's easy, just say her new name, then give her a treat when she looks at you. Do it a bunch of times. Then she'll realize that when she hears the new name something good is going to happen. What are you going to call her?"

"I like 'Nell.' Get it? Cha*nel*, Nell?"

"Perfect! And I think her forever family will probably like it, too." Cora studied his face as he answered.

"Take your time with Cha— I mean, Nell. She probably needs decompression time, right? What's your roomie's new dog's name?"

"Josie." Cora showed him a photo that Abby had taken of the two of them at the shelter.

"Pretty dog! And that's a great photo of you. You're really photogenic."

She blushed. "Nah, it's just the reflected glory of the beautiful blonde next to me."

"Look." Eli nodded toward the couch, and Cora could see Chanel's nose peeking from under the skirt.

"Hey, sweetheart! You okay? Do you want to come see us?" Cora moved to the floor and sat angled slightly away from where Chanel was hiding. The frightened dog crawled out slowly with her head low to the ground.

"Look at her paw," Eli said.

Chanel's front right paw was a tie-dyed rainbow of rusty red near her toes fading to a light pink farther up her leg.

"Poor thing, she must have cut herself and then licked at it. No wonder she's scared."

Chanel made her way over to Cora slowly, favoring her injured paw, and rolled onto her back so that her belly was exposed. Cora reached out to stroke the trembling dog and gently examined her paw.

Eli watched the two of them. "Why is she acting like this? Where's the wiggly dog I met outside? What the hell did Beth Ann do to her?" He sounded angry.

"I really hope Beth Ann didn't do anything *to* her. I think Chanel is reacting to what happened *around* her. Let's CSI a little. Do you see broken glass anywhere? I'm guessing that she stepped in something and cut her foot."

Eli surveyed the apartment and walked into the small kitchenette. "Yup, there's broken glass and blood all over the kitchen floor. There's a lot of blood, actually. Are you sure her paw is okay?"

Cora looked at the wound. "It's a small cut, and it's already clotted. It's probably a mixture of her blood and Beth Ann's."

"How gothic."

"Yeah, I really want to get out of this place. There is some bad juju in here. I hope your apartment is a little cheerier."

Eli walked over and placed a small bowl of water in front of the dog. She barely sniffed it and turned away. "Is Chan— I mean, Nell ready to head out?"

Cora studied the trembling dog beside her. Nell was a shadow of the dog she had met a few weeks prior. Cora hoped that a change in scenery would bring some of her spunk back. "Yeah, I'd say she's as good as she can get right now. Since she's going to be hanging with you for a bit, can you run her outside for a potty break, and I'll unpack the supplies at your place? I want her to get used to you."

"Yup, I'll bring you down to my place and head out with her."

Eli reached down and gently picked Nell up. He tucked her beneath his chin and walked to the door whispering to her under his breath. Cora heard the words *negative energy* and *new start*. She followed him down the hall silently, churchlike reverence feeling appropriate for the moment.

"This is me." Eli swung open the door to his apartment. "I'll do the potty break, you can get her stuff ready." Cora handed him a leash, and they nodded at each other.

After spending time in Beth Ann's dark cluttered apartment, Eli's space felt like it was in a completely different building. How could these two apartments have the same square footage? Eli's apartment was bright and sparsely furnished, with the ubiquitous single-guy futon, contemporary black halogen floor lamp, and a few framed concert posters on the wall. An oversize red Calder-type mobile dangled over the futon. Cora made her way to the metal bookshelf, eager to look at the framed photographs and check out his stacks of books, but she heard the elevator bell chime down the hall. She ran to her supply bag to unpack.

"That was fast!" she said to Eli as he walked in. Nell trotted in beside him. "Look at her, she seems better already."

"Yup. She went out and peed and pooped right away and that seemed to help. So what kind of goodies did you bring for our poor little rich girl?"

Cora held each item up like she was a spokesmodel on a game show. "Dog food! Bowls! A new unisex leash and collar! A bone! A squeaky toy! Treats! Shampoo! And last but not least, a comfy bed."

"That's too much, Cora. You didn't have to bring all of this stuff. What do I owe you?"

"Not a thing. I get so many freebies when I go to dog trainer conferences, I didn't have to pay for any of it. And the bed is a hand-me-down from my collection." Cora placed the navy houndstooth bed on the ground, and Nell immediately walked over to check it out. "It's the least I can do, considering how you stepped up to help her so quickly. And you even had plans tonight." She raised her eyebrows to hint that she wanted to know more.

"Oh, that." Eli grimaced. "A second date–type thing I wasn't excited about. You sort of saved me. Just for tonight, though. Moved it to tomorrow night."

Cora was surprised that she felt a pang.

"I can't thank you enough for doing this. *Nell* can't thank you enough. You're her hero." They both looked down and discovered Nell nestled in the bed, looking up at them with a contented expression. "The next step is a makeover with my groomer friend, then I'll take some photos of her, and we'll start posting her online and around town. I think there's a cute dog hidden under that mess, so she'll probably find a home really fast. You won't be put out for too long."

"Put out? Please, this is going to be great." Eli plopped down beside Nell.

"So . . . do you have any questions for me? Do you feel comfortable with everything?"

"I *got* this! It's me and Nell against the world." He looked down at her. "After a bath, you little cesspool."

"Do you need help? With the bath?" Cora was enjoying watching the connection between Eli and Nell and didn't want to leave.

"I think we're good. I don't want to keep you any longer . . ."

"Well, Beth Ann paid for five lessons and since my student now lives with you—temporarily—I'd be happy to do the final two lessons with you guys if you want."

"That would be great, thank you. We'll just take the next few

days to acclimate and then I'll give you a call to set something up."
Was Eli trying to get rid of her?

"Sure, that works. So . . . I'll just . . . head out, I guess?"

Eli looked up at Cora. "Hey, we make a darn good rescue team. Did you ever think this would happen?"

"I wished her out of that dungeon, and look at her now, living large. Just keep me posted if you need anything."

"You got it. See ya soon." Eli nodded at Cora and went back to petting Nell.

She was used to getting lost in the shuffle, with clients celebrating a new puppy or welcoming home a lucky rescue dog. She knew how to slip out quietly in order to let the bonding continue unimpeded. But this time felt different. Eli and she had just done something momentous together, and she wanted to hang out with him and chart the nuances of Nell's new life. She wanted to answer all of the questions she was sure he had and impress him with her knowledge.

But maybe he was going to invite his date over to meet Nell. Maybe the two of them would give her a bath and end up adorably covered in suds like in a corny but adorable Hallmark movie. Maybe they would sit hip-to-hip on the couch with the little dog nestled on their laps. Maybe Eli would lean over and kiss the girl, marveling at how perfect his life seemed in that moment.

And that was fine.

Because Eli was her friend.

Yes, he's a friend, Cora thought as she walked down the hall, nodding her head for emphasis. *A very good friend.*

THIRTY-TWO

Cora arrived at Toya ten minutes late. She'd read about the glittery Asian-fusion restaurant but had never had an occasion to go. Charlie and Madison were probably regulars. She pulled at the front of her top as she neared the door, worried that it was inappropriate for whatever was going on with Charlie. He had texted earlier in the day to set up a quick "conversation" with her sans Oliver, and even though Cora knew that she needed to keep the meeting professional, the dimly lit restaurant Charlie had selected suggested otherwise.

He had never seen her in anything but her dog training uniform, and she wanted to make sure that she looked amazing, but not so amazing that it was obvious that she was trying. She settled on a loose-fitting black peasant top that left her shoulders exposed. Just enough skin to make him look twice. She paired the top with her favorite slim-fitting jeans that made her legs look extra long, one of Maggie's expensive buttery leather belts from Saks, and a pair of black wedge sandals. She caught a glimpse of her reflection as she walked into the restaurant and nodded, as if to confirm that the attractive woman she saw staring back was actually her.

Charlie was already at the bar when Cora arrived, chatting with the bartender. His eyes widened when he saw her walking over.

"Wow, Cora," he exclaimed, "is that you?"

"What, do I look that different in my uniform?" she asked playfully.

"No, I mean, yes? How do I answer that without getting myself in trouble?"

Charlie seemed flustered, and Cora enjoyed feeling like she had the upper hand for a change. She welcomed the power coursing through her body as she sat down next to him. She was testing Charlie and grading his every move.

The bartender leaned over and broke the tension. "What can I get for you?"

"I want something ridiculous. How about a silly mixed drink?"

The bartender nodded. "I've got just the thing."

Cora turned to Charlie. "So what's going on?"

"Nothing huge, I just wanted to talk to you before the gala. Like, really talk to you and not have to worry about Oliver interruptions."

"Um-hm," Cora said. "So what would you like to talk about?" She knew exactly what he wanted to talk about.

"Well . . ." He paused. "The last time I saw you, for starters. In my bedroom."

"What's left to say about that? I apologized, and we moved on. We're back to a friendly professional relationship, right?"

The bartender leaned over and held out a pink drink in a martini glass before Charlie could answer. "Your 'Blushing Lady.'"

"You've got to be kidding me," she said as she took the drink. "Is it that obvious?"

The bartender looked at her questioningly, and Charlie put his hand on Cora's shoulder and explained, "She blushes. A lot."

"*You* noticed it?" Cora sputtered at Charlie.

"Jesus, Cora, how could I not? You were practically neon the first time I met you. And if it wasn't so dark the last time, I probably would've seen it then, too. Am I right?"

She paused and looked in his eyes. "Actually, no. I wasn't blushing at all."

"I bet I can make you blush right now."

"Go for it."

He leaned in close, put his hand on her knee, and whispered in her ear, "I was rock hard for hours after you left."

Cora jerked away and cupped her hand over her mouth, her eyes wide.

"Excuse me, sir?" Charlie called out to the bartender. "Can you come over here? Look at her, please. Is she blushing?"

He walked over and scrutinized Cora's face. "She is, without a doubt. Bright pink, all around here." He gestured to her cheeks.

"And right here, too," Charlie said as he ran his finger along the side of her neck. Cora shivered, and the bartender turned abruptly, aware that his discretion could impact his tip. She leaned away from Charlie, trying to put space between them, even though their thighs remained touching.

Charlie picked up where he'd left off. "I'm serious. That was, like, the best first kiss I've ever had. But it's complicated, Cora, you have to know that. I mean, the whole Madison thing . . ." He trailed off.

"Yeah, tell me about that." Cora sounded bitter and wondered if she had broken the spell.

"I don't know what to say. I mean, I'm in a long-term relationship with her, and it's been pretty great but . . ."

Cora's heart stopped. *Pretty great? Fail.*

"But what?"

"But . . . I have real feelings for you, too. I tried to ignore them but I can't."

For the second time in just five minutes, Cora felt her cheeks get hot.

"I want to explore this with you, Cora." He reached out and placed his hand on top of hers. "I hope you do, too."

Is this really happening? she asked herself.

"I do," she said quietly, avoiding meeting his eyes. "I thought that was pretty obvious."

Charlie cleared his throat. "But I want to lay it out for you. I'm not one hundred percent ready to end it with Madison. She's been gone for a month, I can't dump her the second she gets home."

Cora narrowed her eyes. *Fail.*

"So anything that happens between us has to stay quiet for now. I'll end it with Madison when the time is right, but I can't do it now, okay?" He smiled winningly at her and placed his hand on her knee.

Cora roused herself so that his hand fell away. "I'm not comfortable with anything happening between us until you guys are broken up."

His smile disappeared like a dry leaf in a bonfire. "Jesus, Cora, why?!" He sounded angry.

"Because that's . . . what I think is right. Girl code, I guess. Do unto others." She shrugged her shoulders to suggest nonchalance, but inside she railed against her own honor code because she desperately wanted to taste him again.

Charlie collected himself. "Okay, okay. I get it. So let's do this: if you get overcome like you did at my house, you have my blessing to jump me. Wait—let's do one better." He held up his hand, as if getting ready for testimony. "I swear the next time we kiss, it'll be because you made the first move. Do you agree to these terms?"

"I agree. Which means there will be no kissing for the foreseeable future." She paused for a beat. "Do you have a timeline?"

"For what?"

"To let Madison know . . . how you're feeling?"

"Oh, that," Charlie answered, sounding as if he had already forgotten about the next step. "Um, not really. Her birthday is next month, so it would be uncool of me to do it before then . . ."

Fail!

Cora snapped. "Listen, I have my own terms, so let's do *this*: rather than sneak around and feel bad about it, let's say good-bye for now. Once you've figured out what you actually want, you can get in touch with me. Okay? That makes more sense to me, since you're sort of up in the air about it."

"Are you mad? You sound like you're mad at me." He cocked his head and looked at her with sad eyes.

"I'm not mad, I just don't want to be the other woman."

Charlie laughed at her. "Oh my God, Cora, never! Something real is happening between us. I care about you. Seriously." He took both of her hands in his.

"Thank you."

"That's all you have to say? 'Thank you'?"

"For now," Cora replied coolly. She downed the rest of her drink in a single unladylike gulp. "I should probably head out."

"Okay, I get it. You're punishing me. But you do still want to come to the gala, right?"

She paused before answering to try to find the logic in the thoughts tumbling in her head. She had just laid down the law about how things were going to proceed between them but she was about to negate all of her tough-girl talk. "That's different. We'll be with a group of your friends, and Madison knows about it. And now we have rules, right?"

Charlie laughed ruefully. "Oh, we have rules, all right. You made that very clear."

He was playing along like a champ. Cora wondered how long the ruse would last. She reached into her pocket and threw a twenty on the bar. "Drinks here are expensive. My contribution." It was a final test. Was he a gentleman? Her heart sank when Charlie didn't hand it back to her. *So many fails tonight,* Cora thought.

"Are you sure you don't want to stay?" Charlie asked, bordering on pleading.

"It's better if I go. We both know that."

He nodded. "I'll walk you out." He turned to the bartender. "Hold my spot, I'll be back in a minute."

He's staying at the bar. Yet another fail.

The street outside the restaurant was empty. They stood staring at each other in silence, uneasy and not sure how to end the conversation.

Charlie turned to Cora suddenly and pinned her against one of the cool marble slabs on the side of the building. He pushed himself up against her and brought his face close to hers. They stood glued to each other, Cora immobilized by the weight of Charlie's body on hers, their lips just inches apart.

"We have a deal," Cora whispered. "You said you weren't going to kiss me." But nothing mattered beside the pressure of his body and the proximity of his mouth to hers.

"I'm not . . . kissing you," he answered, almost panting. His lips hovered just above hers. His hands moved to her hips, and he pulled her even closer to him. Cora's arms hung limply at her sides in a halfhearted attempt to resist what was happening, her head all the way back against the marble. Charlie breathed on her, not moving but somehow bringing his lips closer to hers with each whiskey-tinged breath. She was desperate to cross the impasse, but couldn't. Wouldn't.

"Fuck your terms, Cora," he finally growled and kissed her hard. She kissed him back, embracing him tightly and wrapping her leg around his so that she could feel his entire body against hers. They remained attached, kissing feverishly, until Cora pulled away.

"Oh my God, *je veux te baiser*," she said, breathing heavily.

"What does that mean? Tell me it means what I think it means," Charlie whispered, holding Cora's face in his hands.

She shook her head and said nothing. A group of four approached the restaurant, a young couple and parents, and Cora moved away from Charlie, aware that they looked like they belonged outside a bar at closing time, not outside a restaurant before the sun had even set.

"I'll see you at the gala, then," she said, pushing her hair over her shoulder and smoothing down her shirt.

"Yup." Charlie nodded and didn't look at her. "I've got a car for the night, so we can swing by and pick you up. We'll probably go to the City Tavern Club after. Do you have something to wear yet?"

Focusing on the conversation was difficult with her body lit on fire. "Yes. Well, no, not yet. I have one picked out, I just haven't bought it yet."

He narrowed his eyes at her. "I have to warn you, if you look any better than you do tonight, I'm going to have trouble keeping my hands off you."

"But we have rules," Cora said, her voice catching.

Charlie shrugged his shoulders, gave her a mischievous smile, and wordlessly walked back into the restaurant, leaving Cora alone on the sidewalk.

Fail.

THIRTY-THREE

The check engine light went on right as Cora turned into the Saks parking lot. She was finally picking up the Léger, and it seemed like fate was once again weighing in about what she was doing. She wondered if she'd regret spending so much on a dress when the car repair bill came in.

Darnell was waiting for her when she walked through the main doors in a haze of self-doubt.

"She didn't come with you," he said, crestfallen.

"I tried, believe me, I tried. Maggie's really committed to her bed-in. All she does is watch TV and hang out with the dogs. When I told her I was coming to get the dress today, she said there was no way she's ever setting foot around here again. She's done with this place."

"And me." Darnell sighed, his typical enthusiasm dimmed by the hopelessness of the situation. "Did she tell you what happened?"

"Sort of. What's your side?"

"It was a dumb Darnell joke that blew up in my face. You

know I'm an idiot and I say shit without thinking. I'm absolutely sick about it, and she won't answer my calls or text me back, so I can't plead my case."

"She's stubborn, you know that. But you have to keep trying. She needs you in her life."

"Oh, trust me, I'm not giving up on her. Darnell is *not* a quitter. Now on to you, boo. Is it time to incinerate your credit card?"

Cora nodded and grimaced.

"Well, I have a surprise for you." He disappeared into the back room and returned with the gown slung over his shoulder. "Check this out." He thrust the price tag at her so she could see it was covered in red hieroglyphics.

"Markdowns! I can't read this, what does it cost?"

"I'm going to give you my employee discount, which is thirty percent off, plus the end-of-spring sale price, which is, like, rock bottom, because this dress is now *so* last season, and that brings the price down to . . ." He paused again, working the numbers in his head. "A little under five hundred dollars. Much better, right?"

"Oh my God, so much better! Thank you! And I'm totally impressed that you did the math in your head."

"My dear, when you're on commission, numbers are your life. I run percentages in my sleep. Now let's get you rung up."

Darnell walked toward the register and stared down an attractive woman in a short black shirtdress with a severe ponytail, geek glasses, and gladiator heels.

"Ugh, *Emerson*," he sneered to Cora as they passed the woman. "Maggie's replacement. I bet that's not even her real name. She is the worst." He shuddered.

"No one can replace Maggie, but that gives me an idea. Would you be willing to do my makeup for the gala? We can set it up so that you come to our apartment and we can catch Maggie off guard and do *her* intervention."

"Oh, I love that idea! Like, I'm not coming over to see *you*, Maggie, I'm here to help my girl Cora, just slinging makeup, don't mind me. Then I can woo her and make her my BFF again. And then all will be right with the world."

"Thursday night, can you be at our place at about four? Does that give you enough time to rehab all of this?"

"You're already a goddess, I'm just going to gloss you up a bit. Can I work on that crazy-ass hair, too?"

"I'm in your capable hands, D. In return I'll broker the peace treaty. Oh, and pay you, too, of course."

"Absolutely not. Get me my Magpie back, and we're square. Deal?"

"Deal." Cora leaned across the counter and gave him a kiss on the cheek. "Thanks again."

Cora's stomach twisted. Too late to back out. She had an expensive dress in a zippered garment bag slung over her shoulder. She was going to the gala. Cora closed her eyes and shook her head when an image of Charlie in a tux flashed through her mind.

Strictly professional. From now on.

THIRTY-FOUR

It had taken over two weeks but Cora had finally managed to snag a grooming appointment for Eli and Nell. Her friend Molly's thriving business, Sniptastic, usually required a longer wait, but she agreed to slip Nell in for an 8:00 a.m. groom after Cora sent a pleading text with a photo of the bedraggled dog.

She had arrived a few minutes early so that she could chat with Molly, but the front door was locked when she got there. Molly thrived on self-created chaos, and would no doubt run through the first fifteen minutes of the appointment as if overdosing on caffeine.

Molly was far from the typical groomer. While most of her peers were gruff with both their human and canine clients, made bitter by the physical demands of the profession and the unrealistic expectations of dog owners, Molly's sunny disposition never faltered. Her neon-pink pageboy and multiple tattoos set her apart as well, and gave her an edge that her soccer mom clients hoped would rub off on them if they hung around her enough. Her latest body art was a delicate pink ribbon that laced up the back of her neck like a corset.

Cora wanted to meet Eli and Nell at the salon to introduce them to Molly, but she was also eager to catch up with the duo. She sat on the dirty stoop in front of the salon scrolling through the old texts from Charlie, trying to decipher if what was happening between them was merely a bad idea, or a truly very bad idea.

The door behind her slammed open as if caught by the wind. "Hey, sweetie! Sorry I'm late! Actually, it's one minute before my start time, so I'm technically not late." Molly leaned down to give Cora a kiss on the cheek.

"Hey, been too long!" Cora followed Molly into the bright space, which was crowded with oversize photos of cute dogs and Pinterest-style inspirational quotes overlaid on photos of gauzy landscapes.

"So tell me about this dog and this dude. How do you know them?"

"Long story, but basically he's a client's colleague as well as a different client's neighbor. He's fostering Nell for now, but I'm hoping that he's going to keep her."

"Is he a good dude? Do you approve?"

"He's, like, the best dude. So sweet."

Molly cocked an eyebrow at Cora.

"No, no, no, stop it. We're just friends. He's really nice and totally perfect for the dog. Nell needs a ton of TLC."

"Hm," Molly answered as she folded towels at a breakneck speed.

The bell on the front door jingled as Eli and Nell walked in. He was wearing a blazer, plaid bow tie, and jeans. Cora realized that his geek chic thing wasn't accidental; Eli had a well-defined look. He dropped Nell's leash and she dashed to Cora.

"There she is!" Cora exclaimed, dropping to her knees to greet the little dog. She looked up at Eli as Nell wiggled an overjoyed greeting. "How is she? How are you? Tell me everything! And I'm being totally rude—Eli, this is Molly. Molly, meet the best foster dad around, Eli."

Eli reached out to shake Molly's hand, and Cora watched him for the telltale flicker of interest. Molly's bright hair, tattoos, tight tank top, and pretty face made for an appealingly dangerous conquest that even the dude-est frat bro couldn't resist attempting. The fact that she was a lesbian was usually lost on them until she broke out photos of her girlfriend, which made the most alpha of them pursue her even harder.

"Nice to meet you," Eli said as he shook her hand, adding a slight bow, oblivious to Molly's allure. "Thank you so much for squeezing us in. I can't wait for her to look like a normal dog. I gave her a bath so she doesn't smell anymore, but she still looks like hell. I keep getting side-eye on the street, like it's *my* fault she looks like this."

Molly examined Nell from a distance as Cora fussed over her on the floor. "Wow, I've got my work cut out for me, huh? I can see the mats from here, and what's up with those bald patches?"

"Rough living. Nell survived hard time on a lonely planet," Eli replied.

"Yeah, Cora gave me the overview when she begged me for an appointment. Okay, best-case scenario, what kind of cut do you want? Keep in mind my options are limited, but dream scenario, what do you want her to look like?"

"A German shepherd?" Eli smiled sheepishly. "No, that's terrible, I'm sorry for saying that. I just never imagined that when I finally got a dog, my dog would be so . . . girly. Can you, I don't know, butch her up for me a little?"

Molly let out a brittle laugh. "Are you one of those guys? Won't let your dog wear a pink collar because you don't want people to think *you're* girly?!" She liked to give men a hard time to see how they reacted.

Eli could tell that he was stepping into dangerous territory so he backpedaled furiously, waving his hands in front of him. "No, not at all! I have no problems with pink! No problems with pink! I have two pink shirts!"

Cora laughed quietly at Eli's attempt to avoid Molly's wrath.

"Okay, okay, I get it. You're not one of those guys." She smiled at him. "I'll ask again; what kind of cut, Mr. Pink?"

"I'm afraid to answer now," he said.

"How about I help?" Cora interrupted. "I see Nell with a cross between a puppy cut and a teddy bear. No puffballs on her. Let's keep the body one length if possible, and make the ears and the top of the head fuller."

"You're asking for a lot," Molly said as she examined Nell more closely. She lifted the little dog and ran her hands along Nell's face and body, peering in her ears and handling her paws. "I'll do what I can. But I guarantee she'll look better when she leaves than she does now. I'll trim down those awful tear stains and get her coat back to a version of white." Nell nestled comfortably in the crook of Molly's arm, as if they were old friends already.

"Do I stay with her? How does this work?" Eli asked.

"Nope, it's best if it's just me and Nell. This first groom is going to be really quick because there's not much for me to work with, but as her coat comes back we'll be able to make her look normal. It'll take me about an hour and a half, is that cool?"

"Yup, I can be a little late for work. Thank you again for fitting us in, I really appreciate it."

Eli walked over to Nell cradled in Molly's arms, assumed a serious expression and cupped the dog's small face in his hands. "Don't worry, little alien, change is good. I'll see you in a bit." He kissed her on the top of the head then walked out of the salon, and Molly feigned a swoon behind his back.

Molly pointed at Eli. "Get on that!" she mouthed to Cora.

Cora rolled her eyes and followed Eli out of the salon. She felt spontaneous. "Hey, do you want to grab some coffee while you wait? My next appointment is literally right around the corner from here and it doesn't start for a half hour, so I can help you kill some time if you want."

"That would be great," Eli replied.

They walked to one of the few independent coffee shops left in the city and grabbed a tiny table in the window.

"Coffee is on me," Cora said with authority. "You're doing such a solid taking care of Nell."

"It's no problem, I swear to you. And it's not in my DNA to accept a thank-you for something that requires no thank-you in the first place. Now what can I get for *you*?"

"Well, thank you twice, then. Just a small coffee, black."

"What, no caramel coffeechino chai-spice latte?"

"Nope, I'm the most boring coffee drinker in the world. Like an old man."

"Old men are badass." Eli winked and walked to the counter to place their order.

Cora thought about how Nell would fare during her first visit to the groomer and how much better she was going to look when Eli went back for her. She wanted to see Nell in person postgroom, with the little pink ribbons nestled in the fur on her ears, but she felt like she was being annoying and overinvolved. Then it hit her.

"You said 'when I get a dog'!"

Eli slid in across from Cora with their coffee. "What?"

"Back at the salon! You said 'when I finally got a dog,' and you called her 'my dog'! You're keeping her!"

Eli looked down at the coffee mug in his hands, a smile tugging at the corner of his mouth.

Cora persisted. "Tell me I'm not crazy. You're keeping her!"

"I am, I am. I was trying to think of a cool way to tell you but I'm awful at keeping secrets." He squinted at Cora. "Are you tearing up?"

She wiped her eyes with the back of her hand. "Yeah, I'm such a lightweight when it comes to dog stuff. It doesn't take much to get me going. But this news deserves some happy tears." She sniffled. "I am so, so, so grateful that she's staying with you. It's perfect!"

He rifled through his laptop bag and produced a small cloth handkerchief. "My mom gave me a bunch of these. Chronic postnasal drip. But this one is unused, I swear!"

Cora laughed and dabbed her eyes with the soft square of

fabric. "This is such a relief. I wanted you to keep her but I didn't know if you were ready for a dog. And I didn't want to ask outright. I was sure that I could find her a good home, but that might mean that I'd lose touch with her. Her staying with you . . . well, I hope we'll keep in touch."

"Of course we'll keep in touch," Eli said gently. "I mean, I hope so, too."

"When did you know she was the one for you?" Cora asked.

"The first minute I saw her. I had an immediate connection to her. Which was weird, because I've never been a small-dog guy."

Cora understood the alchemy of a perfect dog-human match.

"Is everything going okay with her? Like potty training and all that?"

"She's perfect. No accidents. And she goes to the door and barks when she needs to go out."

"Speaking of barking . . . ," Cora said with a grimace.

"I forgot to tell you! The barking problem is gone. The *only* time she barks is when she needs to go out. None of that awful nonstop stuff like she used to do. She's totally different now."

"Amazing. But now I feel doubly bad about her life with Beth Ann. Have you heard anything?"

"Nope, nothing. They're cleaning out her apartment. I guess her parents hired a company to scour it down before they try to sell it."

"They've got their work cut out for them."

"I'm still in shock that it was so bad. Beth Ann was quirky, sure, but I never thought she was hoarding." He shook his head.

"Yeah, it's kinda scary how well some people can hide their

true selves." She shrugged and looked out the window at the people rushing to work, wondering how many of them were who they appeared to be.

"Hey, I wanted to ask you something," he said. "This might be prying, because it seems like there's all kinds of secrecy surrounding it, and you don't have to answer me if you don't want to."

"I don't think I'm going to like this," Cora said, grimacing.

"Is ChienParfait your website?"

Her eyes bugged.

"You need to work on your poker face," Eli said, answering himself.

"How did you—where did—?"

"I'll admit that I used to like Boris's show because I didn't know better, but Fran told me what you thought of him. I looked into him when I realized that he was going to be in town and I stumbled on a *Washington Post* video interview with him. Being the nerd that I am, I immediately went to ChienParfait and who did I see on the site but our mutual friend Sydney. I mean, I knew it had to be you."

"So did you hate it?" Cora winced, anticipating the worst.

"Well, it introduced me to a totally different side of you. I mean, you know your dog stuff, but some of the Ershovich posts . . . you get kind of intense. I translated the titles, too. Yikes. Not what I expected."

"Yeah, I get fired up about him. It borders on ranting, huh?"

"No, no . . . it's great stuff. I like the passion. You're not making personal attacks about him, and your arguments make sense. I actually read your entire blog, and you've got plenty of happy stuff mixed in there, too. I like your voice. You should write a book."

"You sound like Fran. I've got plenty on my plate to worry about right now. I did this big—" She started to tell him about the audition but stopped. She was talking about herself too much. "Never mind. Listen, I've got to run. *Please* send me a photo when she's done?"

"You got it. I feel like such a dork but I'm psyched to see what she looks like. I feel like she's on a makeover show."

"Same." Cora paused, unsure of what to say next. She didn't want to leave.

"Hey—Rivera tomorrow night. You going?" Eli asked.

"Wouldn't miss it. You?"

"Yup. I'll text you a picture of Nell's transformation."

"Can't wait." Cora slung her bag over her shoulder slowly and lingered over the last few sips of coffee. She had six minutes to make it to a client who was seven minutes away, but for the first time she thought it would be fine to be a tad late. "Okay, better head out now. Bye."

"I'll see you on the dance floor."

"Ha! Unlikely." She waved awkwardly at Eli and headed out, computing exactly how late she'd be.

She peeked in the window at Eli as she passed. He was staring off into the distance, talking to himself and gesturing with one hand. *Quirky,* she thought. *Nell found her perfect match.*

THIRTY-FIVE

"Does this look okay?" Cora asked Maggie.

Maggie had finally come back to the real world, but even if she'd still been in her funk, there was no way she'd miss a party of Rivera's caliber. Unemployed or not, she was always up for an adventure, particularly when it involved free alcohol and dancing. She looked at Cora's jeans, silky silver racerback tank, and ballet flats with a sneer. "Absolutely not. You look like you're getting ready to mow the lawn. Latin clubs demand sass. They will turn you away at the door if you show up in that, so go find a skirt and some heels. The tank is tit-a-licious, everything from the waist down has to go."

Cora found a short flippy black skirt from her pre-Aaron days in a ball in the back of the closet. A wrinkled mess and it smelled musty, but it was the only remaining sass in her closet. She tried on her strappy black heels and winced at how tight they were in the toes. It was as if wearing flats every day allowed her feet to spread out and grow half a size. She threw on a pair of

Bollywood-inspired dangly silver earrings, a wide black belt, and hobbled to Maggie's room.

"Better?" she asked.

Maggie looked up from her makeup mirror. "*Aiii papi!*" she purred. "Your hair looks great down. But can you dance in those shoes?"

"There's no way I'm dancing. You know it takes a crapload of alcohol to get me on the floor, and my client is going to be there tonight. I'll watch you tear it up, but I'll be sitting the whole night, thank you." It was an excuse. Cora knew that Fran was probably going to be drunk, and the mood was going to be over-the-top celebratory.

"Oh come on! You can't go to a Latin club and not dance! I think it's illegal in some states."

"Nope. Not happening. So this looks okay?" She twirled around.

Maggie laughed. "I can totally see your underwear when you spin—mint green with lace around the edge! But I guess since you won't be dancing, it doesn't matter anyway. You look great. Now go put some makeup on. Oh, and put these on, too." She tossed her a pair of thigh-high fishnets that barely cleared the bottom of her skirt.

"Seriously? That makes the outfit sort of trampy."

"Exactly."

Cora finished getting ready and sat with Fritz on the couch while she waited for Maggie to complete her *toilette*. Josie was with Maggie, watching the transformation. The two blondes were inseparable.

"Are you ready to see some mega *bonita*?" Maggie called from around the corner.

"Yup, hurry, we're late."

Maggie spun into the room and posed like a professional ballroom dancer. She looked phenomenal, perfectly dressed for the occasion, as always. Her black V-neck dress left her back completely exposed. The top of the dress was formfitting, and the bottom flared and fluttered when she moved. Her hair was teased into a hybrid bouffant Mohawk.

"Gorgeous. But you look so dressy. Aren't you worried about being too glammed up?"

"There is no such thing as 'too glammed up' at Café Fuego. Just wait till you see some of the outfits. Now, don't forget, the rules are different in a Latin club. Not everyone who asks you to dance wants to fuck you. Sometimes they just want to dance, so don't be afraid to say yes."

Don't be afraid to say yes. Seemed like good advice.

They each gave Fritz and Josie lipstick kisses on the top of their heads and dashed out the door. After walking a few blocks hoping to hail a cab, they realized the city was jumping and they had no choice but to continue on foot.

"Hey, girls! Girls!" a voice rang out.

"Joe Elvis, it's been a while," Cora called to him as he walked their way.

He assumed his signature stance and belted through the entire first verse of "Girls, Girls, Girls," looking at Cora when he got to the "big and brassy" line and Maggie when he sang the "small and sassy" line, a nod to the height difference between them. He finished and awaited their applause.

"Awesome, as always, buddy." Maggie laughed and clapped.

He whistled. "Y'all are lookin' *fine*! Where y'all going tonight?"

"We're going dancing at Café Fuego. Do you dance?" Maggie asked.

"Nope, nah, I'm a singer. No dancing." He waved good-bye as they finally hailed a cab.

The block surrounding Café Fuego was packed. Clearly, word had gotten out about the invitation-only party, and throngs of gate crashers and wannabes were attempting to talk their way in. The cab couldn't even get close because of the Town Cars and Escalades with blacked-out windows idling out front, so the driver dropped Cora and Maggie off on a parallel street. They jumped the long line and walked up to a young woman in a fashionably distressed Santiago Rivera T-shirt near the front door holding a clipboard.

"Cora Bellamy and guest," she said to the woman, raising her voice over a pounding baseline that seeped through the closed club doors.

The woman scanned the list on the clipboard. "You're guests of Miss Channing, so here are your VIP passes." She handed them two hot-pink wristbands. Cora and Maggie looked at each other with wide eyes but played it cool as they affixed the paper bands to their wrists and walked into the club.

The music throbbed around them, making it impossible to hear anything they tried to say to each other. It sounded like hip-hop with a Caribbean flair and Spanish lyrics. "*Reggaeton*," Maggie shouted in Cora's ear. "I love it!"

The lighting was dim, with red spotlights piercing the shadows like torches every few feet. It was so dark and crowded that

Cora doubted that she would be able to find Fran to thank her for the invitation. The narrow hallway opened up to a packed room ringed with a balcony. Cora could see the musicians setting up their instruments on a stage across the room, and she strained to see if Santiago Rivera was among them, but couldn't find his trademark Panama hat in the throng. The dance floor was already crowded with people gyrating against one another. Maggie was right—there was no shortage of sparkle and glitz. Most of the women wore short tight dresses and heels, and the men wore slim-fitting pants and dress shirts. Now that she was here, she was glad Maggie had forced her into a skirt.

Cora pantomimed drinking, and Maggie nodded. As they threaded through the crowd, Cora noticed men making way for them, nodding as they passed. A man grabbed her hand and swayed his hips in an invitation to dance, but she pulled her hand back, smiled, and shook her head no. "Sorry," she mouthed.

Maggie turned to Cora, pointed to a handsome man standing in front of her, and shouted, "He's getting us drinks, what do you want?" Cora could always count on Maggie to score them a few rounds of freebies. She drew attention wherever she went, and Cora didn't mind hanging out in her friend's shadow. The mix of Maggie's adorable features—pink cheeks, anime eyes, and button nose—with her shocking white-blond hair, mermaid tattoo, and good-time-girl personality made everyone want to be close to her.

"It's a party—prosecco!" Cora pretended to hold a champagne flute.

Maggie nodded and cupped her hand by the man's ear. He draped his arm around her shoulders, and Cora knew that Maggie had already cast her first spell of the evening so she moved away from the crush at the bar and turned to watch the dance floor. The DJ changed the music from the thumping Reggaeton to a more sensual song, and many of the dancers left the floor. The few that remained stood belly to belly, swaying slowly.

Then, as if they all heard a cue in the music that was inaudible to the rest of the room, they began to move in unison, each couple melting together as if they were just moments from stripping off their clothing. The women snaked up and down their partners' bodies in fluid waves. The dancers alternated between tango-like steps across the floor and hip-hop–influenced body rolls, undulating together from their shoulders to their hips, as if they were missing spines.

Cora's eyes were drawn to one couple in particular. A beautiful brunette in a microscopic skirt straddled her equally handsome partner's leg and popped her perfectly round rear from side to side. Her partner flipped her away then twirled her around and around, and her head fell back as if she were exhausted and didn't have the strength to lift it up. Like most Latin-style dancing, even though the man worked the floor like a panther, he was there only to highlight the sensuality of the woman's moves. Cora wondered if Charlie knew how to dance.

She felt a hand on her lower back. "Hey," someone yelled into her ear. She was ready with an apologetic look and a "no, thank you" when she realized Eli was standing beside her. He was wearing jeans and a fitted light pink button-down shirt with the cuffs rolled up, exposing a faint lock-and-key pattern on the inside of the sleeves.

"Hey, Eli, long time no see! Love the pink." The music was still so loud that they had to lean close together and yell into each other's ears in order to be heard. Eli smelled good, like sandalwood.

"Thanks! You look really nice. I've never seen all of this action before." He gestured around her hair.

"Thanks, sometimes I let the beast out. So, that photo of Nell you sent! How does she feel about her new look?" Cora had been stunned by how good the little dog looked.

"Molly is a miracle worker, thanks again for helping me get the appointment."

They stood side by side, watching the soft-core action on the dance floor.

He nodded to the dancers. "Isn't that amazing? It's called 'zouk.'"

"How do you know that?"

"Three sisters, remember? Two of them took dance classes until high school. And my parents love to dance, too. I know more about dance than I care to."

"Can you *do* that? Zouk?"

"Oh my god, no way. I could never dance like that with my sister." He made a face and shuddered.

The music faded, and the DJ broke in. "*Muy caliente! Muy muy!* Ladies and gentlemen, *Tiene un buen momento?* Are you having a good time?" Everyone cheered. "Are you ready to welcome the man of the hour?" The crowd roared. "Okay, okay, Mr. Rivera will be on in just a few minutes. You know he's worth the wait, right?" The entire room screamed in response. "Now back to *bailando!*"

The music swelled again, this time a repetitive three-count beat with a distinct drum pop at the end.

"Bachata," Eli said. "Do you dance?"

Cora shook her head vigorously. "No, not really. Maybe at a wedding after a few drinks, but nothing like that," she said, gesturing to the crowded dance floor. Just then Maggie swooped in with drinks in hand.

"*She* dances," Cora said, pointing to Maggie. "Eli, this is my friend Maggie, and this is Eli, who works with my client Fran. He's the one who is taking little Chanel-Nell."

"Nice to meet you," Eli shouted over the din, raising his glass to Maggie and bowing. She smiled and returned the toast. "So you dance? Do you want to go out . . ." He pointed to the dance floor.

Maggie nodded and turned to Cora. "Do you mind?"

Cora felt an involuntary clench in her stomach, but she shook her head no. "Go for it! I'll hold your drink." She couldn't believe that Eli was so eager to get on the floor that he'd ask someone he'd just met to dance. *I might have tried it if he pushed a little more,* Cora thought.

The handsome dark-haired man who bought the drinks for them walked up as Eli led Maggie to the dance floor. He held out his hand. "I'm Juan. Would you like to dance?" He was short and muscular, with his dark hair gelled into a faux hawk.

Cora balanced both glasses in one hand and shook Juan's hand with the other. "Sorry, no thanks. But thanks for the drinks!" She had a feeling that she was going to be giving apologetic refusals all night.

They stood at the edge of the floor and watched Maggie and

Eli. Cora was curious to see how lanky loping Eli would handle her tiny friend.

The bachata looked like a simple dance; three steps forward, hip bump, then three steps back and another hip bump. Some of the dancers repeated those same movements over and over without any variation, while others added turns, gyrations, slides, and small kicks. Eli started off with just the basic steps, leading Maggie backward and forward rhythmically but without much flair. Cora could tell that Maggie was holding back, keeping her stripper-grade hip bumps subdued.

Little by little, Eli added more flash to his moves, as if he had to feel her out as a partner before he could really get to work. A double turn here, a stutter-step there, until it was clear that Maggie had met her match. By the end of the dance, they'd closed the polite gap between them, and Maggie had her hands clasped behind Eli's head instead of typical partner position.

Cora couldn't believe how good he looked. Sexy, even. The dance floor transformed him in a way that caught her off guard. Granted, he wasn't as fluid as some of the other men on the floor, but for a tall goofy white guy he was peerless.

"They dance well. Are you sure you don't want to get out there and try? I'll be gentle!" Juan promised.

Cora thought for a moment. The music was infectious, the vibe was sultry, and for a change she didn't want to be a wallflower. The prosecco was already having an effect on her, as she'd downed both her glass and Maggie's, and she was about to say yes when the song ended and the lights came up.

"Ahhh, we missed our chance. Later?" Juan asked.

Cora nodded. "Sure, I'll give it a shot. Later, though."

Eli led Maggie off the floor, laughing and dabbing at the sweat on his temples with his sleeves.

"This little lady is quite the dancer!" he said, bowing to Maggie. She fanned herself and offered a courtly curtsy back to him.

"No, *you* are!" Maggie answered playfully. She turned to Cora. "C, you gotta dance with this guy."

Cora imagined herself in Eli's arms and felt her palms go sweaty.

Eli nodded at her. "Yup, you're next. You're not leaving without dancing with me," he said.

Juan grabbed Maggie's hand and dipped her dramatically. "The rest of your dances are mine!"

She laughed, and they walked off together hand in hand, leaving Cora and Eli alone at the edge of the dance floor. Just then the lights dimmed again, and the members of the band walked onstage and started getting their instruments ready, practicing scales on the trumpet and tapping the high hat. The crowd roared, and people rushed to the dance floor.

"We're VIP, let's take advantage of it," Eli said and beckoned Cora to follow. He led her to a cordoned-off area of tables right by the edge of the dance floor and flashed his wristband at the bouncer, who moved out of the way and allowed them to pass.

"There you are, darling!" Fran jumped out of her chair and ran to Cora, plating a kiss on each cheek. Cora could smell the wine on her breath. "You look *gorgeous*! Are you enjoying yourself?" She gestured to Eli. "Did this rake get you on the dance floor yet?"

"Not yet, but it sounds like I have no choice. Fran, thank you so much for inviting me, this is an amazing night."

"It's about to get even more amazing, because here comes Santia*goooo*!" She screamed like a teenager and clapped as the guest of honor came to the stage.

Santiago Rivera, a large man with a close-cropped white beard and a long silver ponytail snaking out the back of his signature hat, walked out to thunderous applause and clasped his hands over his heart. He moved to the center of the stage, took off his hat, and bowed humbly, as if overwhelmed by the love in the room. He positioned himself behind his congas, then erupted into a staccato explosion of sound, and the band embraced his rhythms and segued into his most popular song, "Mi Ritmica Vida."

The sound was twice as loud and three times as vibrant as the DJ's music. Cora could feel the drums pounding in her chest, making her heart beat in time to the rhythm. She surrendered to the music and swayed in place. Looking over her shoulder to give Fran a thumbs-up, she saw that she and Eli were dancing in a small space between tables. Fran was pretty drunk, but Eli was gallantly managing to keep her upright and looking like she knew what she was doing.

Cora checked the dance floor and, sure enough, she could see Maggie in the middle of the action, sashaying around Juan like they'd been dancing together their whole lives. The floor was packed, and though the majority of the dancers were freakishly talented, a few people shuffled off beat and counted their steps as they moved. Cora refilled her glass from an unclaimed wine bottle on a table. A little more lubrication and she might be ready to join the throng in a distant dark corner of the dance floor.

The music changed to a traditional salsa dance, and she felt a tap on her shoulder. Fran wordlessly jabbed her finger at Cora and then pointed to Eli, who stood a few steps away from them. He shrugged, as if powerless about the obvious next step, and offered his hand to her.

"Now?" She looked at Fran, who nodded solemnly. Fran pushed her toward Eli, and he caught her as she stumbled over a chair leg.

"I'll keep the steps simple, don't worry," he said into her ear as they walked to the dance floor. He led her to a small open area directly in front of the stage and right below where Santiago was banging away on his congas. Cora stopped in her tracks with a look of horror on her face at the marquee spot and was quickly trampled by two couples too engrossed in the moment to avoid her. Eli pulled her close, then put his hand on her lower back. She grasped his hand and placed her other hand on his shoulder, surprised by how solid he felt.

He looked in her eyes. "Okay, ready?"

She hoped he couldn't feel her trembling. She nodded.

He held her confidently, stepped toward her with an exaggerated hip roll and nodded to signify that she should step backward with the same hip roll. Cora trampled his foot. It was a disastrous start, but he smiled and nodded at her. "It's okay!"

Eli was a strong leader, using his hands to alternately push and pull Cora's body through the steps. Even though he left a respectable distance between them—far more than what he'd given Maggie—their hips occasionally grazed when she missed the beat. She'd never touched Eli before, except for their first handshake, but here she was in his embrace, with his hand on her back and his pelvis accidentally bumping hers.

Cora stared at her feet to try to stay on rhythm. Eli squeezed her hand to get her attention and leaned in close. She caught a hint of his woodsy cologne again. "Don't look at your feet. Watch the other dancers, that'll help you get the beat, too." He held her gaze for a moment. "Or you can look at me. Just don't look down."

Cora nodded nervously and glanced at the other dancers surrounding them, taking note of the way that the pairs seemed to communicate the moves telepathically. She didn't realize that as she watched the other dancers her own moves were evening out. Her lack of confidence was no match for Eli's strong lead coupled with the pounding drumline, and soon the two of them were dancing in smooth unison. Eli grinned broadly at Cora, and his joy made her smile back and try harder. She switched her hips like the other women and felt her skirt bounce up, probably exposing her underwear, but she didn't care. In his arms, she was transformed, as graceful as the rest of the dancers.

The song ended, and Eli surprised Cora by twirling her into a dip. She felt her skirt swirl up around her hips. The inertia of the move nearly pulled her to the ground, but Eli held her in a rock solid grip. She laughed as he helped her up, giddy from their success. Cora leaned in for an impromptu hug, pressing her body tightly against his.

Eli patted her back and pulled away. "You did great! I knew there was a dancer in there somewhere."

"It helps when you have a good leader," Cora replied. "Thank you for that, I loved it."

Maggie and Juan walked over to them, holding hands and laughing.

"I saw you out there, girl!" Maggie said. "You two looked amazing!"

"Give him all the credit," Cora replied, nodding to Eli. The congas kicked back up and she glanced at him hopefully. "Let's do it again. Want to dance with me, Eli?"

Eli looked up from his phone. "Oh, maybe in a bit? I've got to grab someone who just got here so I'll be back in a few." He walked away quickly, and Cora felt her dancer's high fade.

Juan held his hand out to Cora. "You want to dance? You promised . . ."

She glanced at Maggie questioningly.

"Oh my God, *please* go dance with that animal! I'm exhausted," Maggie said, fanning herself.

Cora took Juan's hand and followed him to the dance floor, weaving through the tightly packed couples. He was a few inches shorter than she was, but it didn't seem to deter him. He arranged her in his arms and started moving.

Cora glanced across the room and spotted Eli walking toward the dance floor with someone, a pretty someone, trailing behind him. She craned her neck and saw the woman reach ahead and grab his arm. He smiled and swept her up in a dancer's embrace, pausing for a moment to find the beat. They started moving together as if they had done it many times, their comfort level with each other more than just that of two excellent dancers.

She brought her attention back to Juan, who had given up on trying any complicated moves, and seemed resigned to ride out the remainder of the song in a predictable side-to-side holding pattern. Cora looked back at Eli and studied his partner.

She was just a few inches shorter than Eli, with a long curtain of blond hair. From a distance she looked model pretty. Cora wondered what else the woman had to offer besides good looks and the ability to follow his capable lead.

"Are you with him?" Juan asked, nodding across the floor to Eli. "Do you want to make him jealous?" He shifted his shoulder back and forth to signify that he was ready to add some flavor to their moves.

Cora was embarrassed that her stalking was so obvious. "Oh, no, not at all! He's a friend. I was trying to see if I know who he's dancing with."

"Ohhhh, okay." He gave her an exaggerated wink.

The song ended, and Cora dropped Juan's hands and smoothed down her skirt. "Gracias for the dance," Juan said to Cora as he simultaneously scanned the crowd. "Now I've got to get back to that Maggie."

"Yeah, she can do your moves justice. I told you I was a bad dancer."

Juan focused on Cora. "What you don't have in steps you have in *animo*. Don't stop dancing, okay? I saw the passion when you were dancing with your friend, so just keep practicing."

"Okay," Cora said. He kissed the top of her hand and disappeared into the crowd, leaving her alone at the edge of the dance floor.

Cora looked around the room and realized that with Eli and the woman, and Maggie and Juan, glued to the dance floor she had no choice but to retreat to the VIP section.

Fran intercepted Cora as she passed the bouncer. "That's Paige," she stage-whispered.

"Who?" Cora asked.

"With *Eli*. They've been 'hanging out,' as he says."

Cora realized that the mystery blonde was probably the date he'd mentioned the night he got Nell. "Oh. Do you like her?"

"She's *nice*. Perfectly nice." Fran paused for a beat. "I hate her."

"Why?" Cora asked, amused by her boozy candor.

"Because she's not *you*!" Fran shouted, exasperated that Cora couldn't follow her logic. "You and Eli belong together. I'm a matchmaker par excellence, and I know you're perfect for each other. But you said you weren't interested, and I let him know. Gently, mind you. He was quite disappointed. Now Paige is on the scene, and he claims they're just friends, but it doesn't look very friendly to me." Fran jutted her chin toward the dance floor.

Cora scanned the room and spotted Eli and Paige on the center of the floor. Paige flipped her long hair as Eli grasped her shoulders and gently led her body from side to side. She managed to look graceful and pornographic at the same time. Eli spun her so that she ended up flush against his body facing out, and they undulated together like snakes. Cora's jaw dropped.

"Wait a sec . . . he said he couldn't do that," she muttered, thinking out loud.

"Mmm?" Fran asked.

"Nothing," Cora replied, nearly shushing Fran so that she could focus. Eli and Paige looked incredible together, and for the first time she allowed the thought she'd been ignoring all night fully into her consciousness.

She was jealous.

THIRTY-SIX

"**S**o what do you want Nell to learn? What are your goals for training?"

Cora was trying to stick to her usual training script, but she wanted to talk about the nature of Eli's relationship with Paige.

Eli paused and looked down at the little dog nestled beside him on his couch. "She's *really* good already. I never knew that I could fall in love with a little dog. You know how we all have a vision of what we think we like, and we stick to it without even questioning why?" Cora nodded. "Well, I always pictured myself with a big dog. Little dogs didn't even register. But then I got to know Nell, and I can't get over how awesome she is. She's smart, she's silly, and yes, she's even cute to me now. Right? Don't you think she looks cute?"

"She's one hundred percent cuter now. I think because she's so happy." Cora leaned over to pet Nell, who flipped on her back to allow full belly access.

"Yeah, we both are," Eli said with a smile.

Cora watched him interacting with Nell and wondered if there was more than just the little dog that was making him happy.

"So why am I here?" Cora asked gently.

"Because I want her to be even better! Plus training is an important relationship step. I read that somewhere . . ." He looked at Cora with a comic intensity, eyebrow cocked.

"Got it, ChienParfait. You're quite the brownnoser."

"All my teachers loved me."

The comment hung in the air. "Let's get started. How about we focus on coming when called today?"

"Perfect, if we can get these lazy bones off the couch." Eli leaned down close to his dog and sang quietly to her as she dozed. *"Nell, Nell, she's been through hell, moved on up to Eli's place and all is well!"*

"You already have a song for her?"

"A song? I have about a dozen already. That's our all-purpose song, but we also have a 'let's go poop' song, a dinnertime song, a sleeping-in-on-Sunday song, and a 'don't worry I'll be home soon' song. Please don't tell anyone and blow my cool-dude cred."

"You'd be surprised how many people have songs for their dogs, it's not as weird as you think."

"Yeah, but are they opera songs?" Eli put his hand on his chest, paused dramatically, and began singing in an impressive baritone, *"Sweet maiden named Nell, fairest lass in the dell, dancing and playing, I am under her spell!"*

Cora stared at him with her mouth hanging open. "Okay, that song was a little weird, maybe keep that one between the two of you."

"Now that I've totally embarrassed myself, it's your turn. Do you have a Fritz song?"

"Of course! Take any song on the radio right now and sub the word *Fritz* in it and you have one of my songs. I don't write my own material for him, I sample. Lots of vintage Michael Jackson, too. 'Fritzie Jean.' 'Fritz in the Mirror.' You get the picture."

The stress of trying to figure out what was happening with Eli and waiting for word about the audition made it difficult for Cora to focus. No news felt like bad news, and she was preemptively disappointed. She wanted to take a few days off and surrender to the couch with Maggie, Josie, and Fritz, but her phone never stopped ringing with new client inquiries. She had hoped that her session with Eli would be more chatting than actual work, but it was clear he was going to make her earn her keep.

"Are you okay? You don't seem like yourself today," Eli said.

"I thought I was hiding it. How can you tell?"

"It's one of my superpowers. I can read auras."

"Seriously?"

"No, not seriously. But I am pretty in tune with people. It's a safety mechanism I developed from working in an office filled with women." He paused. "Sorry, no offense."

"None taken. I get it." She shook her head. "I've just got a lot going on, and it's hard for me to focus right now. But I'm happy to be working with Nell again."

"I think she might surprise you today. She's ready to show off."

Even though the initial lessons with Beth Ann had been a nightmare, Nell had managed to retain the little Cora had taught her. She was an eager student as they added "down" and "come" to her repertoire, and the hour passed quickly.

Eli looked down at Nell, who stood panting at his feet after practicing recalls. "We can be done for today, I think she's cooked," he said.

"Are you sure? We still need to do some leash walking."

"Nah, you need a break, too. Why don't you go home and take a nap or something? Let's schedule our next session and be done for today."

"Nell might be my least accomplished student this far into my program, but if she makes you happy then I'm happy."

Eli stopped and looked at Cora. "Right now, I'm happy."

Cora felt a pinprick of heat on her cheeks. She pulled her phone from her bag and checked her calendar, but not before seeing a text from Charlie that said "Soon . . . XO." She refocused on Eli. "Next week, same day, same time?"

"Works for me," Eli replied.

Cora peeked at her e-mail before putting her phone away. She scanned through the messages, and in the middle of her endless inbox she saw it. An e-mail from Mia Nguyen with the subject line "Next steps."

"Oh my God," she said involuntarily.

"What?"

"I'm freaking out." Cora put her phone down and stared into space, then looked at Eli with wide eyes. "I didn't want to jinx myself by talking about it, but I auditioned for a show. A dog training TV show. I've been waiting to hear if they liked my audition. I just got an e-mail from them!"

"No way! You have to open it in front of me. Please."

"I'm scared."

"Want me to do it for you?"

"No! Yes! I don't know!"

"Hand it over," he said. "I'll be a good buffer, I promise."

Cora gave him her phone and buried her face in her hands. He read out loud, " 'Hi Cora, so nice meeting you,' blah blah blah." He skimmed the rest of the e-mail, his lips moving as he read.

"*Tell* me."

He looked at her with no expression on his face and paused. "Cora Bellamy, according to Mia Neg-I-don't-know-how-to-say-it."

"Nguyen," she said, correcting his pronunciation.

"According to Mia Nguyen, you are one of the final three trainers in contention for *Everyday Dogs*! Congrats!"

"No! Are you kidding? Oh my God! Seriously? Let me read it." She grabbed the phone from his hands and, sure enough, the message congratulated her for her stellar audition and outlined the next steps. Her heart thudded in her chest. It was happening!

"I cannot believe it. I really thought I blew it . . . I mean, the dog fell over in the middle of my demo!"

"Well, you obviously did something right. Congrats." Eli reached out to hug her, and she stepped into his embrace. She ended up nestled under his chin, her heart at ease for the first time in days.

"So great . . . *you*!" Eli said, pulling away and awkwardly patting her shoulders at arm's length.

"Thanks, thanks. I'm in shock," Cora replied, nodding and hot-cheeked.

"Keep me posted, I want to cheer you on. Okay? Text me if anything happens between now and next week. Oh, and can I get your autograph before you go?"

Cora laugh-groaned and waltzed out the door, feeling fizzy.

THIRTY-SEVEN

"Have you thought about something like this?" Cora held her phone out to Maggie, who was sitting in her closet, making piles of clothing and accessories. Josie lounged on a stack of pastel sweaters. Cora wanted to make sure that Maggie was in a positive headspace for her reunion with Darnell, since the gala was today.

"'Institutional Giving Associate.' Huh? What is it?"

"It's a job, Maggie," Cora replied. "The Circle Theater is hiring."

"Theater? Seriously?"

Cora sighed. "Have you completely forgotten your theater roots? Remember, before you got sucked into retail? You getting a job in a theater makes perfect sense."

"I'm not exactly qualified for this," Maggie said as she read the job description quietly. "'Securing support from corporate and government sources . . . grant writing . . . managing the donor cycle . . . stewarding relationships' . . . I've never done any of this stuff."

"Yes, but you got people to part with their money every single day at Saks. Fund-raising is just like sales."

Maggie stared into space. "I guess it sort of is. At Saks I could get an eighty-year-old woman in leather. I could get a twenty-two-year-old in culottes. Everyone I touched spent money." She looked at Cora, her eyes shining. "I definitely could get old geezers and tech millionaires to donate some dollars to a worthy cause like the Circle Theater."

"See? Try it, send your stuff in!"

"You know what's even better? One of my Facebook friends from college works there. We're not super tight, but maybe she could walk my résumé to the right person?"

"Meant to be. Oh, hey, before I forget, I've got someone coming over to do my makeup in a bit." She said it casually, trying to play it off like it was an afterthought.

"Okay, cool," Maggie said, her mind clearly racing toward her bright future as a theater fund-raiser. "Hey, C, thanks for finding this job. I never would've thought of it."

"It's for me as much as for you. I want my happy Maggie back. This sad girl stuff doesn't suit you."

"I know, I'm sorry. I'm moving on. Look, I'm organizing my closet, getting rid of shit that reminds me of that place. I took a shower today. I'm on the road to recovery."

The doorbell rang, and Josie roused herself from her cashmere bed. Maggie had followed Cora's protocol for Josie's front door barking, and now she only let out a few muffled woofs whenever someone came over. Fritz was already dancing at the door when they got there, his nose flush against the seam, inhaling deeply. He looked back at Cora expectantly.

"I know!" she whispered to him. "Uncle D! Shhh!"

Cora opened the door and put her finger to her lips.

"Did you tell her?" Darnell whispered to Cora over an armful of wet sunflowers. She shook her head.

"Sort of. So pretty," she said, gesturing to them.

"Her favorite. Did you know that? That sunflowers are her favorite? *I* know because she's my boo. I pay attention." He shook off his umbrella. "Whoo, it's pouring out there. You picked a bad night to be Cinderella, honey."

"It'll stop. So are you ready to make this happen?" Cora asked him. "She's in a good mood at least."

"I'm ready. I need to make this right."

Cora led Darnell into Maggie's room with Fritz and Josie in tow. She was deep inside her closet, singing softly to herself. Darnell cleared his throat and held the flowers up in front of his face.

Maggie popped her head out of the closet. "Wait—what?"

Darnell lowered the flowers and smiled shyly at her. "I'm so sorry, Mags."

"Oh my God, D!" She dropped the silky blouse she was hanging up and ran into his arms. "I'm so sorry for being such a bitch to you!"

"*I'm* sorry for screwing everything up! I hate myself!"

They separated and fell into a torrent of catch-up conversation, and Cora quietly backed out of the room, smiling at her victory. She walked into her bedroom, Darnell's and Maggie's voices trailing her down the hall, and was once again startled by the luminous gold dress hanging from the ceiling fan like an elegant ghost.

Her excitement about the gala had been tempered by the next steps about the show. The fizziness she'd felt about spending an evening with Charlie was taking a backseat to the new career reality she was facing. The final contestants' video clips were being reviewed by Dalton Feretti and his people any minute, and she would be contacted for a face-to-face meeting with the World of Animals team if they liked what they saw. Cora's stomach twisted as she envisioned Simone—the only client to date to ever truly fire her—taking part in the review process.

Mia's e-mail didn't say who else had made it to the final three, but Cora was convinced that Brooke Keating was one of them. She was a solid trainer with impeccable credentials, and if networking was a factor in securing the position, she'd be a sure thing. Plus, she probably hadn't been fired by Simone Feretti.

Cora ran her fingers along the hemline of the dress. She hadn't seen Charlie since the night of fails at Toya, and even though she simmered when she thought of all the ways he'd let her down that evening, she still wanted to make sure that every inch of her body was exfoliated, moisturized, and perfumed. Just in case.

Darnell burst into the bathroom as she wrapped a towel around her head postshower, oblivious as always to boundaries. "We're back, baby. Reunited and it feels so good."

"It's about time!"

"Thank you for being the bridge, I couldn't have gotten through to her without your help. And in return, I'm gonna make you look *so* good. Johnny Gill is gonna rub you the right way for sure."

"It's Charlie Gill."

"Whatever. Meet me in Maggie's room when you're all lotioned up, her light is better in there."

Cora slipped on a pair of loose shorts and a button-down shirt and joined the party in Maggie's room. Josie and Fritz were mouth-wrestling on the bed, and Maggie was helping Darnell unpack his supplies from a rolling suitcase. He had an arsenal of palettes and tools laid out in formation on clean white towels.

"Oh my God, C, did you hear the latest about Aaron?" Darnell motioned for her to sit on a barstool facing the window. The rain was still coming down in sheets, with occasional cracks of thunder.

She sighed. "Now that the show's over, I've been repurging him. What happened? I thought all failed reality stars are taken out to pasture and shot."

"Yeah, either that, or they leverage their fifteen minutes into something even more stupid. Turns out your boy is quite the singer." He handed her his phone, cued up with a video.

"No, he's not. What is this?" Cora asked Maggie.

She shook her head. "Darnell told me something's up, but I waited to watch it with you."

Cora hit play and the ubiquitous guitar and boom-boom-smash of bro-country music filled the room. She paused it.

"Country? Seriously?"

Darnell nodded. "Wait till you see it. You're gonna die."

She hit play again, and Aaron sauntered on-screen wearing a tattered baseball cap pulled low on his head and a sleeveless Henley unbuttoned so that his hairless chest showed. He reached up to adjust the cap and Cora noticed a new American flag tattoo on the inside of his bicep.

"Barf," she said. And she meant it. His good looks had a new unnaturalness, as if Hollywood had put him through the leading-man machine and spat out a shinier, fitter, less human version of the Aaron she had known. When they'd first started dating, his rugged good looks had been a source of pride for Cora, as if being with such an attractive guy validated *her* attractiveness. Then she started to realize that he used his looks as currency, flirting with anyone who could do something for him. No matter how many times Cora pleaded with him to tone it down, he never did, leaving her to fester as he captivated every waitress, bartender, and bank teller he encountered. Now he was cashing in with a bigger audience.

The video cut to a beautiful ponytailed blonde in a tight white tank top and jean shorts climbing on a dirt bike in slow motion in a bucolic country setting. Aaron started singing.

> *"The way you're hopping on your muddy bike,*
> *makes something in your T-shirt do what I like,*
> *you gun the engine and take off fast,*
> *it's country muddin' time and you're havin' a blast."*

Darnell hit pause. "Do you love it or what?"

"Please tell me this isn't what I think it is," Cora said.

He wordlessly hit play again. The video shifted between scenes of Aaron singing in front of a bonfire surrounded by handsome good-old-boys and down-home sorority girls, and showing the blond object of his affection in various setups, like riding a dirt bike in the mud, waitressing in a crowded bar, and dancing in a honky-tonk. Cora listened closely as Aaron wailed the chorus, eyes closed and head back.

"When you're covered in dirt, I think I'm gonna pounce,
Girl, make your ponytail bounce!"

Cora and Maggie shrieked at the exact same moment. "Noooo," Maggie yelled. "No, no, no!"

"He's making that stupid phrase a *thing*?" Cora asked in disbelief.

"Apparently. You should hear the club mash-up. They played it at Twinkle last night, and I made the connection right away. I was so excited to share this train wreck with y'all," Darnell said, affecting a heavy southern accent. "Now let's forget about the Fairfax cowboy and get to work on you."

Cora groaned and handed the phone back to Darnell. "Only Aaron could turn a throwaway sexist comment into a hit song."

"I bet they started writing it the second the words came out of his mouth. He must have an amazing publicist," Maggie said.

"Writing a song about bouncing titties is a good thing? I thought you were a feminist?" Darnell asked.

"No, the song obviously sucks, the fact that they jumped so quickly and completely repackaging him as a country star is amazing." Maggie looked at Cora. "I still don't understand what you saw in him."

"What I saw in him is exactly what the rest of the world sees in him. I mean, the guy sweet-talked his way out of a scandal and into second place! It's easy to fall for that. The difference is I also saw what was underneath."

"It still didn't stop you from saying yes," Maggie said pointedly.

"Ouch, Mags. But you're right, and when he broke it off he saved me from the biggest mistake of my life."

"*Moving* on, let's not give that loser any more airtime," Darnell said with authority. "I need to get to work." He stood in front of Cora, studied her face, and began painting her with a series of brushes and sponges. After forty-five minutes of primer, foundation, lashes, and sparkle, he nodded approvingly at Cora.

"A masterpiece. Go look."

She didn't recognize her reflection. She looked flawless, airbrushed into glossy magazine perfection.

"Smoky eyes! You gave me smoky eyes!"

"They're seductive. 'Cause that's the goal, right? Maggie filled me in on how you're gonna steal this man away from his woman tonight."

She glared at Maggie. "Hardly. I just want to look like a real girl for a change."

"You don't look real, C. You look like a model," Maggie said approvingly. "Now what are you going to do about the hair? Straighten it?"

"Never! She needs to look like herself. A less flyaway and split-ends version of herself, though." Darnell motioned for Cora to sit down on the stool again. He worked quietly, as if he needed to focus on taming Cora's mass of ringlets. He was done within twenty minutes.

"Voilà."

"Amazing." Maggie sighed.

Darnell had pulled back the hair at Cora's temples and woven it into a deconstructed fishtail braid secured with a tiny Swarovski crystal star clip. The rest of her hair cascaded over her shoulders in fat waves.

"Oh my God, perfect! Not too fussy, not too prom-y . . . I love it! Thank you, D!" Cora bounced into his arms.

"Happy to do it. Now go get dressed. What time is he coming? I need to meet this guy."

"Yeah, no kidding," Maggie said. "I want to see if he's as douchey in real life as he sounds. Judgment is coming!"

"Crap, he's going to be here in a half hour," Cora shouted and ran down the hall to her room.

She slipped the dress on carefully, smoothing her hands up the effortless zipper. Cora had managed to find the perfect pair of sparkly nude heels on a sale rack but had never considered that she might be forced to wear the delicate heels in a monsoon. She didn't have an appropriate coat or wrap for the weather, either, and her lone umbrella was a giant moldering golf monstrosity her dad had forgotten in her car, which was now sitting in a repair shop awaiting a replacement part.

Fritz sat next to Cora and watched her in the mirror as she checked herself out. "Look at us," she said to him. "Beauty and the Beast." She knelt down and leaned her forehead against his. "You will *always* be my prince." His tail thumped on the hardwood like he understood.

Her cell phone buzzed. Charlie. "I'm 2 min away. Rain just stopped. Can't wait to c u."

Cora's fingers trembled as she responded. "Should I meet u downstairs?"

"Nope, coming up. Gotta meet the folks, right?" She wondered what kind of impression he was going to make on Maggie and Darnell. Few were immune to his charms. She paced through the apartment with Fritz at her heels.

She popped her head in Maggie's room. "He's almost here. Be nice!"

"*Damn*, you look hot." Darnell sighed appreciatively. "Don't worry, we'll go easy on him."

They heard a confident knock.

"Wait here!" Maggie ordered. "You need to make a grand entrance, like in the movies." Maggie kissed Cora on the cheek and gave her shoulders a squeeze, as if begrudgingly giving her blessing for what was about to happen. Darnell and the dogs followed Maggie to the door, and Cora watched hidden around the corner.

Maggie swung the door open, obscuring Charlie on the other side of it. "Why hello, I'm Maggie," she trilled, saccharin sweet. She reached a limp hand toward him, and Cora realized she was channeling her southern belle character with the faintest accent. "This is my friend Darnell." Charlie stepped into view, and Cora's heart stopped. His impeccably tailored tux fit like it had been made for him. She hoped she looked good enough to stand beside him.

"So nice to meet you both!" He shook their hands and then looked down at Fritz and Josie, expertly juggling both the humans and dogs to make sure they all got an equal share of his attention. "This must be Fritz, and you're Josie, right?" He reached down to pet them, and Fritz sniffed his leg from a distance. Josie, ever the attention hound, spun in circles in front of him and eagerly accepted his affections.

"So what time will you be dropping our precious Cora off tonight?" Darnell asked, crossing his arms and adopting a square Dad's tone, and Maggie threaded her hand around his bicep.

Charlie laughed and played along. "Well, sir, I'm not sure. Can I call you later?"

Cora didn't know how far the duo would take their farce, so she took a deep breath and stepped into the room before it got out of hand. "Hey, Charlie, I see you've met the crew."

He looked at her and his eyes widened. "Wow, Cora. You look—"

She interrupted him, not wanting to hear his candid assessment in front of Maggie and Darnell. "I take no credit—my glam squad did it."

"Not all of it," he replied quietly, his eyes quickly traveling up and down her body. He walked over to her and hugged her tightly, burying his face in her neck and crushing her chest into his for a moment longer than necessary. He smelled like summer, and the feeling of his light stubble tickling her neck gave her chills. She felt electricity pass between their bodies, and wondered if Maggie and Darnell noticed sparks leaping off of them.

She saw Maggie wrinkle her nose.

Cora started chattering, eager to change the temperature in the room and shift the focus away from the magnetic attraction between them. "Did it stop raining? I don't have the right kind of coat and my umbrella isn't here. Mags, do you have an umbrella I can borrow? Is it muggy out there?"

"Actually, the car has a few big umbrellas, so don't worry about it. And I'll put my jacket down on any puddles," Charlie said with a smile. Darnell threw his head back and laughed, already under

Charlie's spell. Cora looked at Maggie, though, and she could see her friend cataloging every move that Charlie made so that she could dissect him later.

"Okay, then, we're off!" She waved at Maggie and Darnell and placed lipstick kisses on top of Fritz's and Josie's heads.

"Have fun, be good," Darnell replied playfully.

"We're going to dinner so we're right behind you," Maggie called to them as they headed out the door. "Tell Alice Goodwin we send our regards."

Charlie couldn't keep his eyes off Cora as he escorted her to the limo idling in front of her building. They stepped outside into what felt like a solid wall of humidity. The sidewalk hissed irides-cent smoke.

"At least it's not raining," he said with a shrug. "Although see-ing you wet might be a good thing."

Cora shook her head. "This is going to be a long night."

"Hope so," he replied. The driver jumped out of the car and opened the door for them.

"This is the classiest limo I've ever seen," Cora said, not both-ering to hide her wonder. "I bet no bachelorette party has ever set foot in this thing."

"Mercedes S600 Pullman. They call it the 'dictator mobile,' so we're in good company."

Cora climbed into the cream-colored interior. "Wait a second, there are only four seats. You said there would be eight of us total."

"Yup, my crew is meeting us there, but we'll probably all pile in here to get to the after party. I thought you and I could drive around town first and check out the lights."

Cora realized that Charlie's buffer of friends weren't going to be a buffer at all. He was already breaking the rules.

He interrupted her thoughts, placing his hand on top of hers. "You look beautiful."

Cora turned to him. He was staring at her with barely concealed hunger.

"Thank you. You do, too."

He laughed at her.

"I mean, handsome. You look handsome."

"Do you realize that's the first compliment you've ever paid me? I used to get jealous of Oliver because you complimented him all the time."

"I always complimented you on your performance!"

"Oh, sure, you told me I could do a mean down-stay, but you never complimented *me*."

Cora was confused. "Well, that wouldn't have been . . . appropriate. I mean, what would you have wanted me to say?"

"That you were wildly attracted to me because I'm so devastatingly hot."

Cora rolled her eyes at him. "Yeah, Madison would've loved that. *Super* professional."

"I seem to remember someone being exceedingly unprofessional in my bedroom a few weeks ago . . ."

Cora blushed.

"And hey, we're done with training now, so the employee-employer boundaries no longer apply." Charlie leaned toward her, and she caught her breath. "Sorry, but I can't wait any longer. The hell with the pact."

Cora readied herself to meet his kiss, even though it didn't feel right in the fading light of day, sitting behind a driver who was pretending not to watch in the rearview mirror. Their lips were inches apart when the car lurched to a stop. Charlie had to throw his hand on the seat in front of him to keep from falling.

"Sorry about that," the driver said over his shoulder. "The end of rush hour traffic. We're going to be here for a bit."

Cora looked out the windshield and saw a line of brake lights snaking ahead of them, and then peered out her window to orient herself, only to realize that they were just three blocks from her apartment. On the sidewalk, just beyond the row of parked cars, she could see someone struggling with two large dogs.

She looked closer at the filthy dogs and noticed that one of them was being walked on a knotted plastic garbage bag instead of a leash. The other had a belt fashioned into a makeshift leash. "Homeless guy with his dogs," she said quietly. "I always feel so bad for them."

Charlie looked over her shoulder at the trio. "The dogs or the guy?"

"All of them." Cora watched the man struggle to hold on to the dogs. Most homeless people seemed to have a spiritual connection to their dogs, as if the rigors of living on the streets formed a bond stronger than any pampered pet dog could offer its owner. These dogs, though, seemed disconnected from this man, almost as if they were trying to water-ski away from him. The hair on the back of her neck prickled. Maybe they weren't his at all. Was she watching a dog abduction in progress?

She turned her attention to the man. He was a short overweight African American man in a T-shirt with his jacket knotted around his waist. A red jacket.

"That's Joe!" Cora shrieked. She looked at Charlie. "Joe Elvis! I know him!" She started banging on the controls on the door handle, trying to open the window.

"Joe," she shouted out the window once she got it down. He turned in a half circle. "Over here, in the car!"

"Hey girl, I been looking for you!" he called back, grinning widely, as if he wasn't at all surprised to see her leaning out of the limo window. "Lookit at what I found." He gestured to the dogs. "I don't know where they live. They ran away during that storm, I think." The two dogs dragged him toward the limo.

Cora couldn't tell where the mud stopped and the dogs began, but she knew the lean pair were pointers of some sort. Then it hit her.

She was looking at Blade and Hunter Feretti.

Weeks had passed since she'd been at their house, but there was no mistaking them. German shorthaired pointers weren't common DC dogs, and two of them in the same household were rarer still. The dogs radiated the same frantic energy she had picked up on when she met them, but now terror had entered the mix. They were far from home.

Hunter edged toward the car and strained at the end of his leash. Joe was having a hard time handling both dogs, and Hunter's filthy front paws were just inches from the door.

"Whoa, watch the car!" Charlie shouted at Joe.

Joe ignored him. "Can you help me, girl? My aunt won't let me have dogs in the house, and I don't know what to tell these boys. They look real scared."

Cora answered before she thought it through. "Yes, yes, of course I will."

Charlie pulled his phone from his pocket. "I can fix this quickly, and we can get going; we don't have time to mess around tonight. I'll call my guy at Animal Control."

"No!" Cora shouted too abruptly, and Charlie looked up from his phone as if her tone had offended him. She softened her approach. "I have a contact, too, but give me a second." She didn't want to get anyone else involved.

"Sorry, but we've got to move," the driver said, gesturing to the open road in front of him.

"Can you just pull over for a sec?" Cora asked.

Charlie looked at his phone. "Cora, we need to roll, we're already behind schedule."

"I know, I know, but I don't want to leave Joe on his own." Joe stood in the street a few feet from the gleaming car with the dogs pacing and panting nervously. She looked at the driver. "Just for a second, sir."

He edged his way to an open space near a hydrant, and Charlie sighed in frustration. "What can you possibly do to help, Cora? The smartest thing to do is get AC to take over. They come meet this guy, scan the dogs for ID chips, and get them back to their owners. Happy endings for all."

Cora sat in silence, contemplating her next move. These weren't just any lost dogs, these were the *Feretti* dogs. Turning them over to Animal Control would indeed bring them home—no doubt they were chipped—but that would make it a hero-less reunion. Cora knew that Joe would never feel comfortable being associated with their rescue, so that left the position open. If she could get in touch with Dalton Feretti through Mia and Vaughn and hand the dogs off to him in person, it would add a new dimension to her audition. She would no longer be just Cora the dog trainer, she would be Cora the savior of Blade and Hunter.

She turned to Charlie. "You know what? Let me just help Joe get these guys settled, and I'll take a cab to the gala. I'll be thirty minutes late tops, before the cocktail hour is over, I promise."

"Are you fucking kidding me?" he snapped, the smile on his face at odds with his tone of voice. "Cora, it's starting to rain again, you're going to get soaked. And those dogs are filthy. Why can't you hand them off? You don't have to be, like, the personal savior of all animals, you know."

"That sounds kind of weird coming from you," she replied curtly.

"No, what *you're* doing is weird. It makes no sense." He leaned back in the seat and crossed his arms.

Cora couldn't believe how Charlie was acting. "I'm sorry, I just have to do this. Joe is my friend and he needs help. The dogs need help. It's barely sprinkling, I'll grab one of the umbrellas and take care of these guys super quick."

He shook his head again, as if he was worried that his perfect arm piece might be muddy and ruined by the time she got to the gala. "This is insane. But do what you have to do. Whatever."

"I'll be there before you know it. Promise."

Cora climbed out of the car, and Blade and Hunter launched themselves at her.

"Whoa, boys, be careful!" Joe admonished, pulling them away so that they couldn't jump on her.

"I'll see you in a bit. I'll text you when I'm on my way," she said to Charlie through the open window. He nodded but didn't say anything, pouting like a little boy who hadn't gotten his way. The car eased back onto the road just as the sprinkle of rain turned steady. Cora sprinted behind it in her delicate heels.

"Umbrella!" she shouted after it as it pulled away, waving her hands. "Can I get an umbrella?" She saw Charlie's shadow shift in the backseat and the car pause in the middle of the street, but then continue on.

"Well, there you have it. I guess we better walk quickly," she said to Joe as the rain picked up, trying not to think about Charlie.

"I always do," he said with a smile as he struggled to hold on to the dogs.

"Let me take one of them."

"This boy is more chill, he won't get your dress all dirty," he said, pointing to the dog on the belt leash that Cora could now identify as Hunter. Joe looked at Cora out of the corner of his eye. "You look real pretty tonight, girl."

"Thanks, Joe. Not for long if this rain keeps up." Cora was trying to process what had just happened with Charlie and figure out what to do with the dogs, all while attempting to keep dry. The rain subdued Hunter and Blade, and though they walked at the very end of their makeshift leashes, they weren't uncontrollable.

Joe untied his red windbreaker with one hand and held it out to her. "Put this on your head like the church ladies do."

"Thank you, Joe." She stopped and tied the sleeves under her chin so that she looked like "Little Edie" Beale.

"Yup, you look pretty in everything."

They moved down the sidewalk in silence, each concentrating on the dogs in front of them.

"Where are we taking these boys?"

"My place."

"What about taking them to the adoption place, like your boyfriend said?"

"Nope, I have a better idea."

Cora was thankful for the empty sidewalks. The four of them were an Instagram-worthy spectacle, and Cora didn't feel like answering questions about why she was walking mud-covered dogs in an evening gown with a dirty windbreaker tied around her head. Plus it meant fewer witnesses for whatever she decided to do.

"Here we are," she said, stopping in front of her building.

"Okey doke, here ya go," Joe said, handing the trash bag leash to Cora.

"Wait, don't you want to come up?" Cora wasn't sure if she'd be able to navigate the dogs up the stairs in her heels and dress.

"I have to get home now. Can I have my jacket, please? Bye, boys, see you later!" He turned and walked swiftly away as soon as Cora handed him his windbreaker, seemingly uncomfortable breaching their sidewalk-only relationship.

She led the dogs up the stairs and down the narrow hallway, wondering how she was going to manage four dogs in the apartment and remain clean. The golden foil woven throughout her dress provided excellent wicking from the rain, and though she was damp, she hoped that her look was still recoverable. If a fight broke out between her dogs and Blade and Hunter, however, there was no way she'd be able to police it in her gown and heels without getting filthy. Plus, Maggie and Darnell had left for dinner, so she was on her own.

Cora peered up and down the hallway and knew she had no choice. She laced the dogs' makeshift leashes around her neighbor's doorknob and quickly kicked off her heels and stripped off the dress, praying that there would be a traffic lull on their typically busy floor. She ran a few feet down the hall in her strapless bra and tiny thong, holding the dress up in the air with one hand and shielding her naked backside with the other. She stood on her tiptoes and hung it from the exit sign by the stairwell, then ran back to the two puzzled dogs.

"This is going to be interesting," she said to them, quietly putting her key in the lock and ignoring the fact that she was once again exposing her butt to the world. She opened the door and led them in cautiously, hoping that she could race them to the bathroom and close them in before Fritz and Josie roused.

Fritz popped his head out of the family room right as they made it to the bathroom door. "Hi boy, no worries. Just stay right there," she said soothingly. Blade and Hunter spotted Fritz and gave a few tentative whisper barks, as if testing their voices, then launched into a ferocious display. Fritz backed away silently.

"In we go!" Cora sang to them, clinging to the uncomfortable leashes and aware that her response could impact their reactions. The dogs spread their legs and held their ground in front of the bathroom door, raising a terrifying ruckus Cora was sure her neighbors could hear.

The noise summoned Josie, and she jumped in front of Fritz and barked back at them, as if guarding her tired older brother.

"In we go! In we go!" Cora chanted in a chipper voice over the uproar as she struggled to lead the straining dogs through the bathroom door. She didn't know what they were capable of and needed everyone to remain safe. But they dug their claws into the floor and resisted every inch of progress.

She finally got them in and slammed the door behind her. They left muddy footprints and body smears everywhere, even on Cora's legs. She could hear Fritz and Josie inhaling at the seam in the door, trying to assess the interlopers.

"You boys have got me sweating," she said to them as they examined the tiny bathroom, their fury trumped by the allure of new smells. She peered in the mirror. Her rain-smeared smoky eyes now made her look like she'd just woken up after a bender, and the smooth waves Darnell had coaxed from her hair were lost in a mass of frizzy ringlets beneath the unraveling fishtail braid. "Oh no. I think I'm unrecoverable."

She sat down on the edge of the tub, the porcelain cooling her naked butt as she watched the dogs survey the room. Blade, the more skittish of the two, made his way over to where Cora sat and wagged his stumpy tail at her, the plastic bag still coiled around his collar. She reached out to pet him and he took a half step away, tail still wagging. He wanted her to connect but didn't have the confidence to allow her to do so. Hunter pushed in front of his brother and placed his head on Cora's bare legs. She stroked his crusty fur and ignored the dirty stripes he painted on her thighs.

"You two could be my golden tickets," she said to them.

She needed to call Mia—with her help, the handoff would be easy to arrange. She would do her best to fix her makeup and hair and change back into her dress. Wouldn't the story be that much better if she laughingly told Dalton Feretti that she was on her way to an ALPF gala when she discovered the dogs? It would be fine for her to have less-than-perfect hair and makeup, as that would underscore her narrative of being the dogs' guardian angel during the storm. Her heart thudded in her chest as she ran through the scenario.

Nervous, Blade settled down in the narrow area in between the vanity and where Cora sat on the edge of the tub, his head resting on top of her toes. Hunter plopped into a sit beside her and pawed at her to get her to pet him. Despite the stress of the situation, or perhaps because of it, both dogs were glued to Cora in their own way. She wondered how often they were able to just *be* with a person, in silent and companionable meditation, as they were now. How often did someone trace the edges of their soft ears or rub their muscular shoulders?

"Let's get this thing off," she said as she started unwinding the belt wrapped around Hunter's collar. She stopped abruptly when her fingers hit plastic. There, beneath the coiled leather, sat a little black plastic box resting on his throat.

The shock collar.

Hunter wiggled his rear end and panted with his face pointing to the ceiling, almost as if he wanted her to examine it. Cora reached toward him slowly.

"*Ou, chouchou*. I'm so sorry. She hurt you, didn't she?" Hunter flinched as she put her hand on the collar and lowered his head toward the ground as she removed it. Cora inspected the area beneath where the box had sat. Hunter's fur was patchy, and the skin beneath was an angry red. Tears filled her eyes, and she spent a few minutes stroking Hunter, trying to make up for all the wrong that had been done to him. "I'm sorry I couldn't help you."

She turned her attention to Blade. "*Mon loup?* Please let me get it off of you. Please?"

Cora eased off the edge of the tub and sat cross-legged on the ground next to Blade, who opened one eye and peered at her but didn't move away. She reached for him slowly, whispering nonsense baby words. When her hand finally made contact with the buckle on the collar, he jumped up and sprinted behind the toilet. He knew exactly what the collar represented.

Pain.

She sat on the floor, leaning against the tub, hugging her legs to her chest. She knew better than to chase after Blade. It would take time and trust before she could remove his collar, even though it could no longer shock him, because he didn't know it. She pulled one of Maggie's expensive towels off the rack and used it to cover herself, her near nakedness becoming uncomfortable as Hunter tried to drape himself across her legs. Blade watched her from his hiding spot next to the toilet. It seemed like he wanted to get closer, but her breach of reaching for his collar had derailed their burgeoning bond.

Cora envisioned handing them over to Dalton and Simone. Would they notice that they weren't wearing their shock collars?

Would Blade duck his head when Simone reached for him? Would Hunter resist going back out to the yard?

She knew that returning them was the right thing to do from an ethical perspective—they did in fact belong to the Feretti family. She also knew that returning them would be an incomparable coup from a business perspective—how could they *not* want her to host the show after her act of heroism? Bringing Hunter and Blade back was the right thing to do, but seeing the scope of their suffering, both physical and mental, made it feel like anything but.

She picked up her phone to call the one person she knew would help.

THIRTY-EIGHT

"I don't care about the mess, honestly Cora, you can stop."
Eli watched as Cora struggled to wipe the dried mud off of Blade and Hunter before loading them in his car. By now, the sky was pitch-black and misting again. Both of the dogs cowered and backed away from Eli when he reached toward them, so he had no choice but to stand idly by as Cora rubbed them down.

"I just feel bad, they're really dirty, and your car is so clean." She used the towel like a squeegee on Hunter. "I'm not even accomplishing anything, I'm just moving the mud around on them."

"It's okay, just stop. You can detail the interior in exchange for the ride. Deal?"

Cora stood up and sighed. "Deal."

He opened the navy Subaru's hatchback and patted the inside. "C'mon up, pups! Can you jump up? Up up?" Cora was instantly reminded of her bed lesson with Charlie, then his shitty behavior just a few hours prior. She was happy Eli had stepped up to help, like always.

"Not gonna happen," she said as the dogs eyed him warily, skulking near her legs. "I'll lift them." She loaded the dogs in, not caring if the mud got on her T-shirt and shorts.

Eli closed the door softly so the dogs wouldn't startle. "Off we go. Cora and Eli's rescue service is at it again."

"Yeah, I guess we've got quite a thing now, huh?" Cora punched the address into her phone's navigation system. "It's going to take us about an hour."

She sent a quick text to Charlie. "Pls don't hate me, I'm so so sorry but not going to make it tonight. Dog stuff more complicated than I thought. SO sorry." She added a crying emoji to show that she spoke his language. She saw his typing indicator bubbles pop up for a few seconds, then stop. No response. She couldn't believe how angry he had seemed, and how unwilling he was to go above and beyond for animals in need. But she didn't have the headspace to worry about what Charlie was thinking right now.

Like all dogs, Blade and Hunter craved human companionship. Though they were terrified and in an unfamiliar environment with a stranger, they still clung to Cora in the bathroom. She pictured how scared they must have been during the sudden afternoon storm, how many times they must have been shocked as they barked out their distress, and how the thunder and lightning had probably sent them scaling the fence in an effort to escape the noise and find shelter. She wondered how long it was before Simone, or more likely Felisa, noticed that they were missing.

She knew that she had to keep her plan quiet. She contemplated who she could trust with a car to ferry the dogs to their next location—Winnie or Vanessa? Darnell? Fran?—but the people in her DC world were too connected, too incestuous, and she knew that word of her deception would eventually get out. She needed CIA-level secrecy for the plan to work. Once again, Eli came to the rescue.

"I can't believe I'm going to meet Hugh freakin' Brannon!" Eli crowed. "Am I allowed to ask for his autograph, or is that too uncool?"

"Way uncool. He likes to pretend he's a regular guy, so don't act impressed by him."

"I'm curious how you're on a first-name basis with the most powerful tech guru on the East Coast. Tell me the whole story."

"I met him at a rescue facility fund-raiser. I have no idea how I got invited—the room was filled with big-money donors and regular little me. I ran into him at the bar—literally—and we got to talking about dogs and training stuff. I didn't know who he was, but I could tell he was somebody, you know? He had that aura. He told me he was working on his own rescue sanctuary thing. I guess he liked what I had to say, because he asked for my contact info and invited me to be on his rescue's advisory council."

"Are you kidding me? You're on his *council*?"

"In theory, yes. We had one quick e-mail exchange about it, but I haven't heard from him in ages."

"Was it weird reaching out to him again about these guys?" He gestured to the back. "Were you scared?"

"I was *totally* freaked out. But he's doing some great stuff for animals, and I knew he would be able to help. And I knew he would be discreet. He seemed to like that I was vague about Blade and Hunter's origin story. He could tell my secrecy meant that it's a big deal."

"Yeah, the dude clearly likes secrecy. He stays totally off the radar. So will you tell *me* Blade and Hunter's whole story?"

"Nope, the less that people know about them the better. All you need to know is that these dogs need to find a home. A *new* home. Oh, and from now on let's call them . . . Baxter and . . ."

"Horton!"

"Perfect!"

Eli nodded and focused on the road. The rain was coming down hard, and the twisty route to Middleburg was challenging enough to navigate on a clear day.

"You're doing me a huge favor by driving us. I owe you."

"You do, actually. I'm keeping a tally."

The dogs settled into a slumbering knot on the blanket in the back of the car, and by the time Eli pulled up to the elegant gate on an unmarked driveway they were snoring contentedly.

"This place is . . ." Eli trailed off as he peered into the darkness.

"Perfection," Cora said. "I can tell even in the dark. Can you reach the keypad?" Eli leaned out his window and punched the five-digit code Hugh had given Cora into a small keypad hidden in a climbing rosebush.

The huge old trees at the end of the driveway had spotlights at their bases so that the branches were illuminated, hinting at the magic that lay ahead. The metal gate opened quickly and smoothly, a nod to Hugh's tech background amid the countrified setting.

The farther they went down the long driveway the more intricate the lit trees became. Each was carpeted in white fairy lights so tiny that the glow looked like a veil of stars, with long strands of shimmer hanging down intermittently like willow branches. It was hard to tell the actual tree from the sparkly illusion.

"If this is just the driveway, what is the house going to look like?" Eli mused.

The illuminated trees continued for a quarter mile, until they passed under a wisteria-choked brick archway in the middle of an ivy-covered wall. The vintage look didn't match up with the pillared McMansion Cora envisioned Hugh Brannon inhabiting. Once past the wall, Cora realized that her assessment of him didn't take his paradigm-shifting creativity into account.

The driveway opened up to a vast rolling field, as misty and melancholy as a Brontë moor. The house sat anchored in the fog, lit by strategically placed spotlights, a delirious mix-up of styles, with a wood-shingled, dormered barn in the center straddled by a castle-like windowed brick turret on one end and a narrow New England saltbox addition on the other. It was a huge calico cat of a house that couldn't decide if it was country estate elegant or artistically quirky.

"Honey, I'm home," Eli said quietly, in awe of their surroundings.

"Now I'm nervous," Cora whispered.

"About what? You already know he likes you."

"No, what I'm doing is wrong. I'm going to get busted. He's going to figure it out and hate me for what I'm doing. This is insane." She was babbling.

"Cora, stop. Don't question yourself. Even though you won't

tell me the whole story, I think I know you well enough to know that you're doing right by these dogs. It's okay."

She nodded and got out of the car. Blade and Hunter waited quietly for Cora to open the hatchback. She grasped their mismatched hand-me-down leashes and took a deep breath.

"Cora Bellamy, is that you?" Cora saw a dark figure striding toward the car. Hugh Brannon looked like central casting's idea of landed gentry.

"It's me, Mr. Brannon! Nice to see you again. Thank you so much for helping out."

He didn't answer her and instead addressed the dogs. "*Look* at these beauties! Hello, boys, why hello, you handsome dirty dogs." Cora was surprised to see them wiggle their tucked hind ends, as if they recognized a kindred spirit in the man before them. He petted them gently.

"Mr. Brannon, this is my canine chauffeur, Eli Crawford."

Hugh Brannon looked up at Eli, nodded dismissively, and went back to petting the dogs.

"What are their names, Cora?" Hugh knelt beside the dogs, and they nuzzled him, leaving flecks of dirt on his loose white button-down shirt.

"The one on your left is Horton and the other is Baxter." She paused. "From now on."

Hugh finally turned to look at Cora and nodded seriously. "I understand. Why don't you all come in for a moment?" The invitation sounded like a dismissal, as if making it clear that they wouldn't be at the Brannon estate for longer than a minute.

They followed him up the stone walkway and into the barn

section of the house. The foyer had a low-beamed ceiling and was obviously part of the original structure. The walls were exposed brick and crowded with antique paintings of animals, while the floor was an explosion of brightly colored mosaic tile assembled to look like a scrappy stars quilt. The effect was high-end but comfortable country chic.

"Would you like to meet Benjamin?" Hugh asked Cora, as if Eli wasn't even in the room.

"Of course!" Cora replied, readying herself for the appropriate response to either a human or animal "Benjamin."

Hugh turned to Eli. "Wait here with the dogs. I don't know how they might react, and I don't want to scare Benjamin." Cora tossed the leashes to Eli and followed behind their host without a second glance back.

Hugh walked through one of the four doorways off the foyer and into a small anteroom. It had the same low-beamed ceiling coupled with a vibrant black-and-white-check wallpaper that made her feel like she was inside a chessboard. An amazingly life-like carved bulldog, crafted to look like a carousel horse and festooned with a saddle and cabbage roses, stood guard by the unlit fireplace. In the center of the room, next to a red plaid couch, sat a small pen.

Animal, Cora thought, ready to meet either a puppy or a kitten. Hugh reached into the pen and pulled out the tiniest pig she had ever seen, so pink and perfect that it looked like an animatronic creation. Benjamin was dressed for company in a miniature red bow tie that complemented his black spots. He coordinated with the room perfectly.

"Benjamin, meet Cora," Hugh said, holding the pig out to her.

"I've never held a baby pig!" she exclaimed as Benjamin snorted and wiggled in her arms. "Where did he come from?"

"I can't say where, but let's just say that he was destined for the slaughterhouse. Do you eat meat?" Hugh stared at her face intently.

"I, uh, sort of? I mean, not really, but a little?"

"Well, just keep in mind that you're holding bacon in your hands right now," he replied gruffly. "Everyone involved with animals should be vegan."

Cora looked down at the piglet and thought about how to answer Hugh. She opted for avoidance.

"What do you need to know about Bla—, I mean, Baxter and Horton?"

"Absolutely nothing. You said they're young dogs, and they were living outside so their potty training and socialization are probably spotty. That's all I need. I understand that there's some drama related to them, so I won't ask for more than that."

"They're probably chipped, so when you find a new home—"

Hugh waved her off. "To be honest, Cora Bellamy, my 'rescue' is more of a drop-off for lost souls like Benjamin. I had high hopes when I met you, but the reality is that I just can't stand to give any of them up. I'm a hoarder. I have a wonderful staff that supports my efforts, which is why I now have four horses, a blind ass I call Forty-Five, a yard full of ducks, chicken, and geese, a turkey, six goats, three pigs, two peacocks, fourteen incredibly tolerant barn cats, three indoor cats, and, with Baxter and Horton in the mix now, eight dogs."

Cora couldn't believe what she was hearing. "Now I feel terrible—I thought you were going to be able to find them a new home. You're going to get overcrowded!"

"Do I have to spell it out for you? Cora, I can *afford* to take care of all of them and more. I could hire a day nanny, night nanny, and personal chef for every single animal on my property and still bring home a thousand more animals in need. I've created a sanctuary. This is what I was meant to do, not tech. Now, if someone worthy falls in my lap and they're interested in adopting one of my animals, then certainly, we can talk about it. Like you and Benjamin. He seems fond of you."

Cora picked her chin off the top of the little pig's head. "Me? Take Benjamin? Oh, I wish I could, but I live in an apartment and I'm already pushing the limits with my dog and my roommate's dog. Plus, don't these little guys get huge?"

"You're right, there's no such thing as a teacup pig. You're looking at over a hundred pounds of pig in a few years." Hugh reached out to take Benjamin and placed him back in his pen. "Everything is going to work out. My other dogs are a tough pack, but once they welcome in new dogs, it's an unbreakable bond. They'll school those two and show them how we run things here. It'll be fine."

Cora noted that Hugh was speaking with the bravado of someone with just enough dogsense to be dangerous, particularly when she knew how the dogs had reacted to Fritz and Josie. "Are you sure? Do you want me to help with the introductions? I could come back tomorrow and—"

"Not necessary," he interrupted. "I know what I'm doing."

She thought better of trying to correct the great and powerful Hugh Brannon.

"I'm always available if you change your mind," Cora added, the hint of a blush tickling her temples.

"Thank you for saving the dogs from whatever their circumstances were, Cora. I can assure you that they will live very happy lives here on *Le Mûrier*."

"Ah, *avez-vous des mûriers ici*?" Cora asked, wondering if the estate's name was a nod to the nursery rhyme, or if mulberry trees grew wild on the property.

"Oui, they keep the *chevres* very happy," he replied, not even noticing that they had lapsed into French. He paused and stared off into space for a moment. "I'll see you out."

Cora followed Hugh back to the entry hall. Eli was sitting on an intricate wooden throne that looked like it had been salvaged from a castle or a cathedral with the dogs curled up on top of his feet. He didn't look at Cora when she walked in the room.

"Do either of you need the washroom before you go?" Hugh asked. "May I get you some water?"

"We're fine," Cora said, answering for both of them. "We should probably hit the road."

"Indeed," he said distractedly. "I'll take the dogs now." He strode over to them and took the leashes from Eli. The dogs stood up slowly, stretching and yawning.

Hugh turned to Cora. "Cora Bellamy, from this point on, you will never be associated with these dogs again. They are strangers to you, and you to them. Agreed?" It felt like a benediction. He reached out his hand.

"Agreed." She nodded and shook his hand to seal the pact.

"Farewell, Cora, travel safely." He turned abruptly, nodded at Eli, and disappeared through a doorway with the dogs, leaving them alone in the foyer.

Cora looked at Eli and shrugged her shoulders. "I guess that's it."

The two walked to the car in silence, each contemplating what had just happened. Eli opened the door for Cora and bowed deeply. "I am your chauffeur, after all," he said.

"I'm sorry about that—it sounded awful. I was just nervous talking to him. You're so much more than my chauffeur." Cora put her hand on Eli's arm and was again reminded how it felt to dance with him. He shrugged.

"I *am* so much more. I'm also your Beth Ann wrangler, key fetcher, dog rescuer, foster home, blog reader, dance instructor . . . I'm like your personal manservant." His voice didn't sound like he was kidding.

"Wait, you really feel like that?" They stood beside the car, facing each other, the fairy lights from the trees illuminating them.

"Sort of. You consider me your helper dude, like when you need something, oh—call Eli! He can do it! You treat me like I'm your brother. I have enough sisters to know the feeling." He shrugged again.

Cora's palms went clammy. "Can we talk about this on the way home? I feel weird standing here, like he might have surveillance on us or something."

"Yup."

They drove in silence for a few miles. Cora contemplated what Eli had said, and how upset he seemed with her.

"I'm sorry I make you feel used," she said quietly. "I understand why it seems like that, and I feel terrible now."

He shrugged.

"I'm serious."

"I'm over it, Cora. Don't worry about it." His jaw was clenched and his eyes were glued to the road ahead of him.

"Eli, I really like spending time with you. I look forward to it. It's kind of effortless, you know? I was actually hoping that we could spend more time together, like maybe—"

"Cora, stop. Just stop."

"What?"

"Stop playing with me. You've known I had feelings for you. Fran told me she told you, but she said you weren't into me. But I was stupid, I kept hoping that maybe you might . . . I don't know, learn to love me or something, which is why I stuck around and did your bidding. But I finally realized, tonight, that I'll never be anything more than your errand boy. I'm done, Cora."

She was shocked.

"But . . . I do . . ." Cora struggled to put words to the feelings that had been bubbling inside of her for longer than she realized.

"You do what? Love me?" He laughed at her. "Yeah, right." He pointed back and forth between them. "This? This affection is fraternal, not romantic. I get that now."

Cora couldn't process what was happening. She needed him to know he was wrong.

"The night you brought Nell home!" she shouted at him. "I wanted to stay and hang with you guys, but you made it obvious you wanted me to go!" The intensity of her response caught her off guard.

"I thought you were only staying out of obligation!" he yelled back. "Like you didn't trust me alone with Nell!"

"What about Café Fuego? I *know* you felt something happening between us. You blew me off! I wanted to dance with you for the rest of the night, but then that girl showed up and you never stopped dancing with *her*."

"Oh, now you're trying to blame me? Amazing." He shook his head. "Yeah, well, Paige and I used to just dance together, but we've gotten much closer and things might start to develop. So don't feel too bad for Mr. Lonely Heart, okay?"

Cora leaned her head against the window and squeezed her eyes shut to blot out what was happening between them. She'd never seen Eli angry—she didn't think it was possible for Eli to sound stern—yet here she was on the receiving end.

Before she could admit her feelings to Eli, she needed to admit them to herself, and she'd waited until it was too late. He didn't want to hear anything she had to say, so there was no point trying to convince him that Fran had predicted it.

Little by little, the quirky good egg had won her over.

THIRTY-NINE

"**C**an I come in? I'm coming in," Maggie said, knocking on and opening Cora's bedroom door at the same time. Cora had been napping more and more in the week since the Feretti dogs drop-off, finishing her daily roster of clients and retiring to the mountain of blankets on her bed.

"Hey, how did it go?" Cora asked, trying to pretend that she hadn't been sleeping. Fritz barely stirred beneath the blanket.

Maggie beamed at Cora. She looked adorable, a mix of quirky and professional in a high-waisted lipstick-red skirt, faded chambray shirt, and leopard print heels. "Awesome. Amazing. Perfect." She paused for effect. "C, they offered me the job! They didn't even want to do a second interview! I am now the institutional giving associate for the Circle Theater. Pending a drug test, which thanks to a month-long break, I'll pass." She jumped up and down in place, and Josie hopped excitedly beside her.

"Aw, yay, Mags! I'm so happy for you!" She mustered up an appropriate amount of cheer and reached out to hug her friend.

"It's all thanks to you. I owe you big-time." Maggie sat on the edge of Cora's bed. "Oh, and even better—a super hot guy on the Metro asked me for my number on my way there!"

"Whoa, it really is your lucky day," Cora answered with a wan smile.

Maggie stared at Cora for a moment. "What's going on? Is it cosmically impossible for us to be happy at the same time?"

"It sure feels that way. I'm okay, just freaked-out waiting to hear about the show."

"That's it? I've been pretty caught up in my own shit lately, I'm sorry I haven't been *here* here, like, plugged in to you. What else is going on?"

Cora sighed. "You know Eli, my rescue buddy?"

"Of course—I love that dude! Kick-ass dancer. You're working with his dog, right?"

"I was. But when we went on that rescue errand the other night, he told me that I make him feel used."

"Ouch. Did you apologize?"

"Yup."

"So what's the problem?"

"It's complicated, Mags. I've been suppressing it for a while, but I sort of have . . . had . . . feelings for him. And I tried to tell him but he shot me down, hard." Cora's eyes welled up.

"Wait, what? You like *him*? What about Lord Douche?" Maggie had upgraded Charlie from just a plain douche to a titled one after meeting him. Her breakdown of him the day after the gala had been brutal.

"I'm not stupid, I figured out that he was sort of a jackass, but I ignored it. I was *horny*, I'm sure you of all people understand that.

But he was such an asshole about those poor dogs on the night of the gala. And I haven't heard a peep from him since. He didn't even get in touch to see if I was okay." Cora had kept the details of the Feretti dogs vague, only telling Maggie that she and Eli had taken some stray dogs to a rescue and she had missed the gala. "You know, I never laughed when I was with Charlie. I always felt like I had to be the best version of me around him to compete with Madison. But Eli? He made me laugh and he liked *me*. It totally snuck up on me. I didn't even know how I felt. And now it's too late."

"It's never too late! Haven't you ever watched a chick flick? Let's jump in your car and make a mad dash for his apartment, where you climb up the fire escape and profess your love!"

"Eleventh floor. Not happening."

"So he shot you down. He wasn't interested at all?"

"He had feelings for me, at one point. But now he's dating that stupid hot blond chick he was dancing with at Café Fuego." She threw herself back on the bed and blinked away tears.

"Oh, C. We can fix it; once a crush, always a crush, in my book—wait, is that your phone ringing?"

"Probably." Cora shrugged. "Just another client inquiry, I bet. I'll let it go to voice mail." Maggie gave Cora a sour look and jumped off the bed to fetch the phone from her dresser.

"Stop pouting. Only one of us is allowed to be a drama queen, and that's me. Answer it." She thrust the phone at Cora.

"Top Dog Training, may I help you?"

"Hey, Cora, it's Mia Nguyen. Do you have a second?"

Cora's eyes went wide and she put her finger to her lips to pre-emptively shush Maggie.

"Hey, Mia, nice to hear from you! I do have time to chat." Maggie recognized the name and gawked.

"So, Vaughn and I wanted to touch base with you and tell you what's been going on with the show." Cora's heart quickened. Mia's tone sounded upbeat, like she was about to deliver good news.

"We thought your audition was, like, spectacular. And we weren't the only ones who felt that way. Dalton Feretti over at World of Animals thought you have something really special, too."

"Oh my gosh, thank you!" Cora's voice trembled. She gave Maggie a thumbs-up.

"Our final three were just so incredible. Like, we could go with any of you and the show would be a hit."

"Oh, wow," Cora answered agreeably.

"That's why we had to really pick the meat off the bones, as it were." Cora had no idea what Mia meant. "You know, the show is going to get a ton of attention since it's in direct competition with *The Doggie Dictator*, and our trainer is going to have to do quite a bit of media, so we need someone who can handle, like, the *rigors* of live TV and interviews and stuff."

"Um-hm."

"So with that in mind, we had to go with someone else, Cora. We thought you were *so* awesome with Honey, but we were concerned that your, um, *intensity* about Ershovich might leak out. We totally agree with your perspective on him, but we have to keep it completely positive when we're on the record. Does that make sense?"

Cora was numb. "Um, yes?" She bit her lip to keep from crying. Fritz crawled out from under the covers and began licking her cheek.

"Please know that we all really loved you, though! You're super special, Cora!"

Not special enough, clearly. "Thank you, that's nice of you to say." Cora took a breath to steady herself. "Before we hang up, may I ask who you went with?"

"Of course! I think you know her, Brooke Keating."

"Brooke is great. She's going to be great. I'm so happy for her." Cora hoped she sounded genuine.

"I know, right? We're thrilled. I hope you're going to tune in!"

"You bet, wouldn't miss it." Cora played along but wanted to toss her phone across the room.

"Tuesday nights at eight on World of Animals. I'll shoot you an e-mail so you know when it starts airing."

"Awesome, thanks again for the opportunity."

Cora hung up the phone and closed her eyes.

Maggie hopped across the bed and threw her arms around Cora. "I'm sorry, I'm sorry," she crooned comfortingly. Josie jumped up and muscled her way in between them, offering solace and kisses next to Fritz.

"Can this day get any worse?" Cora sobbed.

"Shhh, it'll pass. I promise. Cry it out. I'll get us some ice cream." Maggie rubbed her back.

"I quit."

Maggie pulled away from Cora. "Oh no you don't. Never quit.

Take a minute to lick your wounds, then get right back up and kick more ass. Okay? I'll give you a few days to be sad, then I'm gonna be on you like a flea on a junkyard dog. Got it?"

Cora hiccuped and nodded, then put her head down on the pillow and cried some more.

FORTY

It was the first gathering of the Boozehounds since Cora's audition. Winnie had selected a hole-in-the-wall, locals-only spot frequented by bold-faced names looking to go incognito. A few of the men sitting at the bar looked official and pissed off.

"A belated toast to Cora's valiant effort," Winnie said, raising a glass.

"To Cora," Vanessa echoed, and they clinked glasses.

"Sorry I couldn't be the one to unseat the Hound Harasser. I tried."

"We know you did," Vanessa said soothingly. "I'm so mad that Brooke got it. When does that stupid show go on the air?"

"Not sure, but they're probably well under way shooting by now." It had been over a month since Cora got the news, and she was finally able to think about it without getting depressed.

"You have to admit she's a decent trainer," Winnie said, ever the voice of reason.

"Yeah, but I hate her," Vanessa said. "And I know y'all do, too!"

They chuckled in agreement.

"Hey, at least we like her methodology. It's not like she's going to be choking dogs and forcing them to submit to her," Winnie added.

"I know, I know, she's just so . . . fake," Vanessa replied. "And her client roster! It's like she wants to know her clients' net worth before she'll agree to work with them."

"I think she's had her eyes on the prize the whole time," Cora said. "She knew what she wanted and went for it. I could learn from that."

"Don't you dare," Winnie chastised. "Stay true and genuine and real, okay? The world has enough fakes. Now, if I may, I'd like to shift gears for a moment and brag . . ." She reached down and rooted through her patchwork bag, pulling out a folded newspaper. "Hot off the presses, as of yesterday. My niece's wedding announcement in the *New York Times*!" Winnie was happily child-free, but she doted on her nieces and nephews.

"La-di-da, how big-time!" Vanessa exclaimed. "Those announcements are so silly. Just when you think you've read the most over-the-top one, you look at the next one and it's even worse. Or better, I guess."

"I've never read them," Cora said, reaching for the paper.

"It's a lot of 'daughter of this wealthy scion and son of this land magnate are joining their kingdoms,' but every so often you get a lovely normal couple, like my Bettina and Jonathan. No fancy titles in this one, just a teacher and an accountant who fell in love!"

"Aw, that's so sweet," Cora said as Winnie passed the paper to her. Cora glanced at the rest of the well-named couples in the Vows section and the wedding-related article on the facing page.

The photograph showed a man kneeling in front of a woman in a lush garden, all hydrangeas and dappled light. The article was titled AFTER FLASHMOB PERFORMANCES, THE QUIET PROPOSAL MAKES A COMEBACK. She studied the photo. The woman had her hands over her mouth, as if she couldn't contain her excitement, and it was obvious even in quarter view that the man was beaming at her. Something about the photograph nagged at Cora. She read the caption.

"Madison Perry is overcome by emotion as Charlie Gill asks her to marry him. The scene was witnessed only by the photographer, who hid in the bushes until the couple walked into the garden."

"Oh my God!" she screamed.

"What? What's wrong?" Winnie asked.

Cora choked on how to convey what she was seeing without having to get into the details. "These people—I, I . . . *know* them." She jabbed at the photograph, sputtering. "They're clients. Former clients."

Vanessa peeked over her shoulder. "Cute! Did you like them?"

"I . . . uh, hard to say," Cora answered in a haze as she speed-read the article. She was dumbfounded. The article didn't list a date for the proposal, but it was obvious that it had happened shortly after Madison had returned from her trip, which had been only a few days after the gala. No wonder she hadn't heard from Charlie since she bailed on the evening. He had been planning to propose to Madison all along.

The quotes in the article made her feel nauseated. "I knew I was going to marry her the moment I saw her," Gill said while holding Perry's hand. "She's perfect, and I needed to find the perfect way to propose to honor our relationship. I discovered this spot a year ago and knew this was where it was going to happen."

Cora stared off into space while Winnie and Vanessa chattered, not noticing that she had removed herself from the conversation. The scenario dawned on her slowly; she had been Charlie's last long con, his final "legal" seduction, before proposing to Madison. He had been able to intuit her crush on him from their very first meeting, and had taken advantage of Madison's absence to weaken Cora's defenses one training session at a time. The "total package" comment, the wine, the cute texts, the twilight bed training, and the night at Toya had all been foundation work leading up to the gala, where his con would finally close so he could get married knowing he still had it. That's why he was so angry when she left him in the limo. He wasn't concerned for her welfare or worried that she would miss Alice Goodwin; he was upset that his hard work wasn't going to pay off. Charlie Gill was going to remain unfucked after putting in way more effort than usual.

Cora felt vindicated. Doubtless, she wouldn't have been able to resist him after drinking too much wine and getting caught up in the glamour of the evening, pact be damned, and in his mind he would have won. Screwed the stupid naive girl and moved back to his unsuspecting near-fiancée. He probably had the ring in his pocket when he kissed her last. Cora nodded her head in silent victory.

"You were right, I was blind," Cora texted Maggie, along with a link to the article. "Lord Douche indeed."

She then dashed off an e-mail that came to her faster than she could type, to Madison with a cc to Charlie.

Dear Madison— A warm welcome home and congratulations on your recent engagement! I'm sure your wedding preparations are in full swing but I wanted to make sure that you're pleased with the work Charlie and I did with Oliver while you were away. Oliver was a wonderful student, and your intended was a devoted and attentive teacher! Charlie went above and beyond in so many ways. I am always available for a one-on-one session with you if you have any questions or need clarification about any of my dog training secrets (there are so many!). And it would be lovely to catch up and see your ring! I wish you the best as you and Charlie embark on this wonderful new adventure. Fondly, Cora

Charlie would shit himself over the subtext. Good.

FORTY-ONE

Cora pulled up in front of Fran's office with four minutes to spare, just enough time to park and dash inside. They had traded texts and e-mails in the weeks since the Rivera concert but hadn't found the time to get together and catch up, and Cora was looking forward to a heaping dose of Fran and Sydney. While the visit wasn't purely social—Fran was worried about Sydney's burgeoning leash aggression during their walks around Old Town—Cora made sure to keep her afternoon open so they would have ample time to chat without having to rush.

She walked into the foyer and was reminded of her first encounter with Eli. They hadn't talked since the trip home from Middleburg, and she missed him. She hoped that she would run into him, so she wore her lucky green shirt and tamed her hair into a smooth braid.

"You can go right down, Sydney is expecting you," Lydia said with a smile.

Sydney dashed out to meet her before she was halfway down

the hall. "Hello, my friend," Cora greeted him. "You're forgetting your manners, aren't you," she chastised as he jumped up on her.

"There she is!" Fran swanned out of her office in a flowy asymmetrical print dress and enveloped Cora in a perfumed bear hug. "I have *missed* you, my dear! We have so much to talk about!"

"I know! I missed you guys, too. I'm bummed about his aggression stuff, but at least we can catch up. Shall we get right out there?" Cora glanced around the office, barely hiding her motives.

Fran watched Cora closely. "We're ready, darling. Leash in hand and treats in pocket." She dove in the folds of the dress and fished out a handful of freeze-dried liver. "Even Yohji Yamamoto does pockets now."

The quiet side street in front of Fran's building was a block away from the bustling Old Town shops and restaurants. Cora was surprised by Sydney's walking as they made their way to King Street.

"He's doing great, Fran. I'm actually blown away."

"Oh ye of little faith," Fran chastised. "Believe it or not, we did continue practicing after our lessons ended. He's fabulous on the side streets and in my neighborhood, but when we get to the main drag, he's a nightmare. Prepare to watch him unhinge."

Sure enough, Sydney's demeanor changed the instant they reached the busy road. His body tensed, and his head swiveled from side to side, scanning the horizon for potential targets.

"See? It's like I'm not even here. He goes into the red zone."

"I'd call this pre–red zone. We still have a chance to get through to him at this stage, but once he tips over and starts barking at a dog, it's going to be tougher to reach him."

Cora explained the basics of dealing with Sydney's leash

reactivity as they threaded the sidewalk, keeping a buffer between Sydney and the other dogs they encountered so he'd remain calm. The streets of Old Town were a challenging proving ground, and within a few blocks it was clear that both Fran and Sydney had had enough.

"Nice work, guys," Cora said. "This is just the first step, but I think he's going to do great. He figured it out quickly."

"Yes, yes, yes, we get it, we'll work hard," Fran said dismissively and looked at her watch. "The lesson is officially over now, so let's move on to the important stuff." She peered over her glasses at Cora. "What in the devil is wrong with Eli these days?"

Cora's phone rang, and she used it as a redirect to hide the pink exploding on her cheeks. It was a 212 area code—New York— which meant it was probably a robocall. She stuffed it back in her pocket and looked at Fran questioningly.

"Oh, don't play innocent with me, darling. Something strange happened between the two of you, and he won't tell me what it was. You might think today was just about Sydney, but I had ulterior motives. I'm going to engineer a run-in when we get back to the office so you'll have to face each other."

Her heart surged at the thought of a Fran-mandated meeting. If anyone could fix it, Fran could. "How do you know something happened, what did he say?"

"It's not what he said, it's what he *didn't* say. You always used to come up in conversations with him, and then suddenly—nothing! The second I mention your name, he's busy on his phone or making a quick exit. I just don't understand it. Did you root and run?"

"Huh?"

"Sorry, darling, a little Oz slipped out. Did you two ever get together and . . . you know . . ." She made a lewd hand gesture.

"Fran!"

"Sorry, darling! His reactions about you changed so dramatically that I assumed you two had an unfortunate assignation. I know *something* happened between you. Spill it."

Cora rubbed her forehead and grimaced. "It's not what you think."

The whole story tumbled out in a flurry so circuitous that Fran kept interrupting to get clarification. Cora was careful to avoid mentioning the Feretti dogs specifically, but she told her every detail of the near miss with Charlie, the gala, and how Eli had once again saved the day but felt unappreciated.

"And then . . . I sort of told him that I have feelings for him," she finished sheepishly with her eyes downcast.

"I *knew* it! I am never wrong about these things!" Fran crowed. "I knew it before *you* did! So what did he say?"

"He shot me down before I could even get all of the words out. It was awful. I'm cringing just thinking about it."

"Pshaw, I can make this right, darling! Easy peasy, Franny to the rescue."

"You don't have to," she protested weakly. "I can see why he thinks I'm awful, and he has every right to be upset at me. Let's just try to forget it. It's fine, really."

They stood facing each other in front of Fran's building. Fran sighed. "Darling, you are not awful. This is all a ridiculous misunderstanding, but you have my word that I won't say anything. It will test my limits, but I'll refrain. Aussie's honor."

Cora managed a small grin. "That's fine. Thank you. I've got to run, time for me to hit Rock Creek with my guy. Keep me posted on your progress with Sydney, okay?"

"Oh, you'll be hearing from me," she replied mysteriously, and then disappeared with Sydney into the building before Cora could respond.

Cora checked her phone as she made her way to her car. Two new client inquiries, then a voice mail that stopped her in her tracks when she played it.

"Cora, this is Dalton Feretti from World of Animals. I'm here with Mia and Vaughn, and we need to talk with you. Give us a call back in the next hour or so."

Something happened with Blade and Hunter. He knows. They know. Cora was beside herself. She got in her car and replayed the message twice, trying to figure out if he sounded angry. She wiped her palms on her jeans. Forty-five minutes had passed since he left the message. What was he going to do to her? Have her arrested? Was Hugh Brannon implicated? Or Eli? She had to own up to it and take the fall. Everything was her doing. She swallowed hard and dialed the 212 number.

"Dalton Feretti."

She summoned every ounce of Maggie in her system and spoke with a strong, clear voice. "Hi, Mr. Feretti, this is Cora Bellamy returning your call."

"Cora, hello! I've got Mia and Vaughn here with me, let me put you on speaker. Can you hear us?"

"Yes, I can, hi, everyone." Cora's heartbeat slowed a measure. He sounded cheerful, so unless he was in the business of delivering mob-style ambush attacks, she was in the clear. Blade and Hunter were safely still in Middleburg.

Vaughn took the lead. "Cora, we have an interesting idea we'd like to run by you. We're here at WOA corporate with Dalton today to brainstorm through some challenges with *Everyday Dogs*. We've had some surprising feedback on our rough cuts, as it turns out."

Cora had no clue what he was implying. "Hm, interesting," she said.

"Yeah, the show is a scripted-reality hybrid, and it seems that the scripted part is going fine, but the reality aspect, well, that needs some help."

She still didn't know what he meant, exactly, but she did pick up on the fact that no one had mentioned Brooke's name.

Mia chimed in. "Some of the feedback is that we need to inject some . . . what did they call it?"

"Q-score saver," Dalton mumbled. "We need to make her more relatable."

Mia cleared her throat. "We need to add another voice to the show to maximize the advertising synergies. To bring some warmth to the package. Brooke is really awesome at reading copy on camera and doing all of the scripted content like the interstitials before we go to commercials, but she . . . um . . . has a bit more of a challenge when it comes to interacting with the families. She's just very . . . how should I say it?"

"Formal," Vaughn added. "She's superb with the dogs, but corporate is getting a headmistress vibe when she's working with people. We need some down-home warmth on the show as well."

Everyone paused, and Cora held her breath.

"And we all agree that *you* are the warmth we need," Mia said, breaking the silence.

"What?" Cora wasn't sure she understood what they were telling her.

"You had such a way with Honey, Cora. You stood out from everyone. It was like you could *talk* to her, like, in her language, and she could talk back to you, and you could totally understand her. It was Dr. Doolittle stuff. And you were fun to watch. Very likable," Mia went on.

"That's such a nice compliment, thank you." Cora tensed her body to try to stop the trembling. *Are they saying what I think they're saying?* "So, um, how can I help?"

"Cora, we're asking you to cohost *Everyday Dogs* with Brooke Keating. Would you be interested?" Vaughn said, speaking plainly for the first time in the conversation. "After some media training, of course."

"Are you serious?"

"We are totally serious. What do you think?"

Cora took a breath and spoke the words that she'd known in her bones since Wade's e-mail first appeared in her inbox.

"I would love to host *Everyday Dogs*!"

FORTY-TWO

Fritz was waiting for Cora when she got home. He had taken to sleeping by the door again on the days when Maggie brought Josie to the theater with her. While he enjoyed the occasional respite from his boisterous sister, he clearly missed having her around.

They made it to the park in the golden hour before the rest of the world came home from work and took to the trails. Fritz's tongue hung low, and as always Cora surveyed his body as they strolled to make sure he seemed comfortable. When the sun hit him just right she could see new white hairs hiding in the dark patches on his head.

Cora hadn't told a soul about the call. She wanted to be alone with the news before letting the rest of her world in on it. Was she ready for the scrutiny? The haters, judges, bullies, and trolls who wanted to tear her down for the way she looked or the things she believed? Could she stand the relentless gaze of social media? Was she ready to make her quiet voice heard without hiding behind an anonymous blog and babbling French? And how could she possibly work for Dalton Feretti, knowing that she had essentially stolen his dogs?

She let all of the fear and doubt and anxiety run through her until the only thing she could hear echoing in her head was, "Yes. I can do it."

Fritz slowed down behind her and finally came to a standstill with his nose magnetized to the ground. She walked a few paces ahead, turning her face into the sun to enjoy this feeling of confidence and peace before everything changed.

"C'mon, slow poke," she said, after a long pause but without turning around.

"We're getting acquainted," a voice answered.

Startled, Cora screamed and leaped around. "Who— *Eli?!*"

Fritz was leaning against Eli's legs, grinning while Eli rubbed his shoulders. They looked like old friends, delighted to have run into one another in such an unexpected spot.

"What are you, a ninja or something? I didn't even hear you walk up! You gave me a heart attack!"

He laughed. "I'm sorry, I do walk really quietly. It's another one of my superpowers."

"What are you even doing here?"

"I heard you were at church."

"Thanks, Fran. So much for 'Aussie's honor.'"

"Remember, it's an island of convicts."

"But how did you know I'd be *here*?" She pointed to where she was standing.

"I read your entire blog, Cora. Between the millions of mentions and the photos of Fritz on the trail, it doesn't take a genius to figure out your route. Anyway, I'm in your church because I need absolution." He bowed his head like a pious congregant.

"What are you talking about?"

"Cora, I'm sorry I was so awful to you on the way home from Brannon's house. You didn't deserve that."

"No, I owe *you* an apology. I'm mortified that I made you feel like my errand boy. I'm so sorry. Really. I appreciated everything you did to help me."

They stood a few feet apart, staring at each other in silence. Fritz looked at Cora's face, then at Eli's, then back to Cora's, as if trying to translate what the tension between them meant.

Eli took a step forward. "Do you accept my apology?"

Cora nodded. "I do. And will you accept mine?"

"I will." He put his hand on his chest and bowed.

They stood cemented in place, not sure how to act or what to say next. Eli focused on Fritz, massaging the dog's shoulders like he was cornerman in a boxing ring. Cora adjusted his leash in her hand over and over. The silence became painful.

"Want to walk with us?' Cora asked.

"Sure," he answered quickly.

Fritz high-stepped between them as they set off.

"He's a really handsome dude," Eli said. "The photos on your site don't do him justice. No offense to your photography skills, of course. I just mean he's really good-looking."

"I'm biased, but I agree."

They were talking as if they'd just met, or like Eli was a client and they were in the first minutes of his first session.

Should I bring up the weather? Cora wondered.

"Warm today," Eli said.

"Mm-hm," Cora agreed placidly. Inside she raged. *I need to say something! I need to tell him that I miss being around him. That I want him to put his arms around me and say that he'll never dance with anyone else. That I need his kind of quirky in my life. Don't screw this up again, Cora!*

"Hey, I'm really glad we sorted everything out. I mean, I'm glad we're back to normal," Eli said.

Back to normal? Is that all he wants?

"Yeah, definitely. Me, too. Back to normal." She smiled as she said it to force the feeling into the words.

They walked along silently. The only sound was the impatient jangling of Fritz's dog tags.

"Eli, stop being stupid," he muttered to himself. He took a deep breath, stopped walking, and turned to face Cora. "I'm lying. I don't want to go back to normal. Our normal was torture for me. *This* is the normal I want."

He gazed at Cora for a moment, placed a hand to her cheek like he was asking for permission, and then swept her into a kiss unlike any she'd ever experienced. He wrapped his arms around her, and the feel of him, the smell of him, and the familiarity of his body against hers mixed with his unexpected passion made Cora dizzy. They kissed for a long time, neither one wanting to pull away. He finally loosened his grip on her, looked into her eyes, and sighed.

"Do you know how long I've wanted to do that? And do you know how long I want to *keep* doing it? I mean, that was worth th—"

Cora kissed him on the mouth midsentence, reveling in the way his lips felt on hers. This was exactly where she was supposed to be.

A cyclist sped by and whistled at them, and they laughed at the spectacle they had created. Fritz danced next to them, wagging his tail and grinning, as if he approved of what was happening right above him.

"So this is our new normal?" Cora asked.

"I hope so. Does Fritz like little space alien dogs?"

"Fritz likes every dog. No, scratch that. Fritz *loves* every dog."

"Then let's go to my place and grab Nell and see what happens."

"Yes," Cora replied and reached up to kiss him again. "Let's see what happens."

FOUR MONTHS LATER

"I can't believe it's finally here," Cora said, looking around the patio at the group of beloved people and dogs. "I'm still in shock."

"I'm in shock that Josie won't stop counter-surfing the appetizer table." Maggie dashed over to stop Josie from grabbing an entire tray of stuffed mushrooms, then cupped her hands around her mouth. "Anyone know a dog trainer I can call?"

Cora took a sip of champagne and surveyed the crowd. Fran was sitting next to the glass-walled fire pit, gesturing emphatically at Wade and Rachel with an overfull glass of red wine. Sydney was on leash near her, taking playful nips at Daisy's heels every time she turned away from him. Cora had Fran to thank for the gorgeous venue for the first-episode viewing party of *Everyday Dogs*. Fran had called in a favor with a swanky DC property that was getting ready to close their outdoor dining area for the season, and begged them to allow dogs for the event. The result was a magazine spread–worthy cobblestoned space lit by hundreds of café lights and punctuated with a dozen dogs of all sizes trying to be on their best behavior.

"We did it," a voice said behind her.

Cora turned and smiled at Brooke, who was holding out her champagne glass in a toast.

"Indeed we did," Cora said, clinking her glass. "Thank you for helping me figure out how to be on a show."

The costars had reached a quick truce by the end of the first episode taping, aware that they could either make life easy for one another or make the experience a nightmare. Once the initial posturing and assessing was over, the women became strong allies. They were really different, of course, but working with Brooke was more seamless than Cora could've imagined.

"I've gotta go find Sasha," Brooke said. "I'm sure she's taunting the big dogs and making me look bad." Her Yorkie was incorrigible, but she didn't seem to care.

Cora saw Vanessa beckon from across the patio and point to her feet. There was Sasha, crouched and barking at Vanessa's yellow Lab, Samson. Winnie stood nearby, nursing her beer and watching the dogs with a detached look, making it clear that she was officially off dog training duty and that it wasn't her first drink of the evening.

Cora heard an unmistakable canine snort behind her.

"There you are!" she exclaimed as Eli walked Fritz and Nell to her. Fritz looked dapper in a preppy blue-and-red bow tie that matched Eli's, and Nell was sporting a leather collar with a cowboy boot–inspired thistle motif, shipped all the way from Beth Ann in Texas. "Was it a successful potty run?"

"You know it," Eli said, leaning in to kiss her cheek. "Two pees, and Nell did a nice solid poop."

"Aw, honey, you really know how to sweet-talk a girl."

"So when does this thing get rolling? I've been nervous-drinking all night and I'm feeling it."

"You're nervous? I'm the one who's supposed to be nervous," Cora said.

"*Nervous* is the wrong word. I'm excited. I'm super stoked. We all are." He looked down at Fritz and Nell, and his voice went up a pitch. "Right, puppy-faces? Right?" Fritz danced in place and Nell turned in her happy-dog circles.

As if on cue, the big-screen TV in the middle of the space sprang to life, and the show's cheerful theme song came over the loudspeakers. People clapped and hooted and a few dogs barked along. Cora and Eli settled into a love seat off to the side. Like always, they arranged themselves so they were touching from shoulder to hip. Fritz hopped up beside her uninvited, and Nell stood on her back legs and danced in front of them, her adorable way of asking for help.

Eli leaned over and kissed Cora's neck. "I'm so proud of you, love."

Cora's voice sounded over the loudspeaker as scenes of frolicking dogs played out on-screen.

"This season on *Everyday Dogs*, you'll learn exactly what it takes to build a relationship with your dog that's based on love, compassion, and a little bit of science. You'll understand how to bring out the best in your best friend, and have fun while doing it. We've got tons of laughter, a few tears, and tools that *every* pet parent can use. Are you ready to get started? Let's train some dogs!"

ACKNOWLEDGMENTS

Many thanks to my early readers, Holly Frabizio, Stephen Busemeyer, Nicolle Wallace, and Jennifer Buckley, for blending friendship with editorial rigor.

To Kevan Lyon, my amazing agent, who made my dreams come true.

To Kate Dresser, whose brilliant edits had me shouting, "Hell yes!"

To Molly Gregory, for handling my endless first-timer questions with grace.

To my parents, for their unwavering support of my unconventional life.

And to my husband, Tom, who was my Fav way before "fav" was a thing.